Muskogi Sunset

The Second Creek War of 1836

The Sequel to the Historical Novel
TALLAPOOSA

LARRY
WILLIAMSON

The Ardent Writer Press
Brownsboro, Alabama

For general information about publishing with The Ardent Writer
Press contact *steve@ardentwriterpress.com* or forward mail to:
The Ardent Writer Press, Box 25, Brownsboro, Alabama 35741.

Cover Art and composition by The Ardent Writer Press using public domain images from Wikipedia and Photoshop techniques. Images are of Menewa, a Creek chief, painting by Charles Bird King, one of the lithographs in Thomas L. McKenney & James Hall's *History of the Indian Tribes of North America*, published in three volumes from 1836-1844. The painting is now in the Smithsonian National Portrait Gallery, Smithsonian Institution, Washington D.C. The other photo is of General Winfield Scott by George Catlin in 1835. The background map is of *"Georgia and Alabama", showing county boundaries & Native territories, 1823*, by Henry Schenck Tanner from the Historical Maps of Alabama collection, University of Alabama Department of Geography. Interior maps are by the author, Larry Williamson. Composition and cover are covered by the same grant for noncommercial use noted above.

Photo of Larry Williamson is by Steve Gierhart, The Ardent Writer Press at Tallassee Armory.

Library of Congress Cataloging-in-Publication Data

Muskogi Sunset: The Second Creek War of 1836 by Larry Williamson, Tallassee, Alabama

p. cm. - (Ardent Writer Press-2017) ISBN 978-1-64066-057-1 (pbk.); 978-1-64066-059-5 (eBook mobi)

Library of Congress Control Number 2018939803

Library of Congress Subject Headings
- Fiction/Historical
- Fiction--Social aspects--United States--History--19th century

BISAC Subject Headings
- FIC014000   FICTION / Historical / General
- FIC032000   FICTION / War & Military

OTHER BOOKS BY THE AUTHOR

Tallapoosa

Over the River, Long Ago

Legend of the Tallassee Carbine: A Civil War Mystery

Acknowledgements

Thanks forever to my writing gang, the Auburn Writers Circle, especially Suzanne Johnson, Robin Governo, and Julia Thompson. They endured endless readings in weekly sessions to keep the manuscript chugging along.

Much gratitude to Steve Gierhart, Doyle Duke, and their talented associates at The Ardent Writer Press. They are diligent and dedicated.

Myra Singleton Johnson read the whole manuscript and caught several boo-boos. She is a treasured source.

I must commend John T. Ellisor's epic volume, *The Second Creek War*, as a valuable reference. It may be the only authoritative, comprehensive work on the Second Creek War in existence.

Character Index

Main characters listed by chapter of first appearance

	FICTIONAL	**HISTORICAL**

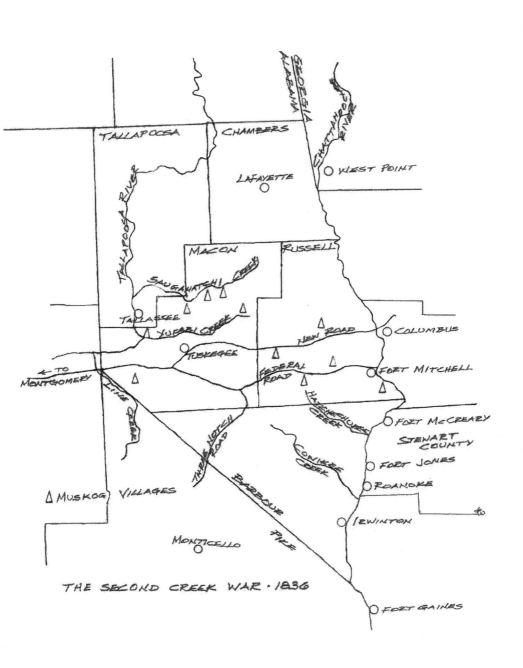

THE SECOND CREEK WAR · 1836

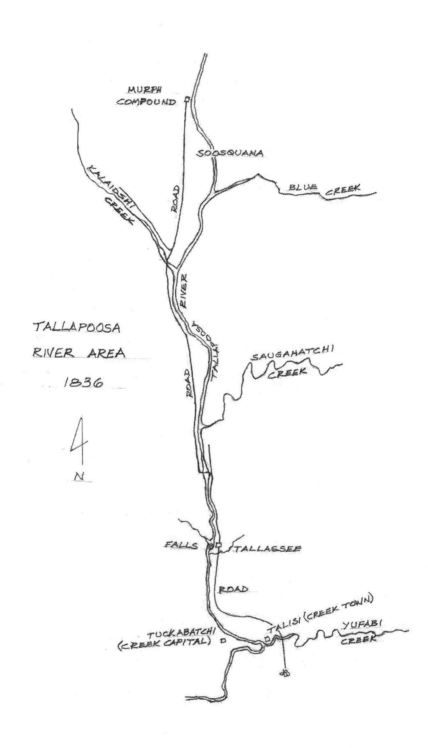

MURPH COMPOUND

SOOSQUANA

BLUE CREEK

KALAIDSHI CREEK

ROAD

RIVER

TALLAPOOSA

ROAD

SAUGAHATCHI CREEK

TALLAPOOSA RIVER AREA

1836

N

FALLS TALLASSEE

ROAD

TALISI (CREEK TOWN)

TUCKABATCHI (CREEK CAPITAL)

YUFABI CREEK

Prologue

Murph Settlement, Tallapoosa River, January 2, 1814

AS A BIG FIERY SUN POKED through the treetops across the river, sounds of activity within the cabin stopped. Dead silence. Saul froze in the middle of the porch, facing the door, unable to move. Cal stopped rocking.

No sound. Nothing. Not even, it seemed, the murmur of the river washing over the shoals. Every movement had been suspended. Long minutes. Long, long minutes.

The door cracked. Then it swung full open. Adelin slowly walked out. She tenderly held in both arms a big bundled blanket.

"Daddy Saul," she sputtered, fighting to control herself, "say hello to your beautiful, beautiful baby daughter."

Saul carefully peeked into the blanket as Adelin began crying, unable to hold her emotions longer. Sleeping in her arms was the most gorgeous baby Saul had ever seen. Everything about her, as far as he could tell, was perfect, right up to a full head of coal black hair.

THE WEEK-OLD MURPH BABY still had no name.

"Cousin Josephus back in Virginia," Cal philosophized, "went six months before they named him."

"Hell, Cal," retorted Saul, "this baby will go nameless her whole life if we can't come up with something better than Josephus."

Adelin thought it wonderful the baby was a girl. "The women here now outnumber the men," she gloated. "What do you fellows think of that?"

Debate over the child's name continued. Saul thought she should have a Muskogi name and pressured Soosquana to select one. She disagreed, with perhaps more head than heart. Her main argument sounded unusually wise and thoughtful.

"This child will surely not grow up in Muskogi culture, if the Muskogi Nation still exists for her. She will be part of the white man's world. So she needs a name from the white man's culture."

"But she will always be Muskogi, Soos. We won't ever let her forget that."

"I know. And she will always be proud, as I am proud. But you and yours will be her people. You are my people now also, even as I will forever remain Muskogi. I think she must have an American name."

Neither parent would yield, so the friendly stalemate continued for several more days. Life at the compound gradually returned to near normal.

Finally, one evening at supper, almost two weeks after the baby had been born, Soosquana sought to break the name standoff.

"Did you know Adelin has another name?" she asked Saul and Cal.

Saul looked at her. "What?"

"Yeah," said Cal. "You mean her middle name?"

"Adelin's other name is Anna," Soosquana continued. She addressed Saul. "You want me to give the baby a Muskogi name? Adelin is my Muskogi sister, is she not? So I pick Anna as our baby's Muskogi name."

"Can't argue with reasoning like that, big brother," offered Cal.

"Why, Soos, how nice," said Adelin, thrilled. "I'm flattered, but I'm sure you can ..."

"Anna it is," persisted Soosquana. "Anna Murph. You like it, Saul?" She smiled at him.

Saul only stared, lost in thought. "Why not?" he finally relented. "Yeah. Anna Murph. I like it, I have to admit. I like it a lot. Does everybody agree?"

All agreed. The remainder of the meal became a celebration of the life and future conquests of baby Anna Murph ... American ... Muskogi ... of the Tallapoosa River country of the Mississippi Territory.

—Excerpted from *TALLAPOOSA*
Chapters Eighteen and Twenty

❖ ❖ ❖

THE FIRST CREEK WAR, culminating in the Battle of Horseshoe Bend in March of 1814, opened Alabama to floods of settlers, most from Georgia and the Carolinas, in search of new, rich lands. The Muskogi Creeks, who had nurtured the land for centuries, harbored deep resentment, for the past and for new intrusions, while newcomers coveted the territory for their own.

The conflict in 1813-14 and subsequent treaties had subdued the Indians while Alabama became the twenty-second state of the United States in 1819. The white man's government now prevailed, and his culture was making rapid inroads. Meanwhile, Muskogis and whites coexisted in relative tolerance.

Until 1836 ...

Chapter 1

East Alabama Wilderness, April, 1836

QUARRELING SQUIRRELS high in the longleaf pines signaled the first faint glimpse of morning light penetrating the forest. Beneath, wrapped in his thin bedroll, Kaspar Brayke opened one eye. Too close for the eye to focus on him, his flop-eared orange-red hound stared back. A dripping tongue quivered in anticipation from the dog's happy mouth.

"'Morning, Rube," grumbled Kaspar. "Least, I 'spose it's morning."

Rube's panting increased at his master's resurrection. The rekindled corpse popped open the other eye, then scruffled his reluctant body into a sitting position, struggling to awaken fully.

Kaspar surveyed his surroundings, though he was confident Rube would have alerted with alarm at any intrusion through the night. He studied the tiny brook below the slope and its opposite bank, then the hill above him. Finally, he scanned the thick foliage on both sides of his site. Satisfied he and Rube were unobserved, he stood and checked the grounds close around, including the dead embers of the modest campfire. He focused on the small spit he had structured from sticks above the fire.

"Rube, did you steal the rest of that rabbit?" Kaspar asked, glaring with mock disdain at the dog, still lying flat with his front legs splayed in front. The dog's already pleased expression brightened as his wagging tail thumped harder against the forest floor. Kaspar was certain Rube smiled at him. "That was to be breakfast, but it's okay. Too much grease with that jack, anyhow." He wrinkled his nose. "And practically all gristle. We'll find a passel of berries along the way for breakfast."

Kaspar tore down the spit and filled in the shallow cooking pit. He covered it with brush and pine needles to return the site to nature and obscure his visit. Rube grabbed the greasy skewer stick and lay nearby to gnaw on it while his master rolled his few tools into the slight blanket and strapped the roll across his shoulders. Next, Kaspar checked his long rifle, reloaded it with a fresh cartridge, reprimed the pan, and carefully lowered the hammer against the strike plate.

"Come on, Rube, time to get moving. If I figure right, we should reach the trading post at the river falls by tonight."

Kaspar hefted the rifle to a shoulder and trudged up the slope to find the faint trail they had followed through the woods since leaving Columbus two days previous. Rube clutched his tasty stick and trotted along.

The new morning, now half gray and half orange, greeted the two at the top of the rise. In the faint light, Kaspar found the trail, took a few strides, and stopped. He unshouldered the rifle and peered through the trees to survey the area on all sides.

"Rube," he announced quietly to the dog, now as alert as his master, "something's burning." He checked the air and detected a whisper of a breeze drifting into his face. He sniffed. "It ain't close, but it is in front of us. Don't get so happy with that stick so's your hound dog senses stop working." He resumed walking, but now carried his iron in a cradle position. "When it gets lighter, maybe we can see where the smoke's coming from."

KASPAR BRAYKE HAD LEFT Charleston three weeks before. He had worked during the winter dressing ship masts at the navy yard after moving over from Nashville, but soon realized the job wasn't to his liking. Rube hated city life as much as he, and that was enough incentive to seek new adventures. Newly posted handbills solicited agents to aid the army in enforcing the Indian Removal Act in Cherokee and Creek country. Seemed a good fit, so he checked with government offices in Charleston for details. He had experienced the Cherokee in the Smoky Mountains of Tennessee, North Carolina, and North Georgia, and didn't care for the hills or the culture. He thought he would prefer the Creeks, so he elected to set out for Alabama in search of the junction points for collecting the Indians.

"You want to find a place on the Tallapoosa River called the Falls," instructed the official in charge at Charleston, moving his fingers across a map spread on his desk. He thumped a certain spot. "There's a trading post on the eastern bluff above the falls, right there. An Army unit is coordinating the operation. Report to the commander and he'll swear you in."

"Yes, sir."

"Do you have a horse?"

"No, sir. I prefer to walk. Don't rightly trust no horses."

"Well, you'll need one for the march west, and for getting around before the departure. The cavalry will loan you one when you get there." He paused. "One more thing, Brayke. This should be an easy thing for you, you liking the wild country and all. The Creeks are friendly now and eager to head for their new homes in the unorganized land west of Arkansas Territory and Missouri. Since Andy Jackson cleaned out the scalawags among them a ways back, they've been quite peaceable. I think you'll like 'em, even if they are savages."

"Yes, sir. I'll leave as soon as I get my affairs here in order."

Brayke's Charleston affairs took less than two hours, so he and Rube trod the westward road out of town at first light the following morning. He stopped in Georgia's state capital, Milledgeville, and propped his sore feet up for two days, then struck out for the small, growing town on the Chattahoochee River called Columbus. He tarried there for three days.

"Son, they ain't told you straight 'bout them damn Creeks," drawled the stationmaster at the town's stagecoach depot. "Them Red Sticks are still prowling around, now more'n ever. They're madder'n hell since Jackson decided to send 'em out west."

"Red Sticks?"

"Them's the mean 'uns, the ones what fought Jackson back in 'thirteen and 'fourteen. Leastwise, their papas fought Jackson. Most of 'em got wiped out. Now their whelps done gone wild, partly in revenge and partly 'cause we want to get 'em outta the way."

"Are they violent?"

"Hell, yeah, they're violent. Been burning farmhouses and crops, even kilt a farmer and his whole family a month or so ago. Attacked one of my stagecoaches here 'while back, but it got away."

"You're right," sighed Kaspar. "That shore ain't what they told me in Charleston."

"So far, they've kept theirselves on the Alabamy side of the Chattahoochee. Hope they stay there." The old man paused, scowled. "Them's real ugly creatures, too, what with their faces all painted up red-like. Look out for 'em, son, when you see 'em like that, and be careful."

KASPAR AND RUBE TRUDGED several miles along the trail. Full daylight revealed the brightest day they had seen in weeks, showcasing statuesque pines, oaks, and hickories in the prettiest and lushest forest of any since leaving Charleston. Easy to see, he mused, why folks would fight over this land. After an hour, they topped a low knoll, from where they spied a black wisp rising in the blue northeastern sky.

"There's our smoke, Rube. Looks about a mile off. Not a woods fire, since that would most likely be white smoke. Could be bad, but it don't seem to be in our path. Too far to the right."

Another hour led to a wide, sandy beach bordering the near side of a broad, shallow creek flowing westward, to the left. The trail pointed straight into the creek, across a sandbar, back into the water, and up the mud bank on the other side.

Kaspar started down the slope, then glanced to the far bank to see a man step from the forest onto the trail. Then another, obviously an Indian like the first. Kaspar stopped and shifted his rifle into his hands, but didn't point it. Rube stepped forward to utter a low growl.

"Easy, Rube," Kaspar almost whispered. "Down, Boy." More men emerged, forming a silent barrier across the trail. Nine total, all glaring at Kaspar, all with scarlet painted faces.

Chapter 2

Near the Tallapoosa River, April, 1836

SIXTY YARDS ACROSS THE WAY, the Red Stick party of nine warriors stood steadfast. Kaspar Brayke knew they were 'Red Sticks' from the descriptions and warnings of people he had talked to at the Columbus outpost. He evaluated his predicament, keeping a firm grip on his rifle but not daring to cock it or shift it from the port position held close to his chest. Half the men appeared armed with muskets and the others with bows and quivers full of arrows. If they meant him harm and charged, he was confident he was a sharp enough shot he could take one out immediately and reload in time to hit another. That would leave seven to deal with in close quarters, if he survived the musket balls and arrows sure to fly his way. The odds loomed bleak.

Kaspar cradled his gun in his left arm and raised the right hand high, palm open. He held his signal of peace for several tense seconds, hoping the party would recognize it as such. Finally, the Indian in the middle stepped aside and motioned for his compatriots to create a narrow slit in their ranks. He glared at Kaspar and waved a hand into the gap.

"Come on, Rube, and behave yourself," Kaspar cautioned. "I think they're letting us pass." He reached down, gripped his dog's thick leather collar, and guided him down the beach and into the water. He could risk no chance Rube would take a dislike to one of the warriors and chomp off a hunk of leg.

The two struggled up the mud bank on the far side of the creek and approached the party. The men glared at him and the dog with unfriendly expressions. Kaspar dared not try to stare them down, but studied each one carefully. As he entered the gauntlet, one warrior pointed down at Rube and chattered excitedly. Most of the others snickered, seeming to find something about the dog fascinating. Rube uttered a low growl, but cut it short when Kaspar shook his collar.

Kaspar cleared the line of Red Stick warriors, but still held onto Rube for another fifty yards. Rube expressed his irritation with a parting snarl, but kept walking beside his master after being released. Kaspar steeled himself against turning his head, using his peripheral vision the best he could to check to the rear and to the flanks as he walked. He wished to gain distance as fast as possible, but knew he must not show fear by hurrying.

"Whew! That was scary, Rube," Kaspar finally dared to mutter. "They must've recognized us as strangers, and not of the fellows they've been feuding with."

After another mile through the forest, Kaspar began to feel safe. His heart slowed, and he became aware of taking a breath for the first time since leaving the creek.

THE YOUNG LADY DISMOUNTED and tethered her horse, all the time eyeing the activity to the south. She climbed the steps to where Perley Gerald, the trading post proprietor, and a friend sat rocking.

"Mr. Gerald, what are they doing across the way? Why is the militia there?" Half the men working to build some kind of wall appeared to be local militia, the remainder civilian.

"Well, hello there, Miss Anna. You ain't been 'round here in weeks. Proud to see you again, Dearie."

"Nice seeing you, Mr. Gerald. And you, Mr. Peavy." She looked again at the construction and gestured toward it. "The militia?"

"Yeah. Thought you and your folks might be concerned 'bout that."

"Seems to me they're up to no good," rattled Sam Peavy. No one knew for certain, but locals guessed Sam's age at many multiple decades. He spat a stream of tobacco juice off the end of the porch. "Can't leave decent folk be."

Gerald ignored him. "Captain Brodnax says the gov'mint means to bring off the Act, his commission being to enforce it. Says an army column will soon reinforce him. Seems the gov'mint don't like Muskogis running 'round loose."

"I'm Muskogi. Are they after me?"

"Naw. You and yore folks are too well set in up the river. They likely won't bother y'all or anybody up 'round yore place."

"Yore pa ain't no Creek nohow, Honey," said Peavy.

"That's so," agreed Gerald. "'Sides, claim is they's not messing with peaceful folk. Just them what's lost thar properties and are making trouble 'bout it."

"You sure? The government has crossed Muskogis before. More'n once."

"No, I ain't shore. Don't trust 'em. But that's what they say. The treaties are supposed to protect our peaceful Indian neighbors."

"Yeah," said Sam. "But them bad 'uns oughta be rounded up and sent off. Some of 'em keep stirring up trouble, all right. We don't need nobody else getting kilt."

Gerald looked at Anna, still standing at the top of the porch steps. "Almost happened last night. You know the Coogan folks farming up near Thaddeus Post? Wallace Coogan?"

"Yes." Anna nodded, a worried expression creasing her face. "Nice family. I've met 'em at least twice."

"They come straggling in here this morning. Seems a war party burnt 'em out last night. Lucky they warn't hurt or kilt."

"That's awful, Mr. Gerald. I'm right sorry to hear that." She grimaced. "Where are the Coogans now?"

"They went on over to the Batson place. Alfred will let 'em set up on his spread till they figure something out."

"When they catch these people, if that's what the army is about, what will they do with them?"

"Hang the worst of 'em and send the rest out west, I 'spose. That's what the law provides for them what don't want to stay here, or can't behave theirselves."

"Well, if they do catch up with the bad'uns, I hope they give 'em a fair trial. They need to leave the good people alone, though," said Anna. She stepped up onto the porch deck, propped her hands on her hips, and turned again to peer at the doings to her left. "Don't like the looks of those walls they're putting up. Looks like a fort."

Gerald changed the subject. "You come down to get some supplies, Miss Anna?"

"Just need a few things, Mr. Gerald, no more'n will fit snug. Let me get my saddlebag." She retreated to retrieve the leather pouch from her horse. Returning to the porch, she started for the front door.

"Go on through, Honey," instructed Gerald. "Melissa's in the back somewhere. She'll help you out."

Sam Peavy directed another stream of tobacco juice off the end of the porch. He and Perley Gerald resumed rocking.

KASPAR BRAYKE FOUND THE RIVER and paralleled its valley for some time, hearing the murmur of the current without seeing the water through thick woods. He passed an Indian village on his left, between the trail and the river, drawing curious looks but no signs of hostility. Gradually, the river sound changed to a low roar, signaling the presence of rapids.

"Rube, we may have found our falls," announced Kaspar to his hound, who trotted alongside but occasionally broke off to chase some frightened woods creature.

The trail emerged from the forest into a modest opening. A new double-ended settler's house, featuring a central walk-through, sat close by the trail. Kaspar crossed a small creek at the base of a steep wooded hill and followed Rube up a twisting course to the top of the rise. Minutes later the trees opened to a broad clearing. As they strode cautiously into the expanse, Kaspar observed a low-walled stockade under construction to his left near the bluff overlooking the river valley.

A hundred yards beyond, near the edge of the bluff, stood a large log building with a wide, roofed front porch. Smaller houses and sheds stood scattered to either side and behind. A neat rail fence enclosed a rectangular yard of perhaps two acres with the structures centered at the rear, overlooking a much steeper, higher bluff than he had just climbed. Below the precipice thundered his quest of the past three weeks, the falls of the Tallapoosa River.

Kaspar walked beside the rails toward a wide opening in the fence. No gate blocked the gap, which implied to Kaspar, 'Strangers Welcome'. This has to be the trading post.

As he was about to step through the entrance, a black horse charged toward him. He jumped back to dodge the horse and its rider, a young woman with hair even blacker and shinier than that of her mount. She wore an irritated scowl on an angelic face, and seemed to notice Kaspar not at all as she reined the steed hard left and cantered off to the north, her long, loose tresses streaming behind.

Kaspar stood entranced, staring after the rider. "Rube," he finally announced, "there goes the most beautiful animal I've ever seen." After a few seconds pause, he added, "Her horse is right handsome as well."

Chapter 3

Tuckabatchi, April, 1836

THE COUNCIL FIRES, which had burned brightly, lessened to a small flame and glowing embers in the gloom of a falling sun. Burning hickory logs, newly sated with sap, crackled and spit sparks high into the air. They accented the anger seething within the Council of Chiefs seated around the fire.

After a long pause, when few of the opposing debaters would look at each other, Head Chief Opothle Yahola drew a deep breath to temper his fury. He speared each Muskogi member of the council with his piercing eye, then settled on one.

"Tuskenea, you must control your warriors, those loyal to you, those putting us at peril. Though you hold no authority over the people of the Muskogi nation, you have much sway over those who commit crimes against whites and Muskogis alike. You must discourage such dishonorable behavior. This Council demands it."

"You have said the same before, Opothle Yahola," said the scowling warrior. "The invaders who steal our lands can't be trusted, and must be banished. You befoul my name. Me! The true chief of the Muskogi Nation. My father was the great Big Warrior, and he anointed me chief as his successor. You are the pretender, Opothle Yahola, with false authority. By trusting whites you commit treason. You do not speak for this Council."

Opothle Yahola bristled. "You spout blasphemy, and I do speak for this great Muskogi Council. I am the legitimate leader of this body, ordained by my mother's tribal lineage and a majority of chiefs around this sacred fire. I work with the leaders of the whites to better our people, because we cannot defeat them. We must continue to mesh our culture with theirs for peace and safety of all. Else, we face destruction." Opothle Yahola paused and stared long at his opponent, daring him to refute the point. Tuskenea remained silent, but retained his scowl. The speaker continued. "I, too, distrust and condemn whites who defile forests and pollute rivers. They are criminals, as are those who seize our land grants by fraud. I also condemn Muskogis who commit murder and pillage. You, Tuskenea, have power over many. It is you who commit treason if you fail your leadership of the rogues who follow you."

Tuskenea leapt to his feet, his hand on the hilt of the knife at his belt. "You betray all Muskogis! I challenge your authority over any man true to the blood."

Opothle Yahola did not flinch. He stood firm in a defiant stance, his arms crossed and his hands near no weapon. As Tuskenea began to slide his knife from its sheath, aged warrior Menawa stood and stepped between the belligerents. No other of the dozen councilors around the fire dared move.

"There will be no violence at the Council fire," spoke Menawa in an even, strong voice. "The Council speaks for peace and good bearing of all Muskogis, those of us of the Tallapoosa and those of the Chattahoochee." He turned and swept his arm around the circle. "And you of the Coosa and the Tensaw and the many streams that nourish our rivers. We are all brothers, natives of this land which has nurtured our fathers and grandfathers for time ever."

Tuskenea let the knife nestle back into its sheath. "All Muskogis respect your wisdom, Menawa. But Opothle Yahola is not a friend of the Muskogi. He has sold out to the invading whites, and I refute the call to invoke the memory of our fathers where this traitor is concerned."

"The great Chief Menawa speaks the truth," said Opothle Yahola, still planted in place. "We must respect his counsel, even you, Tuskenea."

The younger warrior uttered a low growl and took a step toward his adversary. Menawa raised his arms, straight and with palms open, one toward each man. Tuskenea again stopped, furious as Opothle Yahola stared at him with a stone face.

"Again I say, the Council fire must be exempt from violence and discord," spoke Menawa. "Our differences are to be resolved in the glow of its sacred flame. I have but a few years left to me, and I mean them to shine as bright as the sun for the Muskogi Nation. We must act with unity, but civilly, against invading whites who scheme to take our soil and our livelihood, and banish us to strange lands."

MENAWA, NOW NEARING SEVENTY years of age, was a veteran of Creek wars since 1813. He was the leader of one thousand Muskogis at the ill-fated defense of Cholocco Litabixi, the Horseshoe, on the upper Tallapoosa River in the spring of 1814. General Andrew Jackson of the Tennessee militia, centered in Nashville, invaded Creek lands the previous October in response to an attack on the army outpost and civilian settlement at Fort Mims near the Tensaw River in the south of the Territory.

Jackson immediately wiped out several Creek villages in the area of the Coosa and Tallapoosa Rivers before enduring a cold, rough winter. To climax his campaign, he prevailed in the horrible, one-sided, bloody battle on March 27 with aid from a regiment of regular army and another militia contingent from Knoxville. Approximately nine hundred of Menawa's warriors were massacred, while Jackson lost only forty-nine of his own three thousand men. Menawa, in serious condition with several gunshot wounds, managed to save himself by escaping into the river and floating downstream.

Later, as the leader of Muskogi factions fighting to repulse the invasion of settlers pouring over the Chattahoochee River from Georgia, Menawa had opposed with force several dictatorial treaties foisted on his people. Especially egregious was the one known as the Treaty of Indian Springs, negotiated by Chief William McIntosh in 1825 without the sanction of the Council of Chiefs. The treaty ceded vast tracts of Indian land in Georgia and Alabama to the states, a deal which angered militant Muskogi tribes. A party of a hundred and fifty warriors, authorized by the Council and led by Menawa, attacked McIntosh's Georgia plantation, assassinated him and others of his family and allies, and burned his palatial mansion.

A new pact, the Treaty of Washington, replaced the voided Indian Springs Treaty in 1826 and returned some of the property in question. Menawa, more powerful than ever, continued his leadership and enjoyed enhanced respect from all Muskogis, especially by the more militant Upper Creek tribes known as Red Sticks.

MENAWA SAT DOWN, choosing a strategic position between the two warriors. Opothle Yahola again stood then slowly strolled full circle around the fire, meeting each chief's eye. He stopped in the spot where he started and paused another half-minute before speaking.

"I hold no animosity toward Tuskenea. He is my Muskogi brother and a brave warrior of many fights and hunts. My opposition is to his hard line against peaceful settlers. I, too, would rather they had never arrived, never defiled our soil, never polluted our rivers, never compromised our hunts." His voice rose as he delivered his passionate oratory.

Opothle Yahola paused and swept an emphatic hand toward the distant forests. "Now the whites are neighbors, and have been for nigh twenty winters. We have to accept they are here to stay. We must join with those who mean us good will, and work with them to banish the wrong-headed among us, and among them. Violence is ill-founded; we Muskogis will lose all if we follow tragic paths of bloodshed. I call on Tuskenea to join in dealing wisely with our white allies. Else, we perish."

OPOTHLE YAHOLA, a mere decade and a half younger than Menawa, had served as a diplomat and spokesman for the Muskogi Nation for many years. He had traveled to Washington with Menawa to negotiate with Congress, and knew personally governmental leaders in Alabama and Georgia. He had fought on the side of the American army against renegade Creeks fleeing to join Seminoles in the Florida Territory, and to the south of Alabama.

However, Opothle Yahola opposed settlers flooding the territory and strived to quell it as much as possible. He had attempted to purchase land in East Texas to which his people could freely migrate, and even personally traveled there in pursuit of the deal, but did not meet success. Resigned to stay in Alabama and fight, he stood against the violence government policies had inspired, and instead believed in diplomatic compromises. He had accepted that Muskogis could not defeat the United States government and sought to lead his people to learn ways to live in accord with their settler neighbors.

❖ ❖ ❖

TUSKENEA ROSE IN RESPONSE to Opothle Yahola's mixed message, but stood on the opposite side of the fire from his adversary. Opothle Yahola sat down.

"My thanks to the great warrior for his graceful sentiments," Tuskenea began. "He is a leader of the Muskogi in times of righteousness, when he is in tune with our fathers' and our grandfathers' ways. But in these troubled times, he is wrong. The white man, friendly or evil, must be banished from the land of the Muskogis. Our Cherokee brethren to the east and north have not been able to combat the white man's greed. We seem destined for the same fate if we do not fight, and fight with force." He raised a clenched fist and shook it.

"The invader cannot be satisfied. Opothle Yahola is wrong. He says we will perish if we do not follow the white man's ways. I insist we will perish if we do."

❖ ❖ ❖

TUSKENEA WAS INDEED the son of Big Warrior of Tuckabatchi, tribal name Tustanagee Thlucco, the long-time Head Chief of the Muskogi Nation. Tuskenea succeeded his father upon the latter's death in the mid-twenties, but was soon deposed upon discovery he was descended from the wrong maternal lineage, which determined place among Muskogi power. Restored as chieftain by his loyal followers, he was impeached again, and then a third time, and had been fighting since to regain the seat he claimed was rightfully his. Most of his allies were of the Lower Creek towns of Euchee and others along the Chattahoochee, including warring renegades against which Opothle Yahola fumed.

❖ ❖ ❖

THE COUNCIL FIRE SMOLDERED deep into the night as discussion of many current problems dominated. Opothle Yahola and Tuskenea held their anger, though both seethed while leading debates to promote their respective points. Menawa sat with an eye on each, prepared to stymie further violent outbursts and threats.

Little was agreed on this night, or at other Councils concerning white settlers, renegade warriors committing criminal acts, and that cowardly law of the Washington government so affecting the Muskogi Nation.

Many fires would burn before those questions were resolved.

Chapter 4

The Falls on the Tallapoosa River, April, 1836

"**MIGHTY FINE HOUND** you have there, Mr., uh …"

"Brayke, Mr. Gerald, Kaspar Brayke, sir."

"Ah, yes, to be sure, Mr. Brayke. Sorry. A fine hound indeed." Perley Gerald continued to admire Rube lapping water from a pan on the porch of the trading post. "Don't reckon I've seen a red hound before, not quite that red for certain."

"My thanks, Mr. Gerald, for your generosity of this cool water." Kaspar tipped toward his host the dipper from which he drank. "For myself and Rube."

"Rube?"

"For his color. His shade is like that of a ruby stone. But I couldn't name a male hound Ruby. Wouldn't be right. So I shortened it to Rube."

"I say," said Gerald, chuckling, "quite fitting."

"Fine dog, too. He's followed me all the way from Nashville to Charleston, and on over here to Alabama. Never complained once."

Rube finished his refreshment, emptying the pan, and crawled against the porch wall to settle in for a nap.

"You came over from Charleston, you say?" asked Sam Peavy, rocking on the end of the porch. "For what purpose?"

Kaspar gestured toward the construction underway to the south. "Of purpose, I think, to join those fellows. But so far, findings aren't quite as represented to me when I left Charleston."

Kaspar related his adventures on the trails through Georgia and Alabama. He emphasized what he had learned in Milledgeville on the plight of the Creeks and Cherokees in Georgia, and what he was told in Columbus about the Alabama Red Sticks and Euchee rebels. Gerald and Peavy leaned forward when he began his story of the confrontation with the Red Stick party.

"Son, you were lucky," said Gerald when Kaspar concluded. "If those fellows had pegged you as a hunter or a local farmer instead of the traveling stranger you were, you mightn't 'ave been passed through. They can be mean chaps, for shore."

"You must've did right by 'em," added Sam Peavy. "Else they just might've took yore scalp. Yore dog's, too."

Kaspar's mind had strayed. "Who was the young lady what almost run me over out yonder?"

"Ha," chuckled Gerald. "Couldn't help but notice, could you? Pretty lady. That was Anna Murph. She and her folk live 'bout fourteen, fifteen miles upriver. Fine people. Been there maybe twenty-five years now, I guess. Her pappy and uncle were the first whites here, they say."

"She looked mighty peeved. Another step by me and her horse would've trampled me flat."

"Yeah," said Gerald, "Anna has a temper all right." He pointed to the construction site. "Same as what concerns you has her mad. She finished getting her goods from Melissa inside here and came back out to palaver more about what them people's up to."

"What are they up to?"

"Don't rightly know yet, but we think it has to do with removing the rest of the Creeks from around here and sending them out west. By force if necessary."

"They sold me on most of that in Charleston. 'Cept for the force part."

"Half of Anna's family are Muskogi Creek, so the more she talked and watched and fretted, the madder she got."

"She's Creek herself? I noticed her black hair."

"Half Creek. Her pa is Saul Murph, one of them two brothers what first settled a ways up the river. Her ma was a Muskogi princess of some sort, from a village just south of here. She got kilt somehow in the bad doings back in 'fourteen when Anna was but a babe."

"So she's convinced the army means harm to her folks?"

Gerald's face twisted. "Well, I don't think entirely yet, but she don't like the signs. I don't, either. Anyhow, the more she fumed and stared at that thing, whatever it is, the madder she was." He chuckled again. "Finally, she just stomped her foot, almost cussed, which ain't like her, jumped on her horse, and took off. Ho, Mr. Brayke, I'm glad you could get out of her way. Anna's a terror, all right, when she gets riled."

❖ ❖ ❖

ANNA MURPH TROTTED HER HORSE into the midst of a cluster of cabins, barns, and sheds, across a log and plank bridge spanning a brook, and reined up in front of a stable.

"Phonso, will you take care of Toti for me?" She petitioned a red-haired boy of about ten standing in front of the stables.

"You betcha, Anna." The boy grabbed the horse's bridle as Anna dismounted and lifted off her saddle bag.

"Thanks, pal. I'm obliged." She knew Alphonso, her favorite young cousin, would agree to help. Phonso loved horses and never missed a chance to care for them, whether to curry, feed, exercise, or throw down hay. Besides, he worshiped Anna and couldn't refuse her requests.

Anna walked through the dogtrot of the largest cabin and dropped her bag on the kitchen table. She exited the opposite end and headed toward a middle-aged man repairing a fence across the way.

"Pa," she began when she reached him, "do you know what's going on down at the falls next to Mr. Gerald's place?"

"Not entirely, Honey, but I've heard rumors. You just come from down there?"

"Yeah, Pa. Looks as if the army is building some kind of stockade or a fort or something. Mr. Gerald believes it has to do with them capturing Muskogis so they can make 'em live out west somewhere according to President Jackson's law."

Her father scowled. "Black-hearted Jackson!" He cursed. "That sonafabitch already killed too many Indians. I guess he wants to wipe us all out."

Anna usually grinned at her father's reference to himself as an Indian, but today it went unnoticed. Saul Murph wasn't Muskogi, but had lived among them for the past twenty-six years. He and younger brother Cal had traveled from their father's farm in Virginia in search of ideal virgin acreage on which to settle, and found this place on a low bluff overlooking the Tallapoosa River in 1810.

Although the area's first whites, they found friendship among the Muskogis as they built a cabin and a barn, and planted crops. They thrived, Saul being an expert farmer like his father in Virginia, and younger brother Cal a crack hunter. Saul married Soosquana, a Muskogi princess from the downriver warrior town of Talisi, and Anna was born the day after New Year's of 1814.

Andrew Jackson's campaign to subdue and punish the Upper Creek Red Sticks stalled for the winter, but resumed with spring and the arrival of reinforcements. Late March of that year saw the climactic battle at Cholocco Litabixi, a horseshoe-shaped bend in the Tallapoosa. The peninsula hosted a large encampment of Muskogi warriors and their families, approximately nine hundred of whom Jackson's army wiped out. In that fight's aftermath, a patrol of the general's militia searching for Red Stick stragglers threatened the Murph compound, firing a wild musket shot that killed Soosquana. Anna was less than three months old.

Six months earlier, Cal married Adelin Holman, the daughter of a settler the brothers met on the trail farther up in Alabama on their trek from Virginia. At the death of Soosquana, Adelin, already a doting aunt, assumed the nurturing of baby Anna. Saul eventually took another Muskogi bride, Belle, who became a cherished stepmother for Anna and had given her a half sister and two half brothers. Meanwhile, Cal and Adelin had become parents themselves, two boys and two girls.

"Pa," asked Anna, "do you think they'll come here looking for Muskogi people? Mr. Gerald says they're calling them renegades."

Saul Murph spat angrily. He paused several seconds to regain control. "Baby girl," he finally said, "if they do, we'll fight the devilish swine. They ain't taking one citizen away from this community."

Chapter 5

The Executive Mansion, Washington, D.C., April, 1836

The Act. **PRESIDENT ANDREW JACKSON** signed the Indian Removal Act into law on May 28, 1830, after it was passed in controversy two days previously by the United States Congress. Since inauguration, Jackson had advocated its passage, an idea first proposed by some colonial founders. George Washington and Thomas Jefferson championed a program of cultural conversion to Americanize the 'Five Civilized Tribes' of the southeast —- Muskogi (Creek), Cherokee, Chickasaw, Choctaw, and Seminole. Otherwise, they feared, American expansion would push them off their lands or annihilate them altogether. Most settlers and politicians of states sheltering the Five Tribes favored removal.

Jackson proposed Indian removal in his first State of the Union address, that of 1829. The bill did not enjoy smooth sailing, and took another year to pass. A strong contingent in Congress, bolstered by clergy and social activists throughout the nation, opposed the law. Advocates accused opponents of hypocrisy since northern tribes had previously been stripped of ancestral lands with many driven to virtual extinction.

New Jersey Senator Theodore Frelinghuysen and Congressman David Crockett of Tennessee led the opposition. After a long, bitter fight, their efforts suffered defeat. The Senate approved the Act in April by a vote of twenty-eight to nineteen. On May 26 the House followed in a squeaker, 101 to 97.

Implementation of the Act proved an even tougher fight. The State of Georgia had been attempting to take Cherokee lands and evict the natives since 1802, by legislative and illegal means. Several lawsuits and controversial treaties preceded the Removal Act, the passage of which intensified animosities. The conflict reached a peak in the winter of 1832 when the United States Supreme Court, led by Chief Justice John Marshall, decided a case argued before them in favor of the Cherokee Nation. The judgment fazed President Jackson not at all, as he ignored the decision and defiantly continued his policies.

The Choctaws centered in Mississippi complied with the Act peacefully and within months of enactment. A treaty ceded all their lands in exchange for safe passage to new settlements west of the Mississippi. The Chickasaws also agreed to go, but had yet to abandon their homeland pending legal entanglements. The other Nations were resisting, defiantly and often violently. They would not bend to the dictates of an oppressive, illegal government.

No Indian factions were fighting implementation of the Act more fiercely than the Upper Creek Red Sticks and the Euchee rebels of southeast Alabama.

"GENTLEMEN," spoke President Andrew Jackson in his gravelly voice, "the time is dire overdue to move those damn savages from the south of our country. We've dawdled with them long enough, do you not agree?"

"Yes, sir, fully," answered Lewis Cass, Jackson's Secretary of War. "I continue to push toward final resolution, as I have since you were kind enough to place me in this office." Cass, a former brigadier general in the unpleasantries with Britain in 1812-1814, had formerly served as governor of the Michigan Territory. He had been appointed to that governorship by President Madison in 1813 as a reward for his service, and held the post until drafted to his current position by President Jackson in 1831. He had since been Jackson's spearhead in his Indian removal policy.

The President strode across the room, pained by arthritis born of wounds collected long ago in battles and duels. He stared down at Vice President Van Buren, seated in an overstuffed chair swirling his brandy snifter.

"Martin, what should be done next?"

"Mr. President, that is a decision for your vast knowledge and experience. Wherever you lead is surely the wise direction."

Jackson stopped pacing and glared at Van Buren. "Damn, Martin. I'm near the end of my time in this office, and I affirm my refusal to stand again for election. If I didn't think you were the best man to sustain and extend my policies, especially concerning the national bank and the southern Indian tribes, you would not have my blessing to succeed to the Presidency."

"Yes, sir, and I'm most grateful, sir."

Jackson scoffed. "Gratitude is inadequate, Martin, and is a sentiment for weaklings. If you are to be a great President, you must be direct and decisive, and you will certainly be President since the opposition party is in shambles. And frankly, my endorsement carries a lot of weight."

"Yes, sir, I ..."

"Stop 'yes-sirring' me, Martin. Hell, after the November election I'll be yes-sirring you, and it's time you got used to it. This is a tough job, and I didn't get where I am by being weaselly and mealy. You have to face down your opponents. Ha, just ask Calhoun." Jackson grinned then took a deep breath and a sip from his brandy. His reference to John C. Calhoun of South Carolina, his Vice President during his first term, concerned bitter disputes between the two over a number of issues. Consequently, Jackson replaced Calhoun with New York sophisticate and loyal ally Van Buren as his running mate when standing for reelection in 1832. "Now, out with your view on the Indian problem."

"Well, sir, I certainly agree we've tolerated the current situation long enough. Too long, I must say. The tribes have had five years to comply with the dictates of Congress, so I think we must insist on increased cooperation from them."

"Uh huh." Jackson sighed. He turned to Cass. "Lewis?"

"Sir, I had another dispatch from Governor Schley in Milledgeville this morning." Cass shifted his large, rotund frame to a different position in his chair. "The plight of settlers to the west of there, especially over into Alabama, hasn't improved. For certain, hostilities from Creek lands are occurring with more frequency."

"Those are no longer Creek lands, Mr. Cass," sneered the President. "Haven't been since 'thirty-two when the Cherokees and Creeks relinquished all claims of authority. Officially anyway, by treaty, to comply with our Act of 'thirty. The government of the United States is the only authority over those beasts, and they must obey."

"I agree, sir," said Cass. "Please pardon my misspeak. Unlike the Creeks, the Cherokees are peaceful enough, though stubborn. They pretend to be civilized and have now filed another lawsuit. Too, they keep appealing the decisions against them to court after court."

Jackson laughed. "Yeah, does them no good, though, even when they win a judgment. Like I told Chief Justice Marshall when his Supreme Court sided with the Cherokees against the State of Georgia. 'Sir,' I said to him, 'you've made your decision. Now let me see you enforce it.'" He laughed again, pleased with himself.

"However, sir," continued Lewis Cass after sharing the levity, "the Creeks are seeking a different, more violent solution than the Cherokees. Their behavior is increasingly hostile, especially around the Tallapoosa and Chattahoochee Rivers."

"Ah, yes," said Jackson. "Those damn Creek Red Stick savages. Wiped out most of 'em myself in 'fourteen. My mistake was failing to obliterate the pack of 'em. But currently, my good man, what are we about down there?"

"Mr. President," announced Cass, squirming his bulk to a straighter posture, "following your outline and directive of a month ago, my department has instituted new and forceful steps. I have ordered a half dozen or more outposts to be established west of the Chattahoochee River, most between there and the Tallapoosa, for collecting as many Creeks as possible. From those, we plan to shepherd the Indians to the Indian territories, where many of their ilk have gone before, according to law. We are actively recruiting civilian agents to supplement the army in executing the transfer."

"Are we sending more regular army troops? Is there a need for them?"

"I advise against it for the present, sir. Governor Clay of Alabama, in several missives, has requested regiments to be dispatched to bolster his state's militia units. I denied his pleas, sir, as I have those from the Texas militias opposing Mexican atrocities."

"Your reasoning, Lewis?

"Yes, sir. No doubt additional forces would further facilitate removal, but I and advisers in my office believe that would be counterproductive."

"How so?"

"Sir, you are aware of the practice down there of dishonest land speculators defrauding many native property qualifiers and stealing their land grants."

"Quite right. An unfortunate turn. The lands should be acquired by legal means." With a sneer, Jackson added, "If possible."

Cass continued. "It is believed if Governor Clay had more federal troops at his bidding, it would encourage more fraud by further intimidation of those Indians thus far successful in hanging onto their land. Seems best to allow Governor Clay's town militias to play out the process."

"Hmmm, very good, Mr. Cass. I will accede to your good judgment. Please continue to pursue that strategy with diligence, as long as it seems feasible. Your efforts are appreciated and will be duly honored." Jackson stroked his chin. "But I must ask, Lewis, what nearby forces can we marshal if the need arises? Seems to me we may be vulnerable and should strengthen our hand against the resistance."

"Yes, sir, quite right. The army is deficit down there for the moment. But I've alerted General Jesup ..."

"Quartermaster General Jesup? For what?"

"Yes, sir. He's eager for some field duty as opposed to sitting around in Washington. I alerted him he might be needed for a command in Creek country. I must say, he seemed most pleasured at the prospect. Also, General Winfield Scott is in North Florida suppressing the Seminole uprising. We can marshal forces under both commanders within days and send them into the fray in Alabama and Georgia."

"Ah, yes. Then I suggest, Lewis, you ready what sources are necessary to monitor and control the situation. And to mobilize militias as well. More citizen units may be needed."

"Very well, sir. Immediately."

"Order Scott to Georgia as soon as he cleans up that mess with the damn Seminoles, which I wager will be handily done." Jackson scoffed. "He's only dealing with a bunch of runaway, cowardly Creeks anyway, led by some sonafabitch by the name of Osca ... uh, Ossi..."

"Osceola, sir," corrected Cass.

"Uh, whatever." Jackson turned again to Van Buren. "Martin, I direct you to stay abreast of developments. You certainly would be advantaged to see this situation abated before the election."

"Yes, sir."

Jackson sniffed at Van Buren. "Now, gentlemen," he continued, "I've asked Senator King to stop by and meet with us."

"King? May I ask why, sir?" Posed Van Buren. "He has no truck with our views."

"Because, Martin, King is one of the Senate's most powerful members and he represents the State of Alabama. It's true Senator King is often at odds with the policies of this administration, but we agree on one vital issue."

"Ah, yes," mused Lewis Cass, "the Indian removal question."

"Correct," said Jackson. "Senator King is of like mind with us in dealing with those currently savaging his state. I'm consulting him with the confidence he will offer constructive input on the situation."

"Yes, sir. You're quite right, Mr. President."

Jackson threw another scowl at Van Buren. "The senator should arrive any moment, so prepare, gentlemen, to ply his wits. He is an intelligent and learned man, to be sure."

William Rufus King was a native North Carolinian and an alumnus of the University of North Carolina. He gained election to the United States House of Representatives from that state in 1811 when he was only twenty-four, and actually took office more than a month earlier than he was constitutionally eligible by age limitation. He resigned in 1816 to serve as a diplomat in Italy and Russia, then returned to the United States in 1818 to purchase vast acreage in Alabama near Cahawba and build a plantation. Upon Alabama's admission to the Union on December 14, 1819, King was elected as the state's first senator, and had served successfully and powerfully since.

In December, 1835, when John Tyler resigned from the Senate and as its president pro tempore, the duties of that position fell unofficially to Senator William Rufus King. Washington lawmakers believed he would be elected for the record when Congress reconvened in July.

A tap on the door signaled the entrance of an orderly. "Mr. President," he announced, "Senator William R. King begs your indulgence."

"Show him in, Patrick," muttered Jackson.

A tall, wiry, middle-aged man with a high forehead, large hawkish nose, and subdued chin glided through the door and extended his hand. "Good day, Mr. President," he chirped, "I trust you are well today?"

"Welcome, Senator, I'm happy you could accept my invitation." Jackson turned to acknowledge the presence of Van Buren and Cass, who stood and greeted King with handshakes and words of cheer. "Please sit, sir. Would you care to share a brandy with us?"

After a few minutes of idle banter, Jackson broached the meeting's topic. "Senator, you know of the crisis in your home state regarding the Creek populace, and I believe you are in accord it must be resolved soon."

"Yes, Mr. President, I humbly agree."

"I would like for Secretary Cass, as my point man, to brief you on his department's latest developments, and then I would like your ideas." Jackson gestured to Cass. "Lewis?"

For the next twenty minutes, Cass laid out his strategies, outlined developments to date, and projected a rosy future for the southern states and for the Indians following their migration to western lands.

"Sir," concluded the Secretary, "the President, the Vice President, and my department all believe this is the most profitable strategy for all concerned. Do you subscribe, sir?"

King stood erect from leaning over the maps on the table, and drew a full breath. "I do, Mr. Secretary. My state seems to be entering a period of increased conflict, which cannot abide."

Jackson spoke for the first time since yielding to Cass. "We've been patient, tolerant, and generous, but there remains scant confidence the main of those savages can coexist with the fine Americans settling and building that section of our nation."

"I agree, sir," said King, assuming a somber tone. "Just this morning, I received dire news from my state capital." Renewed attentiveness swept over his three companions. "There have been two additional murders at the hands of the Red Stick pretenders, and another farmstead burned to the ground. I tell you, Mr. President, we must act, and act with strength, by military force if warranted. You and Secretary Cass have the total support and cooperation of myself, Governor Clay, and the Alabama state government."

Chapter 6

The Falls on the Tallapoosa River, April, 1836

ONE MORNING, three weeks before the arrival of Kaspar Brayke, Perley Gerald, working inside his building, heard horsemen coming. He walked onto the porch to watch a double column of militia ride through his gate and pull up inside the compound. The officer at the head walked his horse to the edge of the porch, where he dismounted and strode up the steps to extend his hand.

"Good morning, Perley."

"'Morning, John. Not often we see the troops massed up 'round here."

"Yes. Strange times we're having. I have orders to set up government business here at the falls."

"Sir? What business?"

John Brodnax, the captain of the local Tallassee Guards militia company, gestured to his men, which appeared to number about thirty, approximately half a company. "We received orders yesterday by way of a rider from Fort Mitchell." He reached into his shirt and extracted two documents, one sealed with embossed wax. "These are my orders, and this is a warrant for you." He extended the sealed packet to Gerald. "It commands you to let us establish a camp on a portion of your land and construct necessary facilities. A contingent of regulars will soon arrive to take command of the military duties."

Gerald took the document and turned it over twice in his hands. Clearly puzzled, he looked up at Brodnax, then broke the wax seal. He took a long time to read the warrant before again raising his head.

"John, this says you're to establish a post for collecting Muskogi Creeks willing to travel to the Indian Territory."

"Yes, sir, those are my orders. Congress has provided land out there for the Indians."

"Some Muskogis have already gone, thinking it a good move." Gerald's voice held a hint of protest. "Most others are happy here and don't plan to go. As I understand the law, they can stay if they choose."

"Yes, sir, if they're landowners. But there has been violence against citizens by some renegades."

"Are not those 'renegades' also citizens?" Asked Gerald, not attempting to disguise his irritation.

"No, sir, they're Indians. And those bad 'uns are criminals to the United States government, and cannot be tolerated."

Gerald's tone turned cold. "I see, sir. Nevertheless, I fear you will find few Muskogis willing to depart."

"That will be determined, Perley."

Gerald's suspicions rose, accompanied by a bit of anger. "President Jackson's dastardly law, and treaties since, granted land to each Muskogi family. They have the right to live on that land."

"That's true, if they own where they live."

"Many did, but having no business heed they've been cheated of their holdings by white land grabbers."

"Cheated? You term them land grabbers?"

"Whiskey and gambling ruses are hard to resist. Many of these people do not know the ways of American dealings, and are especially open to crooked schemes."

"Perley, I'm mindful of some such doings, but I have my orders. You are my good neighbor, but we seem to stand on opposite sides of this question. I dare say I deem the situation more serious than do you. We have to address the Indian problem."

The door opened and an attractive young woman walked onto the porch. She stood beside Gerald and glared at Captain Brodnax.

His mouth ajar, the captain touched the brim of his hat toward the woman. "Uh," he stammered, "uh, ma'am."

"My wife Melissa, John, a recent arrival from New England," said Gerald. He didn't bother to introduce Brodnax to her, hoping to insult him. "I don't believe you've had the pleasure."

Captain Brodnax recovered from the awkward moment. "Pleased to meet you, ma'am. So, Perley, I should be about my business." He studied the surroundings, rotating his gaze around the vista twice, finally pointing to the pasture near the far south edge of the bluff. "I believe, sir, we shall locate over there."

"What if I refuse?"

"You have no choice. That is the authority of the warrant."

Gerald squeezed the paper he still held. "I see. And you get to opt any plot of ground you choose? Even my prime grazing land?"

"Pretty much so. This enterprise will be to your benefit, and to those good American citizens here who have suffered amongst Indian violence for years. We aim to make these parts peaceful and safe for Americans, something they haven't rightly been since General Jackson opened the territory years back."

❖ ❖ ❖

TWENTY-TWO YEARS HAD PASSED since the massacre. A scant one hundred Muskogi warriors, perhaps fewer, had survived Cholocco Litabixi, the Horseshoe, and many of those had not weathered the hardships that followed. Approximately nine hundred Red Stick warriors perished. More than two decades later, the memory of the slaughtered burned hot within the souls of their sons and daughters.

Andrew Jackson, the American general from Tennessee who had led his forces against Chief Menawa at Cholocco Litabixi, later accepted Chief William Weatherford's surrender of all Upper Creek warriors. One of his first actions upon inauguration in 1829 was to push for the banishment of all native Indians from lands east of the Mississippi River. The United States Congress adopted most of his proposals and placed them into law in 1830.

The odor of spent gunpowder had barely abated from the Horseshoe in 1814 when whites stormed the Territory. The promise of rich farmland and ample resources enticed settlers to carve out farms and communities, even though the Muskogis would own the land for almost two more decades. Settlers initially feared no resistance from the defeated Creeks, who coexisted in grudging peace. Then came the Indian Removal Act and the army's mission to enforce it.

Raids throughout the region began to plague farmhouses, crops, and supply caravans. In the minds of young, virile Creeks, as well as militant tribal elders, the objective was to drive the white man from the sacred ground of the Muskogi and return to the times no man owned the soil, but every man respected it. Most realized that as an impossible goal, but angry warriors at least meant to taste revenge for their forefathers and for the theft of their lands.

Though raiding parties avoided confrontation with army troops, what would later be remembered as the Second Creek War developed into a dangerous time. To protect vulnerable settlers carving lives from the wilderness in building America, authorities decreed steps must be taken to enforce the law.

THE LAW, AND THE UNITED STATES government's Indian Removal Act, had arrived at Perley Gerald's trading post.

"I see them fellas are still at it, Perley," drawled Sam Peavy as he dragged himself up the steps to the front porch.

"Yep. Been watching 'em all week," replied Gerald from his rocking chair.

Peavy studied for a long minute the construction work in progress across the way at the edge of the bluff. A company of regular army had arrived a few days ago to join the Tallassee Guards in the endeavor. "Ya find out 'zactly what they aim doing with whatever thar building?" He asked before settling into a second rocker at the edge of the porch.

"Captain in charge of the regulars claims they're the forward troop to set up a depot here," replied the proprietor.

"Depot? Is 'at what 'at is?" Sam spat a stream from his chaw off the porch.

"Don't know. He said something 'bout keeping up them renegades they catch what been causing so much trouble."

Sam rocked for pensive moments. "You think they're sho' nuff here to make the Indians leave? To send 'em on their way out west?"

"Not all. Just the ones making trouble or unsettled in. The peaceful ones don't have to go, 'cording to all they've told us. The treaties say so. John Highland says the Creeks fitting in with the new settlements won't have trouble."

Thirty-four year-old John Highland McKenzie, his wife Elizabeth, their two sons and two daughters, John's two brothers, and a number of slaves, had migrated from Lancaster, South Carolina, in February. On the arduous trip, the party of nearly one hundred had endured terribly cold temperatures —- zero degrees was recorded in Montgomery during the time — and a measles epidemic affecting the slaves. Forced to set up camp somewhere in the Georgia wilderness for two weeks, the group headed by Elizabeth nursed the patients until they were well enough to continue.

McKenzie, on a previous visit to Tallassee, had bought his plantation site south of the falls on the east side of the river. He had once planned to locate farther west in Wilcox County near the Alabama River, but had been introduced to the Tallapoosa River area by a friend living near Montgomery. He opted for the Tallassee location, which he judged more suited to his needs and desires.

The new log house Kaspar Brayke had passed below the bluffs had been built by John McKenzie. The dwelling was meant to be temporary until he was able to build a substantial plantation mansion for his family. McKenzie had inadvertently placed the structure astride the trail the Indian population traveled on their way to Perley Gerald's trading post and other destinations north of the Muskogi villages along the river. Instead of veering around the house, the Indians simply marched right through the dogtrot through way since it sat directly atop their usual path. The McKenzies, particularly Elizabeth, at first frightened by the intrusion, soon adapted.

John McKenzie quickly became close friends with Perley Gerald, perhaps because they shared the same tolerance toward the Muskogis. The Indians immediately trusted McKenzie as they did Gerald. They had few other allies among whites in the Tallassee area.

Perley Gerald had become the wealthiest man in the region, and one of the wisest. His counsel was sought by Indians and whites alike, and he garnered such respect that he often arbitrated minor disputes between factions. He briefly belonged to the Tallassee Guards, a loosely organized militia of settlers. The Guards were the only local semblance of law enforcement. Gerald's role had been as a liaison with the Creeks, especially the peaceful ones at the Muskogi capital of Tukabatchi, and as an emissary to the state government in Montgomery. However, as hostilities threatened in the wake of

Indian removal and he found his sympathies at odds with many locals, his participation in militia affairs had cooled. He resigned from the Guard. Retaining his status as the area's most respected citizen, he assumed an unofficial position of peacekeeper.

"Lots of them Creeks've been cheated," said Sam to Perley, staring at the construction activity across the way. "They's plenty mad, you know. Reckon that thing they're building's gonna mean more trouble?"

"Could be. But if they're only after the bad bucks, and will leave the good folks be, the situation might improve. Let's hope that's what they're about."

Unfortunately, the situation would not soon improve.

Chapter 7

Near Black's Store, Chambers County, May 5, 1836

HIRAN DAVIS PAUSED FROM HOEING hip-high corn, lifted his straw hat, and wiped his forehead with his sleeve. This is going to be a good crop, he mused, not like last year's disaster.

The winter of 1835 had been unusually cold. Snow covered the ground for several weeks as far south as Columbus, and ice clogged the Chattahoochee, Tallapoosa, and all the smaller streams much of the winter. Due to late planting and sparse growth, harvests had been meager for the few settlers who had established farms years back, but almost nonexistent for the many newcomers who had recently flooded the area from Georgia and the Carolinas. As much as the whites had suffered from crop failures, however, native Muskogis who had lost their lands to speculators and swindlers were devastated. Many faced near starvation, a condition that further stoked growing tensions between whites and Indians.

Davis's gaze dropped from the fluffy clouds floating by to the woods across his field. He briefly admired the lush spring growth until his eye caught a movement among the trees. As he strained to focus, a figure materialized. It was an Indian, whose painted face and long-barreled musket did not appear friendly.

Suspicious, Hiram eased along a plowed furrow toward his house, continuing to observe the man, obviously a Creek, and probably a Red Stick. As he watched, another man joined the first, and quickly several more. Davis walked faster, then as the band started toward him, he dropped his hoe and broke into a run.

"Alice," he yelled, "Frank, Joseph, get everyone into the house!"

A woman, with two small girls at her feet, stepped from the doorway. Another girl, barely a teenager, followed.

"Hiram, what be the trouble?" The lady pleaded to her husband running toward her. She screamed when she spied his pursuers.

Hiram panicked further when he saw several other Indians converging on the house from behind it. His two toddler sons, playing in the front yard, looked up in confusion. The two older teens, Frank and Joseph, sprinted from the side field, where they had been planting cotton.

"Get inside!" Hiram yelled. "Everybody! We're being attacked!"

Neither Frank nor Joseph reached the house. One fell from a musket shot. When the brother stopped to help, a warrior tackled him to the ground and attempted to pin his arms. A companion jumped atop the rolling tandem and slashed the blade of a large knife across the boy's throat. Both assailants howled in triumph as spurting blood bathed them bright red.

Alice managed to herd her other five children back into the cabin and held the door open for her husband. He and four Red Sticks arrived simultaneously. Hiram had no chance.

Alice screamed in terror as she attempted to close the door against the Indians. Behind her a musket shot blasted above the furor. The attackers exploded through the door, overrunning Alice, grabbing the four little ones, and wrenching the musket from the teenage girl. The back of a man's hand slammed against the girl's face, while the other hand grasped a fistful of her hair. He dragged her out the door and threw her to the ground, where a frenzy of Red Sticks already hacked away at Mrs. Davis and the younger children with knives and axes.

The last to die, the girl first had to witness the massacre of her family. She shrieked at the sight and glared wild-eyed at the butchers while cursing their butchery. An ax blow to the back of her head interrupted her final invective in mid-scream.

Their human slaughter done, the dozen-plus warriors raised weapons and voices in unrestrained celebration. A Red Stick straddled each of the Davis parents and sliced scalps from their heads. They held the trophies high as they squealed in triumph. Cohorts busied themselves mutilating the children's bodies by hacking off their heads, which they threw across the dusty yard.

A leader of the pack signaled for a semi-pause among the celebrants. "Gather all food," he ordered in Muskogean. "It is rightly ours, not of the invading whites."

Some of the men had already begun packing as much grain and stored vegetables as they could carry. Others chased chickens and hogs around the yard. The family milk cow, horse, and plow mule were soon harnessed to be led away. Household goods and trinkets were pilfered and the house vandalized.

The pig chase was meeting with little success. One man had an idea. He picked up the headless body of one of the small murdered girls and threw it among the pack of swine. "This will stop them," he declared as the pigs greedily attacked the gruesome morsel, "and should fatten them some. White man's blood will flavor our bacon." He couldn't restrain his laughter and that of his fellows as they moved to capture the animals and lash their feet. They then suspended the pigs upside down from sapling poles for transport.

The attack, massacre, and pillage had started and concluded inside of an hour. The band of Red Sticks carried their treasures and led the livestock away from the Davis farm, heading south.

Above, framed by scattered fluffy clouds, a flock of buzzards already circled.

THE SAME MORNING, a like faction of angry Creeks fell upon the Jones farm a few miles south, near the Macon County line. Like the Davises, the Jones family until recently had enjoyed a congenial relationship with their native neighbors. Even with the widespread land grabs and privations, they still felt little fear, and worked their modest farm in peace.

The Jones cabin nestled within a forest grove of oaks and hickories, with the barn in an adjacent clearing and the fields immediately beyond. When the attackers emerged from the woods, the family's surprise was as stark as their terror. The carnage lasted only minutes.

When the Red Stick band departed the ransacked and looted farm, every member of the Jones family hung from trees ringing the cabin. A different tree for each corpse, some bodies suspended by tethered ankles, others by arms and shoulders.

A sense of peril permeated the region as word spread of the fates of the Davis and Jones families. Other attacks also were reported, though none as gruesome. Panicked settlers all over southern Chambers County and northern Macon gathered their kin and livestock, and flocked toward LaFayette, the seat of Chambers. There they took refuge in the courthouse and began to build barricades to protect the town.

Most of the terrified citizens agreed an all-out war with renegade Creeks had surely arrived.

Chapter 8

Falls of the Tallapoosa River, May, 1836

AFTER TWO WEEKS OF OBSERVATION from afar, Kaspar walked the hundred yards from Gerald's establishment to view the army's project up close, and to report finally to Captain Brodnax. A small column of regulars had arrived days earlier to assume command and to supplement the militia personnel. Kaspar was as curious as he was concerned about the military's assignment, but he thought he preferred to consult with Brodnax, he being a local citizen, rather than the army commander.

The stockade construction wasn't as extensive as it appeared from a distance. The structure of four- to six-inch diameter logs, abutted tightly together, measured no more than fifty feet square. The wall was only eight feet high and not particularly well built, but each vertical log tapered to a sharp point at the top. A small cabin attached to the outside of the south wall, out of sight from Gerald's place. Kaspar would learn later the cabin served as headquarters for the mission and housing for the military officers. A rickety guard tower hovered a few feet above the west wall, between it and the bluff. Past the cabin, several neat rows of bivouac tents quartered military enlisted, civilian agents, and laborers. A rope corral just north of the enclosure penned several dozen horses and mules. A line of wagons paralleled one side of the corral.

In the summer heat, sweat streamed from bodies toiling to finish construction. Civilian and military workers strained and grimaced as they hauled logs and other materials and fashioned them into place. The men had stripped to shirts, hats, and pants, all of which reeked of soaking perspiration. The soldiers wore white but grimy cotton uniform shirts and coarse, off-white trousers. Their pants and riding boots were covered with mud, as the dirt encrusting them had absorbed torrents of sweat.

Cavalrymen not involved in construction topped their shirts with the standard blue tunics and dual white leather shoulder belts crossing at the chest and fastened with heavy brass buckles. The belts culminated at points on either side, one holding a scabbard with a bayonet and the other a leather ammunition box containing composite cartridges, extra powder and flints, and gun cleaning supplies. The shoulders of each officer sported epaulets. A saber, instead of a bayonet, hung from the left side.

"I'm looking for Captain Brodnax," Kaspar informed the first man he encountered, a civilian worker hefting an ax.

The man eyed him suspiciously then pointed. "Over there," he gruffed.

"Captain Brodnax," greeted Kaspar as he neared the officer and offered his hand, "I'm Kaspar Brayke."

"Yes?"

"I came over from Charleston, arriving a few days ago. I'm interested in your operation."

"Oh? Then you came to enlist as an agent? What are your qualifications, sir? Are you familiar with the ways of hostile lands and hostile peoples?"

"Hostile?"

"Could be. Some young bucks around here certainly are hostile, and we don't know what awaits us on the road. Thus, you must be adept at thwarting trouble. I assume you are an experienced man of the wilderness, having tramped all the way from the Carolina coast."

"Yes, sir, I must say I am. I've spent my days in the woods, am more than adequate with my rifle, can sit a horse when I have to, and pride myself in holding truck against most men. Yes, sir, I'm certain I could handle your task."

"Then you are most welcome, and we shall be happy to have you. Shorthanded we are, so we need all the good help we can get. You're joining a noble mission."

"Perhaps. The agency in Charleston convinced me to come over. I did, but I need it straight before I commit to whatever you're doing."

"We're carrying out our orders."

"Which are?"

"Surely you can see the need, sir. We're commissioned to escort Creek dissenters to the Indian Territory."

"Are those some of the dissenters?" Asked Kaspar, pointing to a tight clutch of Indians huddled before a lean-to at the edge of the woods. Three women and an aged man were the only adults in evidence. Several small children played close by.

"To be sure. They're among the first we've collected. We should have enough within a few weeks to ship away the first progression."

"Are the Indians asking to be collected?"

A regular army officer strolled from behind Brodnax. He sniffed with an air of authority. "I can answer that question, sir." He looked at Brodnax. "Who have we here, Captain?"

"This is Mr. Kaspar Brayke, sir. Mr. Brayke, may I present Major Basil Elliot? He is in command of the company of regulars. Major, Mr. Brayke has traveled all the way from Charleston to enlist as a removal agent."

"Well now, congratulations, Mr. Brayke." He reached to shake hands. "Happy to have you."

Kaspar nodded. "Sir. Now, about the natives agreeing to be collected and shuttled west to some foreign soil?"

"Yes, of course," said Elliot with a huff. "Most have no choice. They no longer have a home here, as it is with that family," he nodded toward the lean-to, "or they are not abiding as presentable citizens."

"I see, Major. And for that they must be led away?"

"So holds the law. The President means the Act to be enforced. That's the directive from Congress that says the Indians are entitled to land west of the Mississippi instead of living here at the detriment of civil progress."

"The dut …"

A clamor erupted from the east road, which led into thick forest, across a deep gulch creek, and on to rich forestland and farmland beyond. Kaspar had crossed the creek at another point on his journey in, but had since explored this road and others for short distances. All activity paused and eyes turned to see a soldier gallop his horse from the woods and head straight for Elliot, Brodnax, and Kaspar.

"Major, sir," panted the rider as he dismounted and saluted, "Corporal Moorer, sir."

"Yes, Corporal?"

"Sergeant Pierce sent me ahead to report. We captured two of the renegade Creeks out near Gantt's farm, from the band that's been threatening Mr. Gantt and his farmhands. Sergeant Pierce and the patrol are hauling them in. Sarge thought you might wish to prepare ahead."

"Very good. Yes, Sergeant Pierce used wise judgment. Thank you, Corporal. Dismissed. Care for your mount." Major Elliot turned to an aide. "Lieutenant, see that the stockade is ready to receive prisoners. Post a guard detail and arrange extra sentries for the night. We don't need any surprises from those damn polecats' friends."

"Yes, sir." The lieutenant scurried away, shouting instructions.

After scanning the grounds, apparently to assure the post's good order, Elliot refocused on Kaspar. "Our stockade's first tenants, Mr. Brayke. The beginning of a successful purge, I trust. Now, we were saying?"

"Yes, sir. I believe I was inquiring into my obligations as a civilian agent attached to your unit, should I choose to join."

"Ah, yes. You are to assist in rounding up Indian families willing to travel, and to arrest those law-breaking bucks causing trouble, such as the foul scamps being brought in today. Then we escort them to western parts yet unfamiliar to me."

"Or to me. Interesting, to be sure." Kaspar shifted his attention to the complex. He had noticed there were considerably fewer civilian workers than had been present when he arrived at Gerald's trading post days earlier. However, additional troops had mustered in. "I meant to inquire of the purpose of the enclosure, but I believe that question has been answered."

"Of course. We expect to encounter a number of belligerents, who must be restrained. We shall do so in that modest stockade. Surely, sir, you must have already heard of devilments they are waging in the region?"

"Some. A most interesting setup, Major."

"Then I take it you're ready to join us as an agent?"

"Well, sir, I'm not quite sure. I'm not convinced I wish to commit to your mission."

"Oh, but, Mr. Brayke, I'm afraid you already have. When you signed on at Charleston, that was your commitment."

Kaspar shook his head with a slight grin. "I don't think so, sir. I only agreed in Charleston to journey over here and see for myself. I signed nothing and swore no pledge. When I decide to throw in with your enterprise, if I should do so, I'll be back. For now, though, I must decline."

Elliot and Brodnax could not disguise their anger. "That is a mistake, Mr. Brayke," blared Brodnax. "One which you shall regret."

"Perhaps, Captain. But for now, I feel no regret whatever. Good day, sirs."

Kaspar touched his hat brim with a respectful nod, turned his back to the two officers, and returned to Gerald's store.

SAM PEAVY SAT ALONE on the trading post porch when Kaspar mounted the steps. Rube, snoozing next to Sam's rocker where Kaspar had bade him stay an hour earlier, raised his head to grunt acknowledgment at his master's return, then dropped back to sleep.

"Well, son, did you sign on with 'em?" asked Sam.

"Nope."

"Hee, hee. I knew you wouldn't."

"Did, huh? How come?"

"I already know you right well, fella. I don't see you taking orders much from other folks. Sure can't see you throwing in with the military." Sam pointed at Rube. "Ha, I 'spect this chap is better at following orders than you."

Kaspar chuckled. "You may be right, Sam."

"You gone join 'em anyhow? In time?"

"I don't know. That's what I came here for, but I'm not liking what I'm finding out. I've been told what that law says, all right, and I know them army fellows gotta do their duty."

"Uh huh."

"Something just don't fit, Sam. I need to know more."

Sam sat rocking for long seconds. Then, "Umm. Reckon you could do with a talk with them brothers up the river what Perley and me told you about."

"Yeah?"

"The Murphs. Smartest folks I know 'bout Indian doings. First white settlers in these parts; I believe we told you 'bout that."

"Yeah, you did. I remember."

"If you'd like, I'll ride up with you. How 'bout we leave with the morning dew? Perley'll be glad to loan you a horse."

"Well, uh, okay. I'm obliged, Sam. Meet you here at first light."

A devious smirk crossed Sam's face. "I 'magine anyhow, son, you'd like another look at somebody what lives up there."

Kaspar puzzled for a few seconds, then he and Sam grinned at each other.

Chapter 9

Tallapoosa River, May, 1836

SHORTLY AFTER DAWN, Kaspar Brayke and Sam Peavy
worked down the slopes above the falls into the river valley and
rode north along the eastern bank. Kaspar thought he had not seen
a more beautiful landscape. The high bluffs below the falls gave way
above them to steep but gentler slopes on both sides, forested with
tall, straight pines and stout, never-touched oaks and hickories.
Plants of a thousand genuses poked their colors through the trees.
Three elongated islands immediately north of the falls splayed the
swift stream and split it into four parallel channels to spill roaring
cascades over the precipice of the fall line onto tiers of granite below.

A mile up, an imposing rock cliff jutted from the west into the
river, effecting a slight bend. As the two riders passed by opposite,
Sam pointed to the projection.

"Some say that looks like an Indian's head. I don't see such
myself."

Kaspar sized up the cliff. "Uh, there might be a nose there.
Maybe. But I can't make out much else."

They approached the next shoals two miles farther along. Sam
directed Kaspar toward a ford.

"We'll cross here," he said. "The ground's smoother on up the
other side, making for a more passable trail. 'Sides, there's fewer
cricks to cross."

Kaspar spurred his horse to follow Sam's through the shallow
water then checked to see that Rube had followed. The swift current
swept Rube a couple of dozen yards downstream, but the dog easily

swam to shore, shook loose a spray of water, and sprinted to catch up and explore new territory. Kaspar was certain such outings as this offered unbounded happiness for the dog. For the hour they had been on the trail this bright morning, Rube had repeatedly run ahead, then back, then into the woods to chase a deer or a squirrel, then back into the lead. No doubt, he'd been missing their travels in the wilderness.

Sam laughed. "Rube seems to be having a spitting good time. Glad you let him come with us."

An excited crow chattered nearby, echoing the protests of the family of wild turkeys they had spooked a short way back. The woods lived with a symphony of creature sounds with every mile traveled. Rube rejoiced in coonhound paradise, and his human associates relished the lushness of nature.

As they rode, Kaspar marveled at Sam's horsemanship and stamina. Whatever the old man's advanced age, and it was considerable, Kaspar gathered Sam to be twice the rider as most men half his years, including himself.

After a three hour leisurely ride, the pair began to pass scattered farms and pastures secluded within thick forest and spaced at least a mile apart. A wide creek flowed from the eastern bank across the way. The creek mouth divided impressive farm sites on the slopes of either side, topped on modest ridges by small compounds of cabins, barns, and corrals.

"They call this place Soosquana," Sam explained. "It ain't a town, just a batch of widespread settlements, but they consider theirselves a community. It's centered on that crick over there and the Murph place over here."

"Yeah? How many people?"

"Oh, a hunnerd or so, I 'spose, maybe more. The name came from Saul Murph's first wife, Anna's mum. She was kilt in 'fourteen by a band of Jackson's militia looking to catch stragglers from the Horseshoe fight."

Kaspar looked incredulous. "You mentioned something 'bout that before. Why'd they kill her?"

"'Cording to the Murphs, pure meanness. Never quite got the details myself. Saul and his brother Cal filed murder charges, but nothing came of it. The law warn't 'bout to prosecute a white man for killing an Indian."

"She was an Indian?"

"Shore."

"Oh, right. Anna's mother."

"Uh huh. Saul later married another Creek gal. Both he and Cal got nice families. Anyhow, when other folks began to settle in around here and make alliances with the Murphs, they wanted to name theirselves. Since the Murphs were the leaders and most respected neighbors, somebody come up with the idee of the Soosquana name. The Murphs were right honored by it."

The trail intersected a modest wagon road, which soon led out of the woods onto a wide meadow with a cluster of buildings ahead. A red-haired woman stood near the corner of the closest cabin watching them approach. She appeared to be middle-aged and ruggedly attractive. A man of similar age walked up behind her to await their visitors.

"Welcome, Sam," greeted the woman with a big smile. "This is a pleasant surprise."

"Howdy, Miz Adelin, Mr. Cal. Shore nice to see y'all again." Sam dismounted and nodded to Kaspar, also alighting his horse. "Brought a friend with me. This here's Mr. Kaspar Brayke, newly traveled over from Caroliny. That there's Rube, his dog."

Rube had already begun exchanging sniffs with the several Murph dogs. When all seemed compatible, they trotted off to explore.

The couple fell into swapping bits of personal data and news with their guests. Within minutes, the group had grown to include children and teenagers. Adelin, Cal Murph's wife, began introducing them.

Sam, laughing, raised his hands. "Whoa, Miz Adelin, you're mixing me all up. It's been a while since I've seen most of these young'uns. Catch me up on 'em. They've growed up and I want to know how much."

Adelin checked up with a chuckle, but before she could comply, another couple walked up. She turned to introduce them, but the man trumped her.

"Sam. Wonderful to see you again. You're always welcome, my friend." He turned to Kaspar and reached his hand. "Saul Murph. Welcome, sir."

"Thank you. Kaspar Brayke."

Saul nudged the woman, an Indian perhaps fifteen years younger than he, forward to present her to Kaspar. "My wife Belle, Mr. Brayke. Now, I believe Adelin was about to sound the muster?"

"I was," she said. "Now, the red-topped ones, I confess, belong to Cal and me." She began pointing. "This is Rachel. She's twelve." The girl curtsied. "One of the horse thieves stealing your mounts is Alphonso, age ten. The other is Silas, nine, who belongs to Saul and Belle." The two boys, leading away a horse each, grinned back at them.

"Fine looking lads and lasses," said Sam, "don't you think, Kaspar?"

"Absolutely."

Adelin continued. "These two beautiful girls are Delaine, fourteen, and Louise, the family's baby. She's eight." The two girls, the older raven-haired and the other strawberry blonde, blushed as they curtsied. "Off somewhere else, working I trust, are my seventeen year-old, Matthew, and Belle's Holt, sixteen next week." She opened her hands and grinned. "That's it. I think I got 'em all."

"That you did, dear," Cal confirmed, "except for Anna. Don't know her whereabouts. But I understand you've already met her."

"Well, not exactly," said Kaspar, chuckling at the memory. "But I've seen her."

"Please come, sirs," spoke Belle in slightly broken English, "you refresh yourselves then have meal. You must be tired from ride."

"And we insist on you staying for supper and passing the night with us," added Adelin. She looked at Kaspar. "I want so much to hear of all things back east. You must tell us everything."

While they were eating, Matthew and Holt came in from working in the bean field. Then Anna rode in on her black steed, carrying two full buckets of fresh blackberries. Delaine and Rachel took charge of the berries and carried them to the kitchen of one of the cabins. Alphonso and Silas took Anna's horse away to care for it.

After a meal of venison stew and fresh cider, the Murphs guided Sam and Kaspar around their compound located on a modest bluff overlooking a shoals of the river. They presented with obvious pride several residence cabins, a number of out buildings and storage sheds, and two large barns. Horses, mules, cows, and a few goats loitered in a large corral or grazed in a nearby pasture.

The younger children played with the dogs by tossing sticks for them to chase. The company of children and other dogs was alien to Rube, and he seemed to wallow in the joy.

The adults sat around an outdoor table, and newsy conversation soon switched to the plight of the Indians.

Saul Murph turned somber. "The Muskogis have been done wrong since we came here. They treated us well, and we've tried to do right by them."

"They've been the best of neighbors," added Cal. "Couldn't ask for better friends."

Saul nodded then continued. "Now they're being thrown off their own land. I mean the land of the Muskogi Nation. They don't recognize individual ownership, believing all of it should be open for living, hunting, and growing crops wherever one chooses. We don't consider ourselves owning this property, either. We're squatters, always have been. It's Muskogi ground."

Sam spoke up. "Kaspar here needs some advice. I figured you boys are best suited to give it to him."

"Yeah?"

Kaspar related his quandary. He told of his travels from Charleston, through Milledgeville and Columbus, and on to the Tallapoosa. He revealed what he had learned on the way and how he had become increasingly disillusioned. Then he outlined his conversation with Captain Brodnax and Major Elliot. His original intent was to ally with the army, he explained, but now wondered if that would be on the noble side of the controversy.

"I believe you are right to question, Mr. Brayke," said Saul. "Again, the Muskogis are being wronged. Seems the government wishes to banish all remnants of them. For sure, this is rich and valuable soil and any man would treasure it." Anger flashed across his face. "But, damnit, it don't belong to the government! It belongs to the people who've been here hundreds of years."

"Then," said Kaspar, "you don't accept any of the current Indian policies?"

"Hell, no!" Saul checked himself and breathed deeply. "The United States is a young nation, Mr. Brayke. Alabama has been a part of it less than seventeen years. I doubt we can last as a free country if this is an instance of just government."

"Perhaps the nation shouldn't survive," offered Cal, "not this part of it, anyway. If we were fair, we'd return all this back to the Creeks, and they should kick out every white man."

"Except we would beg them to let *us* stay," added Saul.

Everyone laughed. "The Indians would never ask you folks to leave," cracked Sam.

Serious again, Saul said, "Mr. Brayke, I shan't offer to advise you, but I trust you'll think carefully about giving assistance to forcing my Muskogi brothers off their homeland. This isn't rightful government."

"I agree," said Kaspar. "We certainly need fairer laws, and we don't seem to have them now. I know a little of President Jackson. My first knowledge of him was when he set off on his own with his militia in the winter of 1813, heading to New Orleans where he wasn't wanted at the time. The army intercepted him at Natchez and told him to scat on back home. He did, but some say he left many of his soldiers stranded, to find their way back to Nashville by themselves. Others say not, that he took care of his men. Much in dispute; quite a debacle."

Anna sat up stiffly and acquired an angry grimace. "You rode with Jackson?" she demanded.

"Oh, no, not me. My pa did, but only for a short stint. He couldn't cotton to Jackson's kind of soldiering."

"Humph!" Anna groused. She jerked away from the table and stormed toward the barns, clearly angry.

"Don't mind Anna," Saul apologized. "She gets upset at every mention of Jackson."

"She's always blamed him for her mother's killing," said Adelin. "We do, too. Always will."

"Yes, I heard about that," said Kaspar. "Most regretful."

Fifteen minutes later, as conversation had drifted back to light and pleasant topics, Anna spurred her big black stallion from the barns and thundered down the road and through the forest.

❧ ❧ ❧

EARLY THE NEXT MORNING, Adelin, Belle, and daughters Delaine and Rachel piled high a breakfast of fried eggs, grits, beefsteak, bacon, biscuits, honey, sorghum syrup, fresh milk, goat cheese, coffee, and newly churned butter. Sam and Kaspar feasted fine—Rube, too, on mounds of scraps—then bade goodbye to their new fast friends and began the return journey to the falls.

Secretly, Kaspar sorely regretted they had not seen Anna again since she galloped into the woods the previous afternoon.

Chapter 10

Columbus, Georgia, May, 1836

"GOOD DAY, SEABORN," greeted Judge Eli Shorter, meeting his fellow banker and business partner, Seaborn Jones, for a midday meal at one of Columbus's finest restaurants. They met often in similar settings to review results and receipts of their Columbus Land Company.

After exchanging small talk and ordering their meals, Jones expressed concern. "How are you really doing with your malady, Eli? I'm worried about you."

"Day to day, Seaborn. The doctor continues to research the cause of it, but has yet to uncover the source or devise a wise treatment."

Over coffee after the meal, conversation turned to business, the purpose of the meeting. Each reported recent activities of a half dozen or more speculators and agents in their employ.

"I received four re-certified contracts from Oates in Russell County down in Euchee country," said Jones.

"We need more from those savages. The rebellion of young Euchee bucks, the way they threaten decent citizens, calls for the forfeiture of their parcels. They deserve to lose such land. The soil is too good for the likes of them."

"Only one new grant from that slacker Pohlheimer up in Talladega County. Don't know the why of it."

"Perhaps a new man is required for that region?" Shorter's scowl turned to a smile. "But good news from Tallapoosa County, in the Tallassee town area. Mr. Taggert has conveyed eight prime tracts recently acquired. Exceptional."

"One of our better agents," said Jones. "A hard rider. He is to be commended."

Land agents, most of them unethical mercenaries, some criminal, thrived in the employ of Judge Shorter and other speculators. While whiskey and gambling were the tools the more vicious of them used in the wild, Judge Shorter and his company devised a more devious scheme.

"Hear me, Indian, here's the deal if you want to earn this ten-dollar gold piece." He held the coin for the naïve man to admire. "We're going to the certification office, where I will offer to buy your property contract of three hundred acres for three dollars an acre."

"But I no own that land," he stammered in broken English.

"I know you don't. But you're gonna swear to the official you do. He will certify the purchase, and I'm gonna pay you the nine hundred dollars in front of him as a witness."

"Ni … ni … nine hundred dollars?"

"Yes, but only until we leave the office. When away, you give me back my nine hundred dollars and I give you the gold piece you've earned. You go on your way, and I turn over the contract to my sponsors. Everyone benefits, right?"

Thus, the land syndicate will have stolen the parcel with the real owner not even aware he had lost his property. The scheme was executed perhaps hundreds of times, probably with the subtle nods of most certification officials.

WAR HAD BEEN BUILDING from the passage of Jackson's Indian Removal Act in 1830, or possibly before that. One genesis of the law could have been influence from ambitious land speculators anxious to get their hands on rich Southern acres, occupied and controlled since ancient times by Muskogis in Alabama and Georgia, and by other Indian Nations.

Land contracts were concessions by the Act to Indians who lived on and maintained real property. They were granted ownership of large tracts to do with as they pleased, according to terms of the law. Speculators had immediately swooped in to wrest away those properties by purchase or fraud, too often the latter.

Among leaders of the land barons, at least concerning Creek lands in East Alabama, were Judge Shorter, now aged forty-four, and

Jones, forty-eight. Both were presidents of Columbus banks, and together had formed the Columbus Land Company.

Shorter had been a Georgia state legislator and a Superior Court judge. He moved to Columbus to set up a mercantile business, became a bank president, and started the Columbus Land Company for the expressed purpose of acquiring Indian lands in Alabama.

Judge Shorter was said to be an intellectual giant. As a fellow judge described him, "Amongst the proudest intellects of Georgia, at any period of her history, none more commanding, none more vigorous and subtle in analysis, than that of the Honorable Eli S. Shorter. He is indeed a man of a century."

Despite his reputation, Judge Shorter suffered poor health, and according to advocates of the Muskogi Nation and other opponents, questionable ethics. He and Jones commanded an extensive domain of land speculators and agents who had made them rich, and were making them richer.

Among Shorter's and Jones's associates were Dr. John Scott, Benjamin B. Tarver, and other allies. The company had been buying land from unknowing Muskogi contract holders at fraudulent prices since the early thirties. By the dawn of spring, 1836, Dr. Scott had divorced himself from the Columbus Land Company and begun to reveal correspondence generated by the group. One letter written by Shorter, and divulged by Scott, proclaimed *stealing was the order of the day*. The same letter laid out in detail a scheme by which he and his henchmen had swindled Indians out of their land in Chambers County, Alabama.

Another letter by Tarver dramatically outlined the impersonation scheme. *There is nothing going on at this time,* it read, *but stealing of land with about fifty Indians. Pay them ten dollars or five when certified, and get all the balance back, and get four or five hundred contracts certified with fifty Indians, is all the game.*

The 'game' indeed! Shorter, Jones, Tarver, and associates thieved on a grand scale.

Tarver concluded his letter, *Hurrah boys—here goes it—let's steal all we can. I shall go for it, or get no lands—now or never.*

The conspirators didn't pretend to hide the chicanery. They even boasted to how the federal government would excuse the Columbus enterprise in its anxiety to conclude the execution of the Act and rid East Alabama and Southwestern Georgia of Indians. Thus, the behavior of prominent citizens such as they would be overlooked. It was as if the Columbus Land Company was acting in tandem with the Jackson administration.

❖ ❖ ❖

GOVERNOR CLEMENT C. CLAY of Alabama was furious. He ordered the commanding officer at Fort Mitchell to not only supply him with the names of known Indian perpetrators of hostilities, but also the names of dishonest land speculators. Though Clay was an ardent supporter of Indian removal, he wished it to be done according to law. He resented the criminal acts of cheaters and was determined to cease the practice in his state while continuing the fight against growing hostilities of the Euchee rebels and Upper Creek Red Sticks.

However, Clay was virtually powerless. From his time of ascension to the governorship, he had often appealed to Washington for protection by the army. "Secretary Cass keeps denying us the use of regulars," he ranted to his staff. "He won't even resupply us with the arms and ammunition we need."

"Unfortunate, sir."

"I need not repeat our state militia is woefully inadequate, and we're getting little help from county and town units."

"But, sir, those communities are most at risk from the doings of rogue Indians."

"True. I've so contended with elected officials and militia leaders. They vow to defend their own, but are stubborn to aid with the overall problem."

To the governor, an Indian war seemed inevitable, and Alabama was vulnerable. Never mind most Muskogis remained peace-loving and cooperative neighbors, patience was waning fast in East Alabama.

Chapter 11

South Bank of Saugahatchi Creek, May, 1836

WITH THE ABSENCE OF A BREEZE, smoke rose vertically from an abandoned cook fire before two thatched sapling huts. The flame had died, but hickory embers still glowed. A small iron pot hung above it. A young Muskogi woman and two preteen children busied themselves scrubbing clay pots and sweeping the bare dirt yard with brush brooms.

The woman ceased working and raised her gaze to see a half dozen riders emerge from the woods along the trail paralleling the nearby swift creek. Each man braced the stock of a firearm against his thigh with the other hand reining his mount. Walking their horses into an arc facing the huts with the fire pit between, the group did not dismount. The woman stood erect and scanned each man's face. The two helping children and two younger ones, who exited one of the dwellings, gathered behind her. A dog roused himself from the shade of the nearest house and growled at the strangers. One of the children grasped the nape of the dog's neck to quiet him. The riders and the family remained silent as they stared at each other.

The leader of the horsemen surveyed the area, especially studying the edge of the surrounding forest. Satisfied, he announced in a loud voice, "My name's Taggert. Are there others about or in the houses?" The woman squinted and shook her head to indicate she failed to comprehend. "Do any of you speak English?"

After a long pause, the man next to Taggert said, "Don't seem so, Jonas."

"Hell!" Cursed Taggert. "Didn't think they would. Ignorant savages!" He spat to one side. "Okay, Cullen, tell 'em why we're here."

Cullen rattled a lengthy directive at the woman in her Muskogi dialect. Her perplexed expression grew more twisted while he talked. She shrieked and gestured wildly with both hands as he finished. She yelled what might pass as expletives at Cullen, answering him in rapid, angry bursts.

Cullen grinned at her then turned to Taggert. "She doesn't believe us. Says her man would never sell his land."

"Too bad. Just tell the bitch to get off my property."

An elderly couple ducked from the doorway of the second hut. The woman spoke to them, explaining what Cullen had told her. They looked up at the horsemen, dismayed. The man began yelling, obviously threatening the intruders. He continued for an extensive time, shaking his fist and waving the posse away with both arms.

Cullen's compatriots looked at him for a translation when the old man finished.

"He says he used to bear the white man no ill will, and had stayed home at Tukabatchi when the Americans attacked in 'fourteen. He says he didn't fight Jackson himself, but he wished he had. He wants to kill him now."

The others laughed. A couple of them pointed teasing fingers at the old Indian, inciting him to increase his tirade.

"Sounds like a threat to our President to me," declared Taggert. "So, does he want to fight us instead?" The men laughed again. "Just tell the vermin to get off my property," Taggert repeated, again turning serious.

Cullen relayed the message, infuriating the Indian family to a new pitch. They all screamed at Cullen at once.

"They want proof, they say," Cullen explained.

Taggert scoffed. "Proof?" He hefted his long rifle. "We got all the proof we need right here, I'd say." His men, again amused, echoed his bravado. Taggert shook his head in frustration and fished a document from his saddlebag. He handed it to his aide. "Hell, Cullen, show 'em the paper."

Cullen dismounted and walked past the fire pit to the woman. He unfolded the document and began pointing to it and explaining as he held it before her. The old man strained to see. Both angrily renewed their one-sided argument.

"Did you show 'em the ignorant bastard's mark?" Taggert called to Cullen.

"Yep," the translator replied, folding the paper and walking back to his horse. "They don't dispute the mark. But I don't think they understand it makes the paper a legal signing over of the property. They still want to fuss about it." He chuckled. "You won't believe all the names they're calling us." The group burst with renewed amusement.

Cullen remounted and Taggert received the document from him and returned it to his saddlebag. The Indian family maintained their rant.

"Tell 'em to be gone from here by sundown," instructed Taggert to Cullen. "I'm leaving you in charge, and Horace and Jess with you. See that they move off these holdings. All the way off."

"Where should they go?"

Taggert spat impatiently. A drop of tobacco juice dripped from his chin to add to the stain on his vest. "I don't give a damn. Tell 'em about the army's setup down at Gerald's place. They could go there. Take 'em yourself if they want you to. Just get 'em the hell off my property."

After Taggert issued more orders to the three men assigned to stay, he and the other two reined their horses back toward the trail on which they had come. As they spurred the animals, Taggert checked up and turned again to Cullen.

"Oh," he said flatly, "if that sonafabitch, stupid Indian we 'bought' this place from shows up, shoot 'im."

ACROSS THE SAUGAHATCHI, above its north bank, a pair of keen eyes watched the three horsemen leave. From behind a large boulder a hundred yards away, Nouskuubi had observed through thick scrub and mature pines the entire confrontation between his family and the chiseler Taggert, but could only catch snatches of their dialogue. His wife's fury had sounded through well enough as she wailed at the men. He could tell they had come to evict her, his children, and his parents from the three hundred acres the government's treaties had accorded him.

For his family's immediate predicament he felt deep guilt and remorse. He shook his head again, trying to dispel the last of the whiskey effects from the night before. He couldn't remember whether Taggert's men had made promises or threats to keep him in their camp, but he knew they kept passing him their whiskey jug. For a while, he had enjoyed the party, but it eventually evolved into belligerence. Finally, so inebriated he could barely stand, he wanted to leave. Taggert's men said he could go only if he made his mark on the paper they showed him. Too drunk to remember similar ruses that had recently taken in other Muskogis, he 'signed' the paper.

Before Nouskuubi staggered off into the night, one of the men warned him not to go back to his home lest he be in danger. "We may kill you if you interfere," the man had said. Nouskuubi wasn't clear on the meaning, but it sounded dire. Nevertheless, he had to get home.

Hours later, toward morning as the fog in his head had begun to be replaced by a drumming ache, some remembrance returned. He was horrified as he sorted through the night's events and realized he may have been swindled. Upon nearing his homestead, he decided to survey the scene before showing himself. His worst fear came true as he watched the invasion of his compound.

Now, he silently cursed when he saw three of the thieves linger. He watched them dismount and lead their horses to the edge of the clearing to graze. One of the men walked over and grabbed a pot of water from near the huts and carried it back to refresh the horses. Settling in, the men squatted at a respectful distance to monitor the doings around the two houses as the woman, still screeching, scurried about trying to organize her household.

What should I do, Nouskuubi wondered. *I am such a fool. A damn, damn fool!* He sat down, his back against the giant boulder, and dropped his head in sorrow. Near tears, he pondered his options. He wanted to rush the three men and strangle and beat them, but he was rational enough to realize without weapons he had no chance against their deadly firearms. He was unarmed, having even lost his knife in the night, and the best he could improvise would be a hefty, hickory limb and a handful of stones. Not adequate.

I must leave here for now. Nouskuubi formulated a vague resolution to arm himself, recruit friends and allies, and return to defeat these evil men.

An idea hit him, a reasonable one. *The Murphs at Soosquana! I will go there. Mr. Saul and Mr. Cal will help. They will tell me what I should do.*

Nouskuubi halfway stood and stooped low behind the boulder, careful not to riffle the leaves and twigs around. He checked to assure the big rock and thick foliage would provide cover as he slunk up the slope behind him. Cautiously placing each foot as he crept away, he reached the crest of the ridge and broke into a trot, running north. He would not slow until he reached Soosquana, ten miles distant.

Chapter 12

The Murph Settlement at Soosquana, May, 1836

ALPHONSO AND SILAS MURPH pulled their ponies to a halt when they spied a runner coming toward them from the forest. They waited while the man, now recognized as an Indian, drew near. He stopped before them, exhausted, distressed.

The man looked up at the boys through rivulets of perspiration, his body soaked and pulsating. He tried to talk, but only managed an excited babble in Muskogean. All the Murph children spoke and understood the language, but Phonso and Silas comprehended little of the man's sputtering except garbled "Mr. Saul" and "Mr. Cal." The names were spoken in such a way the boys knew the man wished to see their fathers.

"Silas, you go find 'em," suggested Alphonso. "I'll give this fellow a ride." Silas reined his pony around and galloped away toward the compound. Alphonso reached his left arm to the Indian. "Here, hop on behind me. He'll hold both of us if we take it easy."

The man clasped the boy's arm and struggled to the pony's back. Alphonso gingerly bridled the animal around and walked him after Silas.

Saul and Cal waited for Alphonso and the visitor at the head of the road. Silas stood and fidgeted beside them, holding the reins of his mount.

"That's Nouskuubi," declared Cal as the pony approached with his passengers. "He has a place down at Saugahatchi."

"He looks half dead," said Saul. "Silas, fetch some water." The boy dropped his reins and hurried away. Saul and Cal rushed to help the Indian from the pony.

The brothers led Nouskuubi to a bench and handed him the gourd of water brought by Silas. After drinking most of the container's contents, the man began to babble again, too fast for his hosts to understand.

Saul raised a hand to stop him. "Whoa! I'm not hearing you, friend," he said in his fractured Muskogean. Then in English, "Boys, go find Belle or Anna. They know the language better than any of us."

Alphonso and Silas, who had stood by fascinated, and proud of their part in the drama, tethered their ponies and started to run off.

"No, wait, boys, here's Anna now," Saul said.

Anna appeared from around a far cabin, saw the commotion, and ran to the scene.

"What's happened, Pa? Isn't that Mr. Nouskuubi? Is he all right?"

"It don't seem so, Honey. He's upset and exhausted, and he's not making good sense. See if you can calm him down and understand what he's trying to tell us."

Anna knelt in front of Nouskuubi and gently talked to him. His wild babbling gradually turned into rational conversation as he spilled his story. After a few minutes, Anna looked up with a worried expression.

"He says he's been cheated. A gang of men got him drunk and stole his land, the grant plot the government had allotted him. Then they went to his home to run off his family. He doesn't know where his wife and children might have gone. The men threatened him and he couldn't do anything. So he came up here to see if we could help."

Anna continued talking to Nouskuubi. More information emerged as Saul and Cal agreed they had to help the man, their friend, and pondered what they could do. Other Murph family members had gathered around, and Nouskuubi soon calmed enough so all could understand most of what he said.

"Gerald!" Nouskuubi suddenly blurted. "The leader said something about Mr. Gerald."

"Maybe that's where the family is going," Cal said in an aside to Saul. "The army is taking in a number of Muskogis down there, some say to carry 'em off out west."

"Perhaps," agreed Saul. "I think we need to ride down to Saugahatchi first to check things, and maybe we can track the family from the camp. It's late now, so we can't do anything till morning."

Nouskuubi protested. He insisted they should go immediately, but the Murphs reasoned with him. They convinced him he needed food and rest. Too, no one wanted to risk meeting up with a hostile gang in darkness. They would leave at first light.

❖ ❖ ❖

IN THE MURKY PREDAWN, Saul and Cal rounded the corner of the horse barn intending to fetch their mounts, and one for Nouskuubi, for the excursion to Saugahatchi. They were startled to see Anna standing in front of the barn before four saddled horses, including her own black steed and the sorrel and bay favored by her father and uncle.

"What's this, girl?" asked Saul. "Why are you out here?"

Because, Pa, I'm going with you. Don't try to talk me out of it."

He did try to talk her out of it, with help from Cal, but unsuccessfully.

"Girl, you are the pig-headedest person I've ever known!" yelped Saul.

Anna smiled. "Thanks, Pa. I love you, too."

"Here's Nouskuubi now," said Cal, as the Indian hurried up the lane with Matthew and Holt. Each boy shouldered a long rifle.

We're going with you," called one of the teenagers. "Give us five minutes to saddle up."

Saul and Cal protested anew, but the boys pretended not to listen as they rushed to retrieve their horses. The fathers, exasperated, conceded.

"See, Pa," said Anna with a grin, "there are other folks as pig-headed as I. We just happen to all be Murphs."

Over an hour later, still so early that clouds of morning mist yet hung over the Tallapoosa River when they crossed at one of the shoals, the Murph posse pulled up at a knoll on the south bank of Saugahatchi Creek. Through slits in the woods, they studied Nouskuubi's camp several hundred yards away.

"Seems deserted," Saul decided.

"Three men stayed behind when others left," Nouskuubi stated, information he had repeated several times.

"I don't believe they're still there," said Cal. "But stay alert. They may be around somewhere."

The group cautiously rode to the camp and dismounted at its perimeter. Nouskuubi and Cal walked forward to peruse the site. The others, rifles ready, scanned the nearby woods and the creek area. Nouskuubi checked both houses while Cal studied tracks and the trail into the forest.

"Lots of horses," Cal reported. "Easily the six Nouskuubi counted. Then footprints, several hours old and many of children, on top of the hoofprints. Some horses ran, later ones walked, perhaps leading away the family."

"They will kill them!" shrieked Nouskuubi.

"No, I don't think so," assured Cal, allowing Anna to translate for him to Nouskuubi. "Swindling is one thing, but they won't murder an unarmed family unless provoked. Your family is not going to provoke them."

"They probably took 'em to the army outpost at the falls," added Saul, "at least partway. Could've dropped 'em somewhere along the trail."

"How about we follow?" suggested Cal. "We may can overtake 'em."

"That seems the thing to do, but I doubt we'll catch 'em. They must've traveled overnight. If they made it to the falls, we can find 'em there."

"What if they don't go to the falls?" queried Anna. "Where then would they go?"

"Hmmm, probably angle toward our place," said Saul, "just as Nouskuubi did."

Ten minutes of ideas, discussion, and argument followed. Because Nouskuubi's status was questionable as to his potential danger of harm or arrest, the brothers insisted he should return to the Murph compound. Too, his anger could not be trusted. Matthew and Holt would escort him.

"No!" protested Nouskuubi. "I go with you to find my family. I fight if they try to take me." Anna strained to keep up with his rant and translate it.

All but Nouskuubi understood the folly of such a stance. Finally, after reminding him again his family would just as likely find their way to Soosquana as the falls, he relinquished. He would go with Matthew and Holt.

"Boys," Saul instructed beyond Nouskuubi's hearing, "watch him close, even after you get him back home. If his folks aren't there, he'll take leave if left alone. That would mean trouble for certain."

"Yes, sir. We'll guard him without fail."

Saul, Cal, and Anna would follow the trail in pursuit of Nouskuubi's family. The men preferred that Anna join the boys in returning to Soosquana, but that futile suggestion fell short. Too, she was their best interpreter of Muskogean if they needed it.

Matthew and Holt started back north with their ward. Saul, Cal, and Anna checked their rifles to make sure their cartridges and primer charges were dry. Then they set out along the trail south as fast as tracking allowed.

Chapter 13

Falls of the Tallapoosa, May, 1836

PERLEY GERALD AND SAM PEAVY stood at the south end of the trading post porch and surveyed the army's growing encampment. New families of Muskogis were being added each day. Soldiers and civilian agents circulated among them or stood as sentinels at key locations. The stockade, closely guarded, held a small but growing number of male prisoners.

"What do you make of such, Sam?" mused Perley.

"Don't see nothing good coming outta what they're doing. Right soon they're gone have too many to handle."

"They already 'bout got the edges of the woods lined solid."

"Humph. Many more come and they'll have to set up out in the open sun. Don't see how the army can get all those folks out to the Indian Territory or wherever they aim to go."

"Don't seem right. The Muskogis have lived here all their lives, same as their folks afore 'em, and their'n afore them."

"Long 'fore any o' us got here, 'fer shore." Sam spit a stream off the porch. "When you think they aim to march?"

"Can't be before summer heat lifts. And they sure can't wait on into winter. I hear where they plan to go, winter's lots tougher and colder than here. So, I guess they would aim for early autumn."

"Makes sense. Could be a passel of people by then."

A hail from the front gate caused the two to pivot. Three riders paced their mounts up the lane and halted at the steps, but didn't dismount. Each balanced a long rifle across the front of the saddle.

"Well, hello there, Saul, Cal, Miss Anna," greeted Gerald. "Happy to see you folks."

Saul touched his hat brim in tribute. "Perley, Sam. Obliged to see you."

"What can I do for you today? Come after supplies, did you?"

"'Fraid not, friend. We're here on Indian business. You seen a family come into that camp this morning, or perhaps last night? A mother with four young'uns and an older couple?"

Perley waved to the field across the way. "Such a family might've come. Look out there. New people arriving steady. But I can't say I noticed them you mention. Who are they?"

"You know Nouskuubi up on Saugahatchi Creek?"

Gerald nodded then looked at Sam. "I've met him. Been in here once or twice."

"Yeah, I know him," added Sam. "Nice, hard working fella."

"It's his family we're looking for," said Saul. "They were run off their place yesterday by a gang of land grabbers."

"A lot of that seems to be afoot," opined Gerald. "Where's Nouskuubi?"

"He's safe for now. But he's been threatened to stay away. We came hunting for his folks." Saul turned in his saddle and scanned the vista. "Mind if we leave our horses here, Perley? We want to search through the camp. We can do it better on foot."

LEAN-TOS AND RICKETY HUTS fashioned with brush lined the edges of the woods around most of the outpost's perimeter. A few small, smoky, open fires boiled water or cooked bits of food. Women and children populated the grounds. The only men anywhere were aged or invalid.

The three Murphs, rifles cradled in a non-threatening manner, shuffled single file through the camp, studying each face. Cal led the way, Anna next, with Saul trailing.

"These people look starved," Anna said close behind Cal's ear as they walked.

Cal half-turned his head without diverting his eyes from the search. "Yeah. They don't seem to be getting the best of care."

"The children are just sitting around," she said, "not playing or anything. That's not good." She stopped, pointing. "Wait. Look, that might be them."

A group of Indians huddled on the grass ahead, no shelter close by. They appeared frightened, exhausted, and confused.

"Four kids, a mother, an older couple," counted Saul. "They look as if they just arrived. That has to be them. Talk to 'em, Anna."

Anna approached and squatted beside the mother. The two spoke in Muskogean while Saul and Cal watched from yards away. Into the conversation, Anna looked up at the men and nodded, continuing to listen to the woman. The old couple edged close to hear.

"Halt!" barked a voice from the side. "Stand away, miss!"

A young army regular hurried toward Anna and the family, musket ready at port. Anna stood to meet him, but Saul stepped in front of the man.

"Stop there, soldier," Saul ordered.

"Sir," stiffly announced the soldier, "you are not of this encampment. You have no right to be here."

Before Saul could answer, another voice sounded, less stiff. "Well, now, Private Keller," it gruffed, "whadda we have here?"

A large man stepped around the soldier. He was a civilian, dusty and disheveled, dressed for riding. Several men of similar appearance hovered behind him.

"I have the situation in hand, Mr. Taggert, if you please," announced the private.

Taggert ignored him and approached Anna. "Well, now, looka here. You are a pretty little squaw. I'd take you with me if you weren't a goddamn Indian."

Anna raised her arm, meaning to slap the man. "You vile ...!" Before she could swing, Saul grabbed her wrist and pushed her back.

"Ha!" exclaimed Taggert. "Seems as if the pretty squaw needs a protect ... aaagh!"

Saul's right fist crashed against Taggert's face, sending him sprawling to the ground. His compatriots stepped forward to confront Saul, but Private Keller placed himself between the parties, weapon high and extended at port as a barrier.

"Halt, sirs!" Keller ordered.

"Belay there!" yelled Captain Brodnax, rushing to the scene. "What are we about, Private?"

Taggert, on his feet and rubbing a lacerated lip, interrupted. "Captain, arrest that man! He assaulted me!" He wiped blood dripping from his left nostril.

Brodnax extended an arm with an open palm toward the irate man to restrain him. "Calm down, Mr. Taggert." He looked back at the young soldier, who still stood rigid before Taggert's men. "Private Keller?"

"Mr. Taggert insulted the lady, sir."

"That's a lie!" Taggert glared at Keller. "She's a goddamn Indian! That's no insult! You sniveling soldier, you can't take the side of no Indian!"

"Enough, Mr. Taggert," admonished Brodnax. "Stand aside." He turned to Saul. "And you, sir, are …?"

"Saul Murph at your pleasure, Captain." He gestured to where Cal had Anna blocked, attempting to calm her. "My brother and my daughter."

"Ah, yes, I know you. What is your business here, sir?"

Saul pointed to Nouskuubi's family. "These people are friends. We ask they be released in our care."

"Hmmm, that may not be possible. They seem to be homeless and are, therefore, wards of the state."

"Sir, we have it on good authority their land has been taken from them by fraud. This man …" Saul turned to Anna to confirm what she had learned from the Indian family. She nodded, and he pointed to Taggert. "We believe this man swindled them."

Brodnax looked at the accused. "Mr. Taggert?"

"I bought that property fair and for a good price, Captain. The owner, that squaw's husband, sold it to me."

"You have a paper?"

"Of course." Taggert reached under his vest and extracted a rumpled sheet. He unfolded it and handed it to Brodnax.

The captain took his time studying the document. "Uh huh," he muttered. "Uh huh. Well, this seems in order. Mr. Murph, the paper is proper and legal. It carries the previous owner's mark. It also specifies Mr. Taggert paid him four dollars and fifty cents an acre, a generous sum. That's almost fourteen hundred dollars, sir, a lot of money. Your friend is a rich man."

"Captain, Mr. Taggert paid Nouskuubi nothing," said Saul, fighting to tamp his anger. "Not a cent. He got him drunk and tricked him into signing the paper. Then he threatened him. Taggert stole Nouskuubi's land grant."

"You sonofabitch!" yelled Taggert as he returned the document to his vest pocket. "You can't call me a thief and a liar! Captain, I demand that bastard be arrested."

"Mr. Taggert!" barked Brodnax. "You are to be gone now." He signaled to several armed soldiers, who had been standing by. They moved to escort Taggert and his men from the scene. "And, Mr. Taggert, hear me, you are not to disparage one of my soldiers again, or I'll have you arrested. Understand?"

"You're not arresting him? He attacked me, damnit!" A soldier stepped forward and nudged Taggert to walk. Reluctantly, he stumbled away, ranting and cursing.

Brodnax turned back to Saul. "Now, sir, you should also be off. You aren't welcome here."

Saul gestured to the Indian family. "May I take my friends with me?"

"I fear not, sir. By law, since they no longer own property, they are the responsibility of the government and must remain in our care."

"That, Captain, is a damn injustice!" Saul's anger seethed openly.

"Perhaps so, but I have my instructions. Also, should you know the whereabouts of this Mr. Nouskuubi, please urge him to surrender to us. As an Indian without property, he is now a fugitive and subject to arrest. Now, be off, sir. And, Mr. Murph, stay away from Mr. Taggert."

Saul glanced at Nouskuubi's wife with what he hoped was an apologetic look. "Captain, if only Taggert will soon cross my path again."

SAUL, CAL, AND ANNA STOMPED up the lane to Gerald's establishment. The proprietor and Sam Peavy stood at the top of the steps to meet them. Another man lingered at the rear of the porch on the far end.

The question didn't have to be asked.

"We found them," grumped Cal. "But, no, we couldn't retrieve them."

Saul, red-faced with anger, erupted. "Those damn thieves! I ... I can't fathom this. They're robbing decent people of their lives!"

"I share your sentiments, Saul," said Gerald. "I'm sorry for your failure, but surprised I'm not. I've watched them poor people being herded into that camp for the past few weeks. The army has a lock on 'em from all I hear."

"I can testify to that truth." Saul shook his right hand and grimaced. "I think I broke my finger."

"Oh?"

Cal almost smiled. "Saul smashed in Taggert's face. Do you know Taggert?"

"Yeah, I've met him. A real snake."

"Hee hee," snickered Sam. "I want to hear this story. Hope you smacked 'im good."

Anna had been staring at the man against the porch wall. He hadn't moved or spoken. The others, in their fury, had not noticed him. "Mr. Brayke, are you slinking back there in the shadows?" she accused.

Kaspar Brayke walked forward. He touched the brim of his hat to her. "No, ma'am, Miss Anna. I was listening with interest to your predicament. Mr. Gerald and Mr. Peavy told me of your quest. I'm very sorry the rescue didn't succeed."

"Are you really ...?"

Cal interrupted. "Mr. Brayke, a pleasure again." He extended his hand.

Saul reached with his left. "Sorry, Mr. Brayke, but the right one is beginning to ache something terrible."

"I heard. Hope it was worth it, and I'm sure the fiend deserved it. I haven't met Mr. Taggert, but I've heard much about him, none of it agreeable. He is a snake by reputation."

"Yes, it was worth it. I only wish I had broken his jaw." The anger had not subsided.

"Tell me, Mr. Brayke," demanded Anna, still accusatory, "have you joined this government folly?"

"No, I haven't."

"Are you going to?"

"No, ma'am, I'm not. Can't say I accept anything I've seen of their enterprise."

"That's right smart of you, Mr. Brayke," said Cal, brightening a little. "So, will you be going back to Carolina now, or up to Tennessee?"

"No, I don't think so. The Muskogis' plight has captured my attention. I'm going to stay around a while and see what develops."

Anna stared at Kaspar. She tilted her head with eyes slanted. "Well, I'm surprised," she said with a twinkle, but not quite smiling. "Mr. Brayke, there may be some good in you yet."

Chapter 14

Roanoke, Georgia, May 13, 1836

THE SMALL, ONCE TRANQUIL TOWN of Roanoke sat on the eastern bank of the Chattahoochee River guarding the easiest crossing for forty miles north and south. The Lower Creeks of Alabama wished the ford and the ferry to be open should they need to flee through sparsely populated Southwest Georgia to refuges in North Florida. The townspeople at the instructions of Governor Schley were determined no Indians would flow back into their state from Alabama, and had built a small stockade overlooking the river for protection. Many Muskogis had once revered Georgia's Flint River area as their homeland, and that of ancient forefathers, before being forced to migrate to Alabama. They yet considered it their right to use the river crossing for access.

On this Friday night, sentries scanning the river from the lookout tower atop the corner of the stockade detected motion across the water on the Alabama side.

"Looks like Indians sneaking across," one of the men observed. "Go alert the town. Quietly, now."

Within minutes, all soldiers of Roanoke's sparse militia had reached their pre-assigned posts, a musket or rifle cradled in each man's arms.

"What have we?" asked the militia leader when he arrived at the observation post.

"I count only thirty or so, Tom. Might be more."

"Can't be to good intents."

"Some of them sneaked across up a piece."

"Our guys there should …" A shot from upriver shortened his speech. Then more shots, from both banks. A lull, one final shot then only quiet.

Leader Tom turned to the teenage boy lurking at his rear. "James, go around the back way to the upriver guards and check on 'em. Report any casualties and any Indians penetrating their stations. Be careful, son."

"Yes, sir, I will, sir." He was off the tower and away at a sprint just as firing began against the stockade. The dozen militia soldiers arrayed left and right returned the action.

James was back in ten minutes. "They say no casualties, sir, and no enemy made it across."

"Thank you, James."

"They also report they don't think their rifle balls found a single Indian."

"Seems the case here as well, except we might have wounded two when they came close. That's when they ran like rabbits."

"Shouldn't bother us again tonight, Tom," said the sentry who spotted the intrusion. "I think we beat 'em back."

The town celebrated the victory with pie and cider all around, and music before retiring for the night. Early the next morning, a Saturday, several families loaded carriages and set off to visit relatives in Lumpkin, fifteen miles distance by road, or journeyed to other towns, plantations, or farms. The townspeople were certain the Creeks, having suffered defeat, would not dare attack again anytime soon.

'SOON' HAPPENED THAT SUNDAY morning, May 15. Some families had not yet returned to Roanoke from their weekend excursions, while others relaxed in comfortable homes. Twenty militiamen slept in the cotton warehouse, exhausted from a Saturday of all night partying and celebrating. The stockade was virtually devoid of people.

A large contingent of three hundred Euchee Lower Creek rebels, led by aged militant warriors Neah Emathla and Neah Micco, waded across the Chattahoochee a mile below Roanoke and a mile above, and dissipated into the forest surrounding the town. When each warrior had circled to where assigned, he crept to within yards of the nearest structure.

On a signal, the Euchees attacked. Before the town could react, nine citizens and three black slaves were shot dead while nine more townsmen suffered gunshot or arrow wounds. Most residents fled their homes and survived, though shot at as they escaped into the woods. In the next few days they would stagger into Lumpkin or the upriver post of Fort Twiggs, or perhaps other nearby communities.

Before departing Roanoke, the Indians looted valuables from houses, stores, and a warehouse, and herded away most of the town's horses and livestock. Then they torched the entire town and watched it burn. Also captured and driven back across the Chattahoochee as new possessions were several slaves.

On the verge of calling it a night and a rousing victory, Neah Emathla received a runner reporting the discovery of a steamboat anchored on the near side a short distance downriver. Off went an attack squad of warriors to capture the vessel named the *Georgian*. Fortunately, a crewman who had been in Roanoke when the attack began made it back to the boat with a warning in time for the captain to weigh anchor. The helmsman steered the *Georgian* away from danger to midstream and steamed it toward the downriver port of Fort Gaines, already bloated with refugees from every point of South Alabama under attack, or in danger of attack.

Roanoke's Friday night victory had not been a victory at all. The attackers that night carried a dual mission, to probe the town's defenses and to lull them into a false sense of security. The ploy worked, for Neah Emathla and Neah Micco and their Euchee legions enjoyed the real victory that weekend, a significant one in the fight to preserve freedom for the Muskogi Nation.

Chapter 15

Federal Road, May 16, 1836

"**DRAG THAT WRECK ONTO THE ROAD.** Be ready when the next coach shows." Tuscoona Fixico, head chief of the Russell County town of Wetumpka, directed his warriors to set up the ambush. "See to your weapons. Fresh powder, primed and ready."

With the barrier of a demolished stagecoach, logs, and brush in place, the warriors secluded themselves in the adjacent woods to wait and to repeat their carnage of the previous three days. Thus, the source of the wrecked stage; several more lay strewn along the road, accompanied by at least a dozen bodies of coach drivers and passengers.

Tuscoona Fixico's ambush was being schemed along New Road, about twenty miles west of Columbus. New Road was that branch of the Federal Road that deviated northwest from an intersection thirty miles east of Montgomery to access Columbus. The main road had evolved since 1805 from a mere trail devised to carry mail between Washington and New Orleans. The stretch through East Alabama and West Georgia from Montgomery to Milledgeville crossed the Chattahoochee near Fort Mitchell on the Alabama side. The New Road spur connected the growing populations of Montgomery and Columbus.

On Friday, May 13th, near the ambush site being prepared, a band of Tuscoona Fixico's warriors pursued and stopped a stagecoach en route from Columbus to Montgomery. They killed the passengers, the driver, and two horses, and wrecked the coach. They stole the mail pouches and stripped the bodies of valuables.

During the next two days, the warriors burned and looted all stagecoach stations between Tuskegee and Columbus. On Sunday, the fifteenth, they ambushed and destroyed two more stages, killing and looting more passengers and leading away the horse teams.

A warrior galloped from the direction of Tuskegee to the west to where Tuscoona Fixico waited. "Two miles away," he gasped, excited. "Two large coaches, many horses, many passengers."

"Brothers, conceal yourselves," ordered the leader. "Save your powder until you hear a signal from me. Be true with your shooting. Let every white feel our wrath; no one escapes."

The management of the Great Western Stage Line had decided to remove all company livestock from Alabama in the wake of increased attacks. This excursion from Montgomery to Columbus, deemed safe with two four-horse team stagecoaches traveling in convoy, led a large number of horses tethered behind. Aboard the two vehicles rode sixteen passengers, at least half of them armed guards employed by Great Western.

Around the road bend rattled the first coach. The driver, a Mr. Green, reined his team sharply upon sighting the obstruction.

"Hark, passengers, trouble on the road!" he yelled. "Be spry! Might be Indians."

A frightening whoop filled the air, followed by a crescendo of others, as Green reached for his long rifle. He fell dead by a shot through the heart before he could cock it. The guard perched beside him cradling a rifle at the ready fared little better, firing a wild round before perishing.

By then the second coach had halted. "Get out!" yelled a passenger. "Run! Into the woods!"

Amid gunshots and terrifying yells from the attackers, screaming passengers either vacated the coaches or were pulled out. Some died where they sat, hardly realizing they had been ambushed. The attack was swift and precise.

Warriors chased escapees through the forest, catching and slaying most. A messenger reported to Tuscoona Fixico, "One or two escaped deep into the trees, I fear."

"Continue to seek them! No man of the whites shall fail to taste our revenge. We own this land, and whites shan't again travel this road!"

At least one man, a paying passenger and not a guard, known only as Mr. Lackey, fought valiantly. Mr. Lackey of Georgia was an agent for an orphanage. He had been to Montgomery to collect a sum of fifteen hundred dollars to benefit his charity, and was returning home with the money. After wounding one warrior and fighting another hand to hand, he succumbed to a blow to his head from a rifle stock and a knife thrust to his ribs. The Indian with whom he fought lifted the orphans' largesse and issued a triumphant war scream over Mr. Lackey's body.

Assailants stripped every corpse of valuables, money, and personal effects. They seized mailbags containing official federal and state correspondence, but also considerable money, bank notes, and government securities. At least two dozen of Great Western's finest horses they were attempting to extract from the state were herded away for use by the marauding rebel warriors.

The two large stagecoaches were overturned and, along with as much accompanying debris as the attackers could gather, were piled into the road to block it further. There would be no more traffic on this white man's road for a long while.

An escaping passenger, a Mr. Innes, armed only with a muzzle loading pistol and limited powder and ball, straggled through the woods. He dared not pause to rest for miles, as he heard pursuers not far behind. He couldn't tell how many, and cared not; he just had to find a refuge. Hours later, after dark, exhausted and discerning, he had eluded the hunters, at least temporarily, Innes stumbled into a swamp and hid among thick reeds. There he stayed the night, afraid to move, not sleeping, hoping his weapon's load wasn't too damp should he need to fire on an adversary.

At dawn Innes judged the pursuit had ended, though he remained vigilant as he charted his way back to civilization. "Maybe I can make it to Columbus," he reasoned. "That must be the closest friendly place." He must not return to the road, however, but would have to make his way through thick forests.

Two days later, Mr. Innes staggered into Columbus, hungry and haggard, more dead than alive. He yet held the pistol, still ready to use if necessary.

Columbus citizenry rose in arms upon hearing Mr. Innes's tale of the atrocity. Fearful of such attacks spreading into Georgia, militia squads made ready to march into Alabama in vengeance and to points along the Chattahoochee from West Point down to Fort Gaines. Georgians must protect their own from marauding savages, they proclaimed, and prevent the worst of the criminal Creeks from escaping into Georgia from Alabama.

The war that had been stewing for a half-dozen years had finally reached the citizens of Alabama and Georgia, whites and Muskogis. Governor Clement C. Clay exploded over news of the stagecoach ambushes.

"What the hell is happening down there? Those outlaws will be hanged for this!" he raged. He addressed his aides and military heads gathered in his capitol office in Tuscaloosa. "Send two companies of state cavalry to the Federal Roads. Indian control of those routes cannot be tolerated." He paused, then pivoted and flailed his arm in a wild gesture. "And get a company over to Lafayette in Chambers County to protect those poor farmers. Bah! Don't any of these so-called county militias do anything anymore?"

"One more thing," Governor Clay stormed at his aide. "Draft another letter to the President and the Secretary of War for my signature. Urge them in the strongest terms to send a regiment of regulars to Montgomery or to Fort Mitchell. If these stagecoach attacks—against the United States mail service at that, damnit—doesn't stir their sense of outrage ... Damn 'em to hell! Jackson and Cass used to be my good friends. And they used to possess sane wits within their heads!"

Chapter 16

Murph Compound, May, 1836

ON A DRIZZLY MID-MORNING, a dozen Muskogi warriors walked their mounts along the lane leading into the Murph place. They hailed Saul and Cal with raised arms signaling peace. The Murph brothers, walking out to meet them, acknowledged with like signs. Sensing no threat, most of the family joined the visitors.

"Greetings, friend from old times," said Saul. "You are the notable Jim Boy, are you not?"

"That I am," answered the leader in near perfect English. "It has been many days since I supped with you." The Indian dismounted and approached Saul and Cal.

"You are most welcome here," said Saul. "But what brings you our way?"

"Mr. Gerald at the falls said you would like to talk with me. You are an honored friend of Muskogis, so I could not pass the chance to converse with you."

"Well, yes, I was down at Mr. Gerald's place last week, and he repeated a rumor that you were thinking of riding with the army on their campaign against the Euchees."

"Only partly true, my friend. I beg the opportunity to explain my motives."

"That would be most welcome." Saul gestured to Jim Boy's companions, still mounted. "But first, please have your men dismount, and we can all convene to the house for comfort." He pointed to the huge grins Alphonso and Silas were hiding behind. "These two gentlemen will be happy to care for your horses, while we escape from this weather." The drizzle had increased to a steady sprinkle, and more threatened.

Several men alighted and, though not without suspicion, surrendered their reins to the boys, who joyfully led two horses each toward the corral. Three warriors followed with the others. Then Phonso and Silas took charge until all were safely penned, fed, and watered. The Murphs guided their guests to the large breezeway between the pantry and the kitchen, where tables were in place.

Jim Boy, as a fierce, young Red Stick warrior, may have been the one person most responsible for starting the first Creek War, which culminated in the Horseshoe massacre. In 1813 he led the Indian party carrying a cache of British-supplied arms from Pensacola when they were accosted at Burnt Corn Creek by a settler posse fearful of the Red Sticks. In revenge, he joined Head Chief Red Eagle, or William Weatherford, in attacking Fort Mims near the Tensaw River. Virtually all residents, military and civilian, were butchered, which infuriated whites and brought General Jackson down from Tennessee, General Floyd over from Georgia, and others. Floyd burned Jim Boy's birth town of Atasi on the lower Tallapoosa.

Jim Boy denied being present with Menawa's fated force at the Horseshoe—Red Eagle certainly wasn't—and had mellowed with the maturity of his years. He still retained the authority of a chief, the respect as a fearsome warrior as he gradually accepted the inevitability of white settlers, and had made friends with many.

The Murphs and guests sat at the several tables, or stood or sat against the walls of the dogtrot breezeway while a meal was prepared. They chose to postpone serious discussion until they had eaten, in favor of catching up on families and events.

"Nine children!" marveled Cal. "My, you've been busy, sir."

"That's wonderful, Mr. Jim Boy," said Adelin. "You must be proud."

Jim Boy beamed. "Most certainly, but I believe you Murphs have produced as many." He looked around the crowd, counting children.

"Only eight, and that's two families combined," corrected Adelin.

Anna changed the subject. "Sir, I believe your Muskogi name is Tustennuggee Emathla, is it not? Do I pronounce it correctly?"

"Why, yes, my dear, it is, conferred on me as an honor. But you may call me Jim Boy, or even High Head Jim as some do. I'm impressed you know the Muskogi name, and you say it well."

Saul peered at Anna with a tilted head and narrowed eyes. "Tuste … uh, Tustne …?"

"Tustennuggee Emathla, father," she enunciated slowly.

"How do you know that, daughter?"

Anna grinned. "You forget, I too am Muskogi. I know things, and I talk to many brethren. Tustennuggee Emathla is a renowned chief."

After the meal concluded, most of the Indians chose to nap where they sat or to explore the barns and fields. Belle and the younger children cleaned up the remains of the meal, while Mathew and Holt left to care for chores. Saul, Cal, Adelin, Anna, and Jim Boy gathered around a table to broach the debate.

"You wish to know why I have chosen to ride with the white man's army?" began Jim Boy.

"Yes, you are an honorable man and a respected Muskogi warrior chief," said Saul. "We are curious of your motivation."

"There are two reasons, which I hope you can embrace. I do not trust the white army, so I must ride with them to protect my brothers who deserve to be protected, and to guard against persecution by the whites. I can do this justly as one within the army's campaign, but cannot by looking on from outside. If I do not monitor their tactics, I fear the army's tendency to abuse."

"Won't you have to follow their orders?" asked Cal.

"Only those orders I find prudent. I refuse to be a soldier, or swear any oaths. I shall cooperate on those things I find helpful, but remain free to ignore or oppose anything I judge wrong."

"You will fight against your own blood?" asked Saul.

"Only those who draw weapons on me and my men. I mean to appease those who are reasonable, instead of arming against them, and convince them of peaceable solutions."

"Peaceable, sir?" countered Anna, showing an edge of anger. "Forcing them to leave their homeland and travel a hard road to some unknown place westward?"

"That is unfortunate, but we have lost that battle, I fear. Resisting further only spills more blood."

Anna frowned, but argued the point no more.

Saul pondered a few seconds then, "You said you claimed a second cause."

"Yes, of those Muskogis, Red Stick or Euchee, who have committed crimes and atrocities. I wish for them the proper punishment. They dishonor our people, and their deeds must be accounted. They need to be gone from our midst, and I want to be there when justice finds them."

"The whites are more violent than the Indians, aren't they?" asked Adelin.

"Perhaps, but no one can be excused of crimes against another. I mean to help search out and arrest the Muskogi renegades guilty of murder and plundering."

"That is a noble goal," said Cal. "Can it be done without more bloodshed?"

"It *must* be done. They bring shame to me and all Muskogis of proud heritage. If more blood is spilled in the quest, that is the unfortunate cost."

"I see you are but a dozen strong," ventured Saul. "Even with your great leadership, can so few make a difference?"

"Oh, sir, but we are not so few. I am backed by more than two hundred warriors who share my goal of ending these conflicts. More of like sentiments await among the peoples of Upper towns. For certain, we mean to make a difference."

The debate continued for a while longer before evolving back into personal narratives and remembrances. Soon, Jim Boy decreed it was time to depart. "We must now reluctantly leave the company of good friends. Many blessings of the sacred spirits for your hospitality, Murph family."

The threatened storm never materialized. Rain clouds had moved on, and the sun now peeked through cracks of high fluffy formations. Jim Boy's Creek warriors said their goodbyes, mounted, and rode away to seek destiny.

Chapter 17

East Alabama, May, 1836

CONFLICT HAD FESTERED since the enactment of the Indian Removal Act in 1830. Muskogi land grant holders and speculators bent on annexing their parcels for their own enrichment had constantly fought in courts and county certification offices. The relative peace, though always contentious, evaporated in January when hostilities burst open with raids by both sides out of fear of the other. This was thought to have been the true beginning of the war, already popularly known by whites as the Second Creek War, the first having been in 1813-14, concluding with General Andrew Jackson's near annihilation of the Upper Creek Red Sticks.

However, the two Creek Wars, and their causes couldn't have been more different. In the first one, violence was confined to Alabama; this time it was widespread in Georgia, Alabama, and the Florida Territory. Opponents were easily defined before, that of the U.S. military versus Red Stick Muskogis. Now, Red Stick holdouts, Lower Creek Euchee rebels, and defrauded land grant holders faced off against mainly disorganized, poorly equipped, and incompetently led county and municipal militia units, with a few regular army detachments on the perimeter of conflict or scattered thinly within. In 1813, fighting broke out with both sides seeking revenge against the other, traced to the Burnt Corn Creek and Fort Mims massacres. By contrast, current raids and battles were rooted in white immigrants' quest for Indian properties, and resistance by both sides to share the land.

❖ ❖ ❖

WHEN PRESIDENT JACKSON signed his removal bill into law, he could have predicted a coming Indian war, and he probably did. As 1836 began, conflict was inevitable, brought on by greed, fear, and political bigotry by whites, and a passion to defend their homeland by most Muskogis.

Bowing to concerns of the white citizenry, the Georgia legislature on December 24, 1835, had passed an act to prohibit any Creek from entering the state unless for a legal matter and accompanied by a white person—a *respectable* white person. The law also said no Georgian could hire a Creek to help farm their crops, a common practice until then. Since many liquor establishments existed along the Chattahoochee to sell or barter booze to Indians, Georgians would no longer be allowed by law to trade with them.

The law was not scheduled to take effect until February 1, 1836, but zealots decided they would begin enforcing it immediately. Some began to shoot Indians on sight on both sides of the river without provocation.

"Hell, might as well plug 'em already, now that it's gonna be legal. Why wait till February?"

"Yeah. A dead Indian now means a month less of trouble."

Below Irwinton, Alabama, just north of Fort Gaines, a white mob of more than a half-dozen dragged an elderly Creek from a cotton field and executed him. From that point, among incensed Lower Creek Euchees, the attitude was revenge in kind for every affront.

Sometime in mid-January, a boat patrolling the Chattahoochee south of Columbus happened on a small band of Creeks from Chehaw sleeping at a riverside campfire and fired on them. Most of the campers were killed. When a party of fifty warriors crossed over from Alabama to retrieve the bodies, Georgians panicked. Inflated reports of five hundred warriors reached Columbus. John H. Watson gathered twenty-two armed men and led them fifteen miles downriver to Bryant's Ferry to confront the Indians on January 26th.

The Creeks, far fewer than the posse expected, were about to cross back into Alabama and wanted no trouble. They raised a white flag, which Watson ignored and opened fire. The Creeks sheltered in a ravine and shot and killed two of Watson's men, whereby the remainder broke off the fight and raced back to Columbus.

The incident kicked off several more skirmishes up and down the Chattahoochee and over into Alabama. The Battle of Bryant's Ferry came to be recognized as the real beginning of the Second Creek War.

ON THE SAME DAY as Bryant's Ferry, January 26th, a party of warriors, perhaps sixty in number, invaded the plantation of Lewis Pugh in Barbour County, Alabama. Pugh's overseer, Jacob Herron, climbed to the roof of one of the houses.

"Got a good bead on 'em from up here, boss. Here they come now. Got one of the devils in my sight."

When the first of the raiders thundered onto the grounds, Herron fired off his first shot. As he attempted to reload, a sharpshooting attacker shot him off the roof. Less than a half-hour later, the warriors had also killed Pugh, his farmhands, and five slaves.

The following day a party of twenty settlers arrived to assess the carnage. A few Indians still tarried on the premises.

"Looks as if most of the stinking cowards took off after the killings," observed the posse leader on approach. "Let's get the murdering sonsabitches!" he ordered as he initiated the attack.

But the main body of warriors had not fled. Camped nearby, they heard the firing and came running and drove off the settlers, killing two.

Now the raiders fled east toward Cowikee Creek, along the way burning a store and the homes of a Mr. Martin and a Mr. Murphy. By now, a contingent of militia known as the Barbour Rangers, led by Colonel Wellborn, rode in pursuit. The posse of twenty-two Rangers caught the Indians at the confluence of Cowikee and Martin's Creek and launched into a thirty-minute battle. After losing one man and being overwhelmed by a superior force, the militia abandoned the fight and fled through the swamp.

"I'm telling a truth," one man stated later, "I had to run to the eye-brows to get away from them devils what was chasing me."

A few other militiamen suffered wounds, including Wellborn himself who had the tip of a forefinger shot off with a musket ball, and one of his lieutenants who lost an arm.

FROM THE ONSET of serious hostilities in January, other raids by whites and Creeks occurred during the following few months. Some Alabamians schemed to steal Muskogi land grants guaranteed by the Indian Removal Act, while others sought to protect peaceful Indian neighbors and friends. Angry Indians, especially those of disenfranchised Upper Creeks and rebelling Lower Creeks of the Euchee region, steeled themselves to resist the white man's control. Many militant Creeks doggedly held onto the elusive belief the squatters from the east could still be expelled from ancient Indian tribal lands. They were determined to see that momentous day.

Indians attacked from anger or revenge, while local militias typically made a show of protecting their communities. Some militia units coalesced into viable companies, but most stayed small and independent, and were often led by a local politician with no military experience or savvy. The latter forces, when confronted by an enemy, often fired only a shot or two before retreating and running back home.

By the dawn of spring, 1836, most settlers tried to stay neutral and peaceful, and isolated themselves as much as possible. Muskogis, though granted home properties by the government, were being cheated out of their parcels by speculators. The ones knowledgeable of the scammers' methods resisted, many by violence. All Muskogis feared the threatened removal apparently coming soon.

Chapter 18

Milledgeville, Georgia, May 28, 1836

WITH THE CONFLICT GAINING momentum and threatening to edge into Georgia, Governor William Schley welcomed Brevet Major General Thomas S. Jesup and Major General Winfield Scott to his state capital of Milledgeville.

General Jesup, the army's civilian Quartermaster General in Washington and a career brigadier general, had been brevetted by Secretary of War Cass and sent south to share command of federal troops. General Scott was fresh from Florida's Seminole War, where he had suffered a string of setbacks, and came to Georgia to team with Jesup. The two met in Augusta and traveled together to Milledgeville to counsel with Governor Schley.

"Gentlemen, I believe our strategy is in accordance," concluded Schley in conference with the generals. The three found they agreed almost exactly on the proper plan to defeat the Indian hostiles for good. They would march to Columbus, where General Scott and Governor Schley would command half the regulars, bolstered by county and municipal militias. They would scatter part of their charges along the Chattahoochee at key crossing points from West Point up north to Fort Gaines in the southern extreme. Scott would take the main force down the river to the area of Irwinton, Alabama, to stage the major campaign.

General Jesup was to take the other half of the regulars and march to Tuskegee to join them with Alabama troops. Those forces would be mustered into federal service. From there, Jesup would head south to join Scott near Irwinton, and to combine forces with

General John W. Moore of the Alabama Guards, already in control at Irwinton.

The plan, when all would be ready, was for the combined force to sweep north as a mighty wall, wiping out all hostility as they marched and fought. When the Upper Creek towns were reached, resistance theoretically would have been weakened to almost zero.

❖ ❖ ❖

ON MAY 30TH, scattered groups of citizens stood along the streets of Columbus to welcome their governor and two generals riding at the head of a column of regular army troops. Some cheered as if the company represented redemption from the troubles plaguing their region. Other townspeople stood and stared, not convinced enough help had arrived.

A few bystanders jeered the parade, exhibiting frustration found throughout the region. "Bah! You ain't gonna do nothing 'bout them savages, Governor, are you?" "More soldiers to protect *you*, Mister Schley?" "Courage, Governor, which you ain't got none of!" "Whatcha doing in Columbus? Get on out and kill some damn Indians, why dontcha!"

Governor Schley and his companion generals assured city officials solutions were at hand. However, before the team could replenish necessary supplies and muster into federal service needed militia units, Schley received troubling news.

"Damn," he swore, waving a newly received dispatch at the two generals, "that sonafabitch Clay is going to foul up everything. This letter says he has established a military hub in Montgomery, commanded by himself."

"Has he a military background?" asked Scott.

"Not a whit, I'm certain. But seems that won't stop him. He plans to March his forces toward Fort Mitchell on June 5th to attack Creek villages south of there."

"That cannot be. Too early. Such an expedition will force us to splinter our placements before we're ready. Besides, we need his contingency to join ours."

"I can leave for Montgomery tomorrow," said General Jesup. "We have to convince him to delay."

"I'll have a letter to him ready for you," promised Schley. "We should ask for a postponement until, uh, when should we be prepared to strike?"

They agreed June 15th would be the date they would request of Clay. Early the next morning, with Governor Schley's missive in hand, Jesup rumbled out of Columbus down the New Road with a company of one hundred twenty regulars in tow.

Jesup found the principle unit of Alabama troops camped near Tuskegee, awaiting orders. On the route, he had to pass several Muskogi villages known to be hostile, including that of the aged but still fierce Neah Micco. A few miles south, near the Federal Road proper, lay Neah Emathla's town, its eighty-six year-old chief still one of the most feared rebel leaders.

At dawn Jesup broke camp and cantered toward Montgomery on the main route of Federal Road after it intersected New Road, but didn't get far.

"Ho up the column," signaled the general halfway to Montgomery near Line Creek, as he reined his mount to a sudden stop. A company of cavalry meeting them filled the road ahead. At its lead rode Governor Clay himself.

The two men dismounted on the spot, compared goals, and plotted their best strategies. They found each other compatible, amicable allies, and agreed on most points. Clay was especially pleased to hear Jesup's goal was to eradicate all hostile Creeks and expel the remainder of the tribes from the state.

Clay was impressed with Jesup, and confidently transferred command of his troops over to him and returned to Montgomery. With the regiment came Major General John H. Patterson, the Alabama commandant from Huntsville, who would now serve as Jesup's second in command. According to the master plan, Jesup, after acquiring the Alabama troops, was to turn the column south to rendezvous with General Scott and General Moore at Irwinton and commence the campaign.

Before leaving the area, General Jesup rode to Neah Micco's village to again bargain with the chief, to give the old warrior a chance to peaceably turn himself over to authorities and save his town from destruction. The two had been negotiating for weeks about convincing the headman and his townspeople to surrender to a removal camp for emigrating to the western territories. Neah Micco wavered about the conditions they might endure, but after long discussions, the chief consented to end his holdout and comply.

"We not wish to go, but life in Alabama is lost," he decried to Jesup and his aides in a spatter of broken English. "Living under white man's government and Old Jackson's tyranny worse than anything awaits us in new land."

The surrender of Neah Micco and many of his warriors depleted significantly the leadership of hostile forces.

Chapter 19

Boykin Plantation, Georgia, June 3, 1836

"CAPTAIN," PANTED A MESSENGER after galloping into Captain William A. Carr's militia camp on the previous morning of Thursday, June 2nd, "Indian trouble!"

The dusty, sweaty man dismounted as another soldier grabbed the horse's bridle. Captain Carr strode forward. "Yes? What report have you?"

"Sir, scouts at the river have detected Creek activity on the far bank over from the Boykin Plantation near the ferry. A slave family left behind to look after the place told 'em 'bout it. The darkies said the Indians are making a whole passel o' canoes."

"Hmmm," thought Carr aloud, "one or two canoes could be innocent enough, but why a large number?"

"For no innocent purpose, I warrant," added Lieutenant Saunders, Carr's second in command.

"They must mean mischief coming over on this side of the river, or perhaps to raid the ferry. Soldier," Carr addressed the messenger, "can you ride farther?"

"Yes, sir, if I can borrow a fresh horse."

"You shall have one." He gestured to the man holding the tired mount. "See to it immediately." Carr turned back to the messenger and asked the route to the Boykin estate. Then he instructed, "Carry your same message to the camps of McCrary, Parham, and Brown, with the addendum that I, Captain Carr of the Crawford Volunteers, request we all gather at Boykin's as soon as possible."

IN STEWART COUNTY, Georgia, twenty-five miles south of Columbus, the Boykin family plantation graced the plain atop a long slope leading down to the Chattahoochee River several hundred yards distant. The stately mansion stood empty. The family and other planters along the river had fled to Macon or Columbus or other locales a month earlier in fear of Indian activity, especially from across the way in Alabama. The irate evacuees, plus locals still bravely hanging on at their homes, had appealed to Georgia Governor William Schley for aid. The governor instructed Colonel John W.A. Sanford of the Georgia Militia Command to marshal enough forces to quell the threat. Sanford, in turn, called for most militia companies over central Georgia to assemble in Columbus, but instructed Captain Carr of the Fort Twiggs community in Crawford County to gather several units and march to Stewart County to protect its residents and the nearby ferry.

❖ ❖ ❖

BY EARLY FRIDAY EVENING, militia forces in the area had diverted to Boykin's. Most hailed from Crawford County, some from Sumter. Captain McCrary brought only thirteen of his company, Captain Parham even fewer, as the bulk of both units were engaged as sentinels some miles south. Sergeant Major William M. Brown, in command of his own Crawford militia force, arrived with several dozen woodsmen and marksmen.

Captain William A. Carr, one of Crawford County's more prominent citizens, had been able to raise a large company of over sixty volunteers, more than other militia leaders in and around the county. His wife was Virginia Hawkins, daughter of the late Benjamin Hawkins, the long-time Indian agent respected by whites and Creeks alike in both Georgia and Alabama. Carr was considering standing for election to the legislature the following year. Whether motivated by patriotism or ambition, a military venture would be valuable to his campaign.

When it seemed no additional forces would join them, commanders assembled their various contingents in the Boykin mansion garden.

"To fight effectively," suggested Captain McCrary, "we must be a unified force. We are now merely a collection of several."

Captain Parham stepped forward. "I nominate Major William Brown to lead us," he announced, omitting the 'Sergeant' prefix

Brown normally carried by choice. Militias were free to designate whatever ranks they thought appropriate. Though Brown was a respected, able leader, he apparently preferred the modest rank of a senior non-commissioned officer. "He's the most qualified and has military savvy."

"Aye!" "Aye, aye!" "Hear, hear!" echoed a dozen voices.

"If Major Brown ain't our commander," loudly spoke a soldier in the pack, "I dare say we ain't going to the river tomorrow. Am I joined by all?"

Another clamor of agreement and assents.

"Any objections?" asked McCrary. He paused to hear mumbled support from all around, as if dissent would be damnable.

McCrary looked directly at Captain Carr for his reaction and read none. Apparently, Carr's men would march with him, but they didn't trust him to lead a fight. "Then it's settled. Major Brown will direct our fortunes. May the Higher Power bless us with success. Major?"

Brown stepped forward. "So be it. I have complete, unquestioned command then, as it must be in battle. We shall headquarter here and camp in the yard and fields and see what morning brings."

Major Brown stationed sentries at key points on the slope overlooking the river, and around the perimeter of the big yard. He then divided the men into three groups. Captains McCrary and Parham would merge their small squadrons and supplement them with a dozen and a half of Carr's troopers. Lieutenant Bradford would join them. Captain Carr would lead the remainder of his company, aided by Lieutenant Saunders. The third unit would be comprised of Brown's own militia and the small unit from Sumter County, led by Lieutenant Robertson.

"Rest well tonight, men," Brown instructed when organization was complete. "See to your horses, weapons, and equipment. We must be prepared for whatever awaits us."

AT DAWN, NOTHING HAD CHANGED. Fresh sentries had been rotated in place every two hours throughout the night and none reported movement on either side of the Chattahoochee. After a hurried breakfast, Brown bade the three companies make ready and stand by.

An hour passed, then the better part of another when a scout hustled into the yard to seek Major Brown.

"Sir, there's activity directly across the water. We heard commotions and saw a few Indians through the trees."

"How many?" asked Brown.

"I should wager, sir, a large number they have to be. We heard 'em working back in the woods with much industry. John Causey stayed in hiding to observe while I hurried to you."

"Thank you, soldier. You've done well."

Brown gathered his officers. "Captain McCrary, take your company to the left, far enough to assure the enemy cannot outflank and surround us. And be sure to protect the ferry."

"Yes, sir."

"Captain Carr, you do the same on the right. You have the upriver station, therefore you must be more diligent of a force floating from above you and crossing."

"None will get by us. Be certain of it," promised Carr.

"I'm confident, William, you will permit no such. My company will take the center and meet any major charge on its front." Brown paused, studying each face. "Have your men check for ample and serviceable powder and lead. When you reach your stations, deploy them with appropriate spacing, advantaging yourselves behind adequate cover. Stay out of view of the opposite bank and fire no weapons until you hear my own. Your signal to commence action will be my first volley."

Major Brown saw to the orderly departure of the two flanking companies, then led his own down the slope, assuring stealth as much as possible while spreading the men. He stopped thirty yards short of the water line and checked the cover of each man. They hid behind trees, rocks, and logs, further using brush to seclude their positions from the opposite shore.

Nearly two hours passed. Noise of activity bustled in the trees across the way, but sight of an Indian was rare and brief. Brown found it impossible to determine the size of the Creek force, but concluded they had considerably more personnel than he. Too, he knew they would be a fearful opponent. These weren't the same Lower Creek tribesman of several decades ago, most of whom had remained neutral or even sided with American forces under General Jackson in defeating the Upper Creek Red Sticks in 1813 and '14.

At a quarter to eleven, the edge of the forest on the west bank rustled. A half dozen Indians appeared, carrying a large canoe fashioned from a hollowed tree trunk. Garish painted designs decorated the canoe and the face and toned body of each man.

"Be alert," whispered Brown to those within hearing. No need, for his entire line had manned their weapons and already selected targets. "Wait till I fire."

The Indians worked the canoe to the water while a second contingent emerged from the woods with another. When both crews were side by side in clear view and about to step into the canoes, Brown carefully aimed.

Blam! Less than a half second later, *Blam! Blam! Blam!* up and down the line. Shouts of excitement rang out. Clouds of gunpowder smoke swirled into the trees. Only scant seconds of silence interrupted the din while riflemen reloaded. Then the faster marksmen fired their next shots. Yelling continued. The Creeks began fighting back as their own muskets and long rifles barked. Shooting grew constant as reloading speeds became staggered.

"Cease fire!" ordered Brown after a half dozen rounds as the Indians receded deeper into the forest and stopped firing. The shooting gradually abated as word bounced among the trees and rocks.

Smoke cleared. Across the river, three Indians lay in splotches of blood. At least one was alive as he squirmed and pitched in agony. In the new silence, shooting from both upriver and down was heard. The other two companies were experiencing action.

Two unarmed Indians sprinted from the woods and picked up their wounded comrade. Mercifully, no militiamen shot at them. They escaped safely with the casualty.

"Are all well?" yelled Brown, looking to his right and left to check his troops. All affirmed their good health. "Reload and check your weapons. Keep a sharp eye and pick your targets. They aren't through with us yet."

In minutes, the enemy had found cover and resumed firing, now more accurately while presenting themselves as tougher targets than before. The battle had evolved into each side attempting to pick off the other's marksmen from one to two hundred yards away across the broad stream.

"Major Brown!" sounded an excited voice from behind, fifty yards up the slope. "Major Brown, Captain Carr begs your presence at the house!"

Brown laid his rifle aside and rolled to see Carter Cleveland wildly signaling from the cover of a big oak tree.

"Cleveland," Brown yelled back, "this is a damned pretty time to send for a man as engaged as me. Tell 'im I'll be there presently."

Cleveland scrambled back up the hill and Brown again tended to the battle as shots continued to fly above the Chattahoochee. The action had settled into a relatively low-key battle.

"Got another'n!" "Missed 'im, damnit! Had 'im dead in my sights, too." "Hit one! The rotten savage!" Gunsmoke choked the trees while troopers cursed misses and cheered perceived hits. They were confident they had killed or wounded at least one more Indian, possibly three, in addition to those felled by the initial barrage. Shooting on the left flank by McCrary's company had picked up, but on the right the firing had dwindled.

Five minutes later, Cleveland returned. "Major Brown," he shouted, "Captain Carr says he has to speak with you now. It's urgent, he says."

"Damn!" Brown blurted to Lieutenant Robertson. "Carr must have been shot. I'll go to him and see to his condition. You direct our men until I return."

Brown scampered to the top of the slope, keeping as many trees as possible to his back for cover. Cleveland met him.

"Major, we've had a casualty. Crossland of Captain Carr's company. They brought him to the house."

"Is he alive?"

"He was when I saw him, but it don't look good."

"Captain Carr? Is he wounded?"

"No, sir. He ain't been shot, but he ain't hisself."

Brown turned the rear corner of the house and stopped, mouth springing ajar. "What the hell is this?" he demanded. Twenty or more men had exited the gate with knapsacks on their backs. More than a dozen others busied themselves in and near the house gathering gear and shouldering their own knapsacks. "What are you men about?"

"Captain Carr declares we have to leave, Major," one man answered.

"Damnation!" Brown boiled. "You goddamn cowards! Put down those packs and get back out there and fight, or I'll blow your damn brains out!" Some of the men cowered, others held steady. The stench of burned powder, sweat, and fear hung heavy. "Where's Captain Carr?"

"There, sir."

Carr bobbed amongst the men near the breezeway to the house, but had not yet retrieved his personal gear. Brown rushed to him.

"Captain Carr!" Brown stormed. "Why did you send for me? And why have you deserted your post?"

"Major, should we not leave this place? The Indians are crossing the river above and below my position. They will soon have us surrounded."

"Damn you! I'll drain out the last drop of my blood before I allow those blasphemous Indians to whip me."

"We're almost out of ammunition," claimed Carr.

"More is on the way, and reinforcements," answered Brown, fighting to hold his anger. "For now, we have ample powder and cartridges."

"We should go away from here!" insisted Carr, his voice rising. "Those savages are going to overrun us. One of my men was already shot!"

"I suggest you get back to your area," Brown fumed, "and post pickets where you think the Indians are crossing. Hold them there, damnit! I must return to my company. Damn you, Carr, you do the same!"

Before leaving the garden, Brown asked Carter Cleveland of Crossland's condition.

"He died, sir. Sorry."

"Damn shame. Other casualties?"

"None, sir, that I've determined."

Brown worked down the slope to regain his position. Only a few more volleys followed before the Creeks suddenly ceased firing and fled deeper into the forest. The battle seemed at a finish, but Brown ordered his troops to hold their ground.

Shortly, some warriors ventured out of the far woods to recover their fallen. They made a show of being unarmed as they crept from the tree line.

"Hold your fire, men!" shouted Brown. "They deserve to retrieve their dead."

With the bodies thus gathered, and those counted previously, the final total of enemy killed numbered at least six. Some insisted as many as ten. Other Indians surely had been wounded. The only militia casualty had been the death of W.J.K. Crossland, a young cavalryman of Captain Carr's Crawford Volunteers.

Major Brown sent a squad across the river to destroy the canoes manufactured by the Creeks, and their facilities and tools to forestall future industry. After a few days of vigilance and scouting, Brown and his officers ascertained the Creeks had abandoned the area for good. They gathered their forces and marched north to join other Georgia militias assembling at Columbus under Colonel John W.A. Sanford. All shared the sentiment that further Creek atrocities threatening from Alabama must be repelled.

Chapter 20

Near the Tallapoosa River, June, 1836

THE NOON SUN BURNED HOT. A red-tailed hawk lifted from a hickory tree at the edge of the river bluff as three men on foot emerged from a pine thicket and walked to stand on the lip. One led a mule on a tether, and all three carried long rifles, plus skinning knives strapped to their sides.

"Whew!" blurted Cal Murph as he sought the best place to sit on a nearby granite boulder. "This may be the hottest day of the summer."

"Hot all right," agreed his nephew Holt. He grimaced. "The deer know it, too, and are staying somewhere in the shade. Not a sign of the varmints all morning."

Matthew, Cal's son, chuckled as he wiped sweat from his forehead. "Naaah. They're just running away from your ugly face, Holt."

"But I 'spect they had a good laugh from their hiding place when you fell in that bramble thicket back there. I know I did."

Holt and Cal laughed. Matthew scowled. "I tripped. 'Twarn't funny."

The Murphs had departed the compound early in the morning, hoping to harvest a large buck, perhaps two. They traveled upriver to hunt in more unspoiled forestland than that near their farm. The mule accompanied them to haul home the prey. So far, the morning had proved fruitless and frustrating, thus the mule yet traveled light.

Cal found his comfortable perch on the rock and addressed the others. "Fetch our victuals, boys, and the canteens. We ain't doing good with the deer, so let's take a rest and eat our fare."

Holt tied off the mule to graze then retrieved a leather bag of food and three canteens from the animal's back. They had refilled the canteens at a small, swift brook a half-hour back, and the mule had drunk his fill.

As the hunters lunched on smoked beef, crumbly cheese, and cornbread, they enjoyed the river vista, a scene witnessed numerous times by the Murph family. The bluff gave way to a narrow, flat apron of riverbank below. The crystal water flowed with a gentle current that gained momentum in stretches, but then rolled over shallow shoals, such as the crossing three miles above the falls. Several varieties of birds played above the water and the forest.

A pair of large birds soared high above. One glided lower and circled over the river. It leveled off a few yards above the water and headed upstream from a distance below the Murphs' position.

"That's a golden eagle," declared Cal. "Watch him catch his lunch."

At midstream, the eagle dipped directly in front of his human audience, skimmed the surface, and lifted away a large bass. It flew to a stately oak on the opposite bank, where his mate joined him to share the meal.

"Amazing," said Matthew. "They're better hunters than we are."

"Better fishermen, too," added Holt. "And they do it without lines and hooks."

Cal grinned. "Oh, they have hooks, for certain. You don't want to meet up with them big hooks on their feet. Sharper'n your knife, I wager. Just ask that poor fish he speared."

Twenty more minutes of nature study passed, including watching a pair of large turtles cavorting in a quiet inlet, flocks of birds flying upriver, and a school of crappie navigating the clear water. With the food finished, Cal stirred from his boulder. "Let's go, boys, there's bound to be a deer waiting for us somewhere in the woods." He gathered his canteen and started toward the mule.

"Wait, Pa," beckoned Matthew. "Look." He pointed upriver.

The three turned their attention to an Indian canoe floating around the far bend—then another. Others followed.

"I count eleven," said Cal. "Wonder where they're headed."

"Maybe to the camp at the falls to surrender to the removal agents?"

As the flotilla neared, Cal refuted that theory. "No, if that was so their families would be along. Notice, those are all warriors. I see weapons with them, too. They aren't about to give in to them skunks down there."

"Then where do you think, Pa? What you reckon they're about?"

"They show markings of the Hillabee and Oakfuskee villages. In the old days, them fellas' papas warn't to be trifled with. Red Sticks all. More'n twenty years back they fought Jackson some'ing fierce. Whupped his butt, too, up at Emuckfau and Enitachopco Creeks. A pity more of 'em warn't at the Horseshoe fight."

"But where are these fellas going now?"

"The only places they might get to by water is Tuckabatchi or the Creek village Talisi."

"Both are down past the falls, Pa," said Matthew. "How they gone get canoes past that?"

"They'll have to tie up short of the falls, on the west side for sure. Then they might portage around them and relaunch far enough down not to be discovered by the camp folks. That, I fear, would be risky. Or they could walk on down the west bank to Tuckabatchi. There, if they mean to join them tough fellas over to Talisi, they can ferry across at some point. A passel of ornery Red Sticks over there, too, like theirselves."

"You reckon they aim to fight, Uncle Cal?" asked Holt.

"Appears they're prepared for it, and for certain learned how from their papas. I 'magine, like most of the old Red Stick villages, they've seen too much of what's going on and wanna do some'ing about it. Joining the tribes downriver, or the villages over along Federal Road, might get 'em into the fray."

The canoes glided past and within minutes became dots on the water. The Murphs watched them until they turned the bend a half-mile downriver. They continued to stare in silence for minutes, as if pondering the Indians' fate.

"Let's go, boys," ordered Cal. "There's a big fat deer waiting for us back in the woods. He can't hide from us all day. Fresh venison will taste good tonight."

Chapter 21

Along the Chattahoochee River, June, 1836

WHILE GENERALS SCOTT AND JESUP were busy gathering their army in Columbus and East Alabama, Indian rebels trying to escape to Seminole country in Florida were committing mischief. Under attack were several of Governor Schley's river crossing outposts. On one occasion, a group of warriors crossed the Chattahoochee only a mile from Fort McCreary and looted and burned a plantation belonging to the Brewster family. The marauders then continued their trek to Florida to join their Seminole cousins.

ON JUNE 3RD, the same day as the Boykin Plantation battle, a party of Eufaula Creeks, a faction who had until now been friendly, passed through the southern Alabama county of Pike. They encountered an elderly farmer named Pugh and his two sons working their fields.

"Ho, white man, you give corn and water to us," the leader demanded.

"Sorry, friend, no corn. But you may draw all the water you need from my well."

"Corn! We hungry, white man. You feed!"

"I tell you, we have none. The yield was poor this year and what little we harvested is all gone. The only corn left is forage for the livestock."

A voice from behind the spokesman boomed, "You lie, old man! All white mans lie!" The angry speaker raised a musket from around his leader and fired. The man fell, badly wounded.

One of the Pugh sons, standing nearby, raced for his rifle at the edge of the field. He only made it halfway. Another musket shot felled him sprawling in the newly plowed soil.

The other son, a hundred yards across the way, already had grabbed his rifle and aimed at one of the Indians who had taken a few menacing steps toward him. His shot missed, and by the time he reloaded, the attackers had fled along the road leading eastward. He ran to his father and his brother, checked their wounds, and helped them to the farmhouse. There he barricaded the house and turned the victims over to the womenfolk of the family for treatment. The patriarch suffered a critical but survivable torso wound, while the son had a shattered knee, which would leave him a cripple.

AN HOUR LATER, the same band of Eufaulas traveled Three Notch Road and intercepted a large family driving their cattle herd south, hoping to move away from Indian troubles of recent weeks. A battle ensued, in which brothers Thomas and Peter Watson and Peter's son-in-law were killed. A friend accompanying the family received a musket shot in the mouth, but survived. He and the remainder of the family escaped through the forest and made their way to Monticello, the Pike County seat, for refuge.

The Eufaulas herded their stolen cattle farther south to the headwaters of the Pea River. There they joined Muskogi rebels gathering as a united force for the expected coming attacks by the Georgia and Alabama armies.

ANOTHER JUNE 3RD INCIDENT occurred upstream from the Boykin plantation, where a band of fifty warriors, probably some of the same ones from the Boykin attack, raided the Watson plantation and kidnapped three Watson slaves. This Watson family had no known connection with the Watsons assaulted on the same day in Pike County in South Alabama.

ON JUNE 4TH AT IRWINTON, 125 state militiamen, divided between Alabamians and Georgians, loaded onto the steamboat

Metamora and sailed upriver. Each man concealed himself aboard so to be unseen from the river banks. Captain William C. Dawson had been tipped off that a force of a hundred fifty rebel warriors waited in ambush for the Metamora's regular patrol voyage.

Dawson had been commissioned by General Scott to cruise the Chattahoochee back and forth between Irwinton and Columbus in search of Indian float craft, such as canoes and rafts. The object was to curtail Creeks crossing from Alabama to Georgia. Dawson was also to detect signs of impending attacks on river settlements, and warn residents of such.

"Stay hidden, men," urged Dawson. "Get comfortable and keep your ammunition dry from the river spray. This could be a long trip." His contingency this day consisted of far more than his usual crew of a dozen or so soldiers, aside from the boat crew.

Two miles north of Roanoke, Indians opened up from atop a low bluff on the Georgia side. Musket balls rained down on the boat from the rebels' first volley. Shooting abated for a few seconds while the attackers reloaded."

"Now!" shouted Captain Dawson. "Fire at will!"

A hundred twenty-five soldiers arose from concealment as one and returned a fusillade of lead. In the ensuing action, an unknown number of Indians were mortally wounded, several tumbling off the bluff upon being hit. No soldiers were killed, and only a few suffered minor hits.

Thus, by ambushing the ambushers, Dawson achieved a badly needed victory for the military and settlers on both sides of the Chattahoochee.

※ ※ ※

SHEPHERD'S PLANTATION lay four miles north of Roanoke and six or eight miles south of Fort McCreary, one of the outposts. Another outpost, Fort Jones, was a mere two miles north of Roanoke and equidistant south of Shepherd's.

On June 9th, a large militia unit from Gwinnett County, commanded by Captain Hamilton Garmany, camped at Shepherd's Plantation.

"Captain," panted a frightened sentry runner from an outlying guard post, "we've spotted Indians. Coming this way. Lots of 'em, sir."

"Thank you, soldier. Sergeant, ready the troops. Alert for possible action. Get the m ..."

Garmany's orders were clipped short by a volley of musket and rifle fire. Three men fell before anyone reacted to take cover or return fire. Then two more. And others as militiamen scrambled for shelter of any kind.

Garmany had set up camp in the open away from the farm's buildings, so he and his men were easy targets for marksmen firing from the woods. An hour into the battle, half the company had been killed or wounded. Few casualties among the attackers could be confirmed.

Fortunately, mounted scouts from Fort Jones heard the shooting and rode to the fort to seek help. A messenger was sent north to Fort McCreary for reinforcements as a cavalry company was hastily assembled and dispatched to Shepherd's.

The embattled Gwinnett force, on the verge of being overrun and annihilated, cheered as the Fort Jones cavalry rode in with rifle fire raking the woods.

"Yay, it's them chaps from Jones fort. Jolly good fellows!"

"I began to fancy we might be goners. Now we gonna turn things."

"Huzzah! We gonna get them savages now, boys!"

With cover from the fresh weapons, men who had not yet escaped the open field, but had huddled the entire time in ruts or behind stumps, were able to make it to one of the barns. The battle settled into a standoff with the help of the new arrivals.

After two more hours, the Fort McCreary contingent thundered onto the scene. Within minutes, firing from the forest lessened then ceased, the battle over. The Indians seemed to have been magically absorbed back into the safety of the pines.

"You men are most certainly welcome," stated a relieved Captain Garmany as he greeted his rescuers at the battle's conclusion. "I don't reckon we shall have lasted much longer by our own merits. We were low on ammunition, and we lost too many good men, I fear."

Captain Garmany and his survivors counted the dead and wounded, and prepared to transport the wounded to the nearest medical care at Fort McCreary and the fatalities to Columbus.

Upon reporting to General Scott in Columbus, Garmany insisted he had been assailed by over two hundred Indians, though he admitted they were concealed by the forest for most of the battle.

The report was relayed to Governor Schley, who was weary of reports of troops fleeing from battles without offering a good fight, and of exaggerated numbers of Indians. Some were inflated even from minor skirmishes and sightings. He scoffed at Garmany's estimate of two hundred. "Likely not so many," he noted with sarcasm. "Instead, that would do very well for thirty or forty."

Indeed, some run-ins with Indians in previous weeks, in the face of increased fear, seemed to generate estimates of the foe by multiples of two or higher. Most such numbers were easily refuted, however, usually by a lone dissident with a more reasonable and believable report.

In one instance, a company of Monroe County militia ran from the Creeks at a place called Turner's Field. They insisted their pursuers numbered at least two to three hundred warriors. However, one of the militiamen, Thomas J. Stell, countered the claim.

"I only saw twenty-five or thirty Indians. Our officers refused to stand and fight, and we ran like scared rabbits for Fort Jones."

When Stell was queried by an editor of the Columbus Enquirer, he represented his view of the war with clarity: "Worse and worse—just had a fight with the Indians—got whipped."

ALARMS HAD RENEWED all over the region, especially in river communities and outposts on the Georgia banks and the farms and small settlements in Alabama. Upon hearing of the massacres of the Davis and Jones families, citizens in Chambers County and surrounding areas of Alabama panicked and headed for the county seat of Lafayette or nearby forts for safety.

The attack and burning of Roanoke happened only a week later. The town was destroyed and its survivors scattered to many points of West Georgia. With Roanoke's demise, rogue Indians gained control of a key river crossing.

On the same weekend came the stagecoach robberies and murders along the Federal Road between Montgomery and Columbus. The deaths of nearly two dozen passengers and drivers, the destruction of several coaches, and the theft of thousands of dollars in cash, mail, and personal possessions could not be tolerated. Also, the coach company rued the loss of dozens of prime horses driven off by the ambushers.

The attacks caused the Federal and New Roads to be void of stagecoach traffic and mail delivery for weeks.

Chapter 22

The Executive Mansion, Washington, D.C., June, 1836

A SQUIRREL SCAMPERED across the walkway clutching an acorn in his teeth, and sprinted for an elm tree. He had stolen his treasure from the adjacent oak. A chattering friend in the elm cheered him on, urging him to elude the approaching humans.

Andrew Jackson raised his cane to mimic a trusty rifle and took a pretend shot at the fleeing rodent. "Pow! Got 'im!" declared the tall, grizzled President in triumph.

Secretary of War Lewis Cass uttered a congratulatory grunt. "Nice shot, sir. I bet you got your share of those critters in your day."

"My day? This is still my day, Lewis."

"To be sure, sir."

The two strolled through the arboretum at the rear of the executive mansion. A guarding soldier followed at a respectful distance, his musket slung from his shoulder.

"We would've starved back in the winter of eighteen and fourteen if not for the little beasts, them and rabbits and any other creatures we could shoot or trap. We were stuck in the damn Alabama wilderness with no help coming. Didn't take us long to clean out the deer when our supplies ran out, so we scrounged for anything that moved."

"Must have been an ordeal, sir."

"Aw, I've seen worse, and that situation could've been more frightening. Still don't understand why the Indians didn't kill us off that winter."

"How's that, sir?"

"Did you know at one point we were down to fewer than fifty men? The Creeks were madder'n hell and they had at least two thousand warriors. There we were shivering in our little make-do fort, simple targets. But for some reason they left us alone."

"Why, sir?"

"A true mystery at the time. Later, we surmised they had spent all their time and effort that winter structuring the barricade at the Horseshoe. You should have seen it, Lewis. A magnificent, elaborate breastwork. A marvel of defense, even if they did build it in the wrong place."

"But surely they must have known of your weakness."

"I'm certain they did. But I suppose they thought we expected reinforcements at any time, and that kept them away. Also, the Creeks had this strange superstition they were indestructible, even immortal, if they fought on their sacred ground. Ha, our flimsy Fort Strother was hardly sacred ground."

"You did get your reinforcements, sir, am I right?"

"Oh, yes, we did. Governor Blount finally succeeded in recruiting and sending two thousand militia from Nashville under General Thomas Johnson, and another two thousand from Knoxville, commanded by General George Doherty. That was sufficient manpower to go after the Creek savages, but it was really the Thirty-Ninth who saved our butts. They had arrived a little earlier."

"Colonel Williams's regiment, as I recall."

"Yes, a crack unit, bless 'em." A wry grin lit Jackson's face. "Reckon who was a junior officer in that outfit? Our old friend, Samuel Houston, that's who."

"Sir?" expressed Cass in surprise. "Is that a truth?"

"Most certainly. He was a twenty-one year-old third lieutenant with Williams. The Horseshoe was his first action, and would you believe, he took an arrow in the leg and two musket balls in his shoulder, and he never stopped fighting till the cause was won."

"Most commendable, sir."

"Yes, then Sam grew to be a fine soldier and a rouser of a character. He was a good congressman, too, as he sided with my administration on most key issues."

"But not on the Indian removal question, sir?"

"No, regrettably Sam didn't see the good of it. He lived with the Cherokees as a teenager."

"I've heard that."

"He still respected them and, worse, defended them. However, I should like for him to yet be around, even if I would have to tussle with him on the issue. But, lo, there was that unfortunate bit with Congressman Stanbery, and so Sam had his fill of Washington and ran off to Texas." Jackson turned to Cass. "What is the latest from down there of Houston's exploits?"

"Sir, we continue to receive dispatches relating details of his success at the San Jacinto River in April." Cass snickered. "Apparently, when Santa Ana and his Mexican forces were put to flight, they galloped all the way back to the Rio Grande and have been of slight nuisance since. That seems to have ended their war."

"Frightful shame, though, about the business at that mission fortress in San Antonio de Bexar in early March. Many brave men killed, including my old Tennessee critic in Congress, David Crockett. Did you know he, too, served with me briefly in Alabama in his scout days?"

"No, sir, I didn't. Yes, the mission siege was quite a tragedy. Colonel Travis had recruited an elite brigade, but even they couldn't sustain forever in the face of five thousand of Santa Ana's best. But, apparently, Houston embraced the situation and turned it to his favor." Cass chuckled again. "Sir, I do believe our maverick congressman is a true hero down in that wasteland. I understand now he contemplates a run for president of his new breakaway republic."

Jackson smiled. "I say, brave little Third Lieutenant Samuel Houston has gone far." He sighed. "But now we must address the business of this pleasant little stroll, Lewis, your report of developments from the Indian problem down south. I must say, my patience is wearing."

"As is mine, sir. Work with the Cherokees in East Tennessee, North Georgia, and the Carolinas has progressed rather peacefully. They keep throwing lawsuits at us, but they have no purchase."

"And the Creeks?"

"Would they were dealing in lawsuits, sir. I fear those bloody beings prefer musket balls."

"Are they fighting?"

"Of a certain, and it's waxing worse, desperate in some quarters. General Scott and General Jesup are preparing a major campaign designed to end the war. Governor Clay in Alabama and Governor

Schley of Georgia have banded together and called out their militias. As the majority of tribesmen in Georgia have already moved westward, most of the resistance is in Alabama. Still numerous raids and threats by uncooperative renegades."

"And Scott and Jesup are going to remedy that?"

"They pledge so, yes, sir."

"You say the Georgia situation is stable?"

"Not for certain. Governor Schley fears trouble spilling back into Georgia and has ordered citizen forces to mass in Columbus. He has established posts to man key routes and river crossings."

"How many men has he marshaled?"

"Up to twenty thousand perhaps, according to the latest dispatch."

"That is impressive, Lewis."

"Nevertheless, there have been skirmishes in Georgia near the Alabama border. On June third, a mob of murderous Creeks from across the Chattahoochee River—that's the state divide between Alabama and Georgia, sir."

"I know, Lewis," said Jackson, annoyed. "I spent many hellish days in that territory."

"Yes, sir. Sorry, sir. Anyway, the savages charged across the river and attacked a Georgia militia detachment protecting the estate of a planter named Boykin, and a nearby ferry."

"The outcome? Casualties?"

"A victory, sir. Our boys set them running back over the river and through the forest. Lost only one man, praise the Lord. Enemy kill totaled up to ten or more, others wounded."

"Good, Lewis. Send Governor Schley our congratulations and gratitude."

"Yes, sir. But there's more. A scant week later, not far from Columbus, there was another attack. Details are scarce, except there were more casualties this time. A number of militiamen killed, others wounded, at a place called Shepherd's Plantation. The Indians may have attacked from ambush."

"Regrettably. It does seem, though, Georgia will be able to confine most of the trouble into Alabama. The smaller the area in which we have to chase the vermin the better, I say."

"Yes, sir, and there have been other skirmishes, most of a minor nature, but still casualties and property theft."

"Yes. Very well, Lewis. Keep me informed. Now, how goes the collection of those destined for western territories?"

"Most of the depots for gathering the Creeks are in East Alabama, and all are operating to advantage. From accounts, we are on schedule."

"Can they move by early fall? I need them gone by election day."

"Yes, sir, we think so. Some might be shipped out before autumn."

"Think it for certain, Lewis. Does Governor Clay require additional aid to clear his state?"

"He claims such, sir, but my staff is skeptical. I regularly receive dispatches from him requesting additional arms, plus a regiment of regulars."

"Does he need them?"

"Not by my considered judgment. He seems to boast a substantial state militia. Also, with the Scott and Jesup campaign, we lack the troops to supply further forces."

"I subscribe to your wise counsel, Lewis. Send Governor Clay and Governor Schley my compliments and our good wishes for forthcoming successful ventures."

"Yes, sir."

Another squirrel skittered across the path and zipped up an oak without altering stride. He perched on a low limb and twittered mockingly at the intruders. President Jackson and Secretary of War Cass stopped and stared at the creature.

"He has no regard for the Presidency, sir," said Cass.

Jackson turned to the soldier trailing behind. "Grant me the loan of your musket, Sergeant. I'll show you how to dispatch a quarrelsome critter."

A glint of horror painted the soldier's face. "Sir, I'm not allowed to give up my firearm to anyone, not even to you, sir."

"You're not giving it up, son, you're loaning it to me. Too, I'm your boss and I know more about firearms and soldiering than anyone else in this horrid town." Jackson extended his arm and wiggled his fingers at the confused man. "Now, give it over."

Jackson took the musket, handing the soldier his cane in exchange. He examined the piece lovingly. "It is properly loaded and primed, I assume?"

"Yes, sir."

The President, momentarily reverting over two decades to his soldier persona, faced the tree and cocked the musket's hammer and strike plate. He shouldered the weapon into firing position and searched for his target. Then he raised his head and peered over the musket.

"Where'd the little bastard go?" he demanded.

Cass laughed. "He ran, sir. Ran and hid. I believe he knows your reputation."

Chapter 23

South Alabama, June 14, 1836

GENERAL JESUP SOON FOUND his newly acquired Alabama contingency, few of whom were professional soldiers, full of problems. Most were not enthused with military procedures and balked at routine menial tasks. "We came to fight Indians, not dig latrines," they complained. Too, most would not agree to an enlistment of more than three months, hardly enough of a stint to complete the job. Governor Clay had not gifted him with a battalion of Alabama's best.

"Hell, I'm not gonna spend my life out here in the weeds tracking damn smelly Indians," voiced a common complaint. "They can have my three months, but then, by God, I'm going home."

AFTER NEAH MICCO PROMISED to surrender his townspeople and himself for emigration, only a few key war chiefs remained among belligerent Upper Creeks. Aged Neah Emathla was one, another being Tuskenea, the late Big Warrior's son. Tuskenea still quarreled with Opothle Yahola for the disputed Head Chief position of the Muskogi Nation. For his personal security, he claimed neutrality in the removal fight, but his hostility had not abated. He railed against his Muskogi people who had deposed him three times, against the white invaders, and against the armies and cheats scourging his homeland, and he adamantly refused to agree to Jesup's terms.

Tuskenea looked to the future, with his eye on joining the Seminoles in Florida if the white armies prevailed in Alabama. If

Opothle Yahola emigrated to the west with the majority of Muskogis, Tuskenea's fortunes with them in that desolate place would be dim. And he certainly couldn't remain in his ravaged homeland dominated by hostile foreigners.

Warrior chief Tuskenea would sit tight and monitor events, looking for better times and profitable advantages.

HAVING BIVOUACKED for several days near Tuskegee with his regulars and Alabama militia, both cavalry and infantry, Jesup broke camp and traveled eastward on Federal Road, accompanied by several bands of mounted Upper Creeks, including the followers of the old Red Stick Jim Boy. The general had received their alliances at Tuskegee and welcomed them to the fight against the rebel Euchees and other hostile holdouts.

Before turning south to meet General Moore at Irwinton and await General Scott, Jesup meant to restock his provisions at a settler fortress just north of the road called Long's Station. As he approached, a forward scout galloped to meet him.

"Sir," the man blurted, excited, "there's nothing there."

"Nothing where, soldier?"

"At the outpost, sir. I saw no one, and it appears the wall is down."

"Damn! That can't be right. Something's afoot." He turned to a lieutenant. "Send patrols left and right. See to it the area is clear."

When the general and his column reached the site, they indeed found it destroyed and desolate. The stockade walls lay flat, broken, scattered. Adjacent huts and sheds were in splinters. Not a morsel of food or forage remained, not in the fortress nor for a radius of miles. The settlers who owned and operated the station had apparently fled in fear before the attack.

Jesup called his officers together. "Gentlemen, we must push on to Irwinton without delay. The stores we expected here at Long's have been pillaged, so we are low on provisions with no means of resupply. However, Neah Emathla's town lies on our way. I plan to overcome it and hope to find supplies we can use within. We shall pause at Big Spring to refresh and organize for the attack."

A company of friendly Upper Creeks, led by Jim Boy, rode ahead to Big Spring, a popular natural oasis halfway between Neah Micco's town eight miles to the north and Neah Emathla's on the south trail. As they rested at the spring and waited for Jesup's column to catch up, they were surprised by a small group of Indians coming into the clearing.

"Lo, that's Neah Emathla," whispered a warrior to Jim Boy.

"Yea, it be. He means no harm, his family being at his side. And looks but few warriors with him for protection."

"What should we do?"

Instead of answering, Jim Boy rose and approached to greet the old, much respected headman. "Peace, my friend."

Neah Emathla returned the salutation and, not suspecting danger, entered the midst of his former allies. His family followed, but several of his warriors, being suspicious, hung back.

At the proper moment, Jim Boy faced Neah Emathla and proclaimed, "Honored chief and mighty warrior, though my friend, you are now my prisoner. I must surrender you to the army commander General Jesup, who follows shortly on our trail. He will fairly treat you and your people, and provide the comfort you deserve."

Neah Emathla made no protest and offered no resistance. However, two of his warriors escaped into the forest and headed for the village to warn Neah Emathla's townspeople.

General Jesup, upon arrival, was happy to receive his newest prisoner. Having Neah Micco in custody already, he now possessed the two most influential Muskogi leaders of the region.

Jesup expected reinforcements from more Indian defections, and from a company of North Alabama militia, so he chose to await them at Big Spring before attacking the village, now that it had been alerted. He decided his two day's rations would not permit him to reach Irwinton, so he penned a letter to General Scott. He explained his reasons for deviating from the master plan, and told of the capture of Neah Emathla and his plan to attack the headman's village. Additionally, he insisted he must return to Fort Mitchell for resupply. He asked Scott to assure an ample cache of corn and other provisions would be waiting for him.

IN COLUMBUS, General Scott exploded with anger. Though he hadn't yet received Jesup's letter, he heard about his exploits from a citizen traveler. He proceeded to write a return letter, in which he spared no venom. After expressing his fury about Jesup's changes, specifically of his planned attack on Neah Emathla's village and his projected return to Fort Mitchell, he added new orders. *I desire you instantly to stop all offensive movements (if you are in command) on the part of the Alabamians until the Georgians are ready to act, say on the 21st instant, when the greater number of them will be armed and ready for the field.*

❖ ❖ ❖

WITHOUT GENERAL JESUP'S permission, Jim Boy left camp with a large group of warriors and several white militiamen, and headed north to Neah Micco's village. There he found no defenses, as most of the town's militant warriors had joined Neah Emathla's forces upon their own headman's capitulation with removal. What he did find, surprisingly, was an accumulation of luxurious trappings such as nice furniture and fine china, undoubtedly stolen at some point from plundered settlements and farms. Better, Jim Boy's gang discovered much food, especially beef, pork, and bacon. The men sat down and feasted on the spoils before returning to Big Spring and presenting Jesup with a dozen new prisoners.

❖ ❖ ❖

UPON RECEIPT OF SCOTT'S LETTER while still encamped at Big Spring, Jesup judged it unwise to heed the order, though Scott was his superior officer. His Alabama troops were eager to fight, and he felt the Indian allies relished a taste for blood and could not be restrained.

On the morning of June 18th, Jesup launched his attack on Neah Emathla's heavily fortified town, its defenses designed by the crafty old headman himself.

"I'm impressed," Jesup stated to General Patterson as they surveyed the village. "This resembles Menawa's fortress at the Horseshoe I've heard stories about."

"For certain, sir. I've visited the site. Quite much alike."

Jesup sent his Indian allies south of the creek, while he planned to advance from the forest in a pincers maneuver. But the Indians moved prematurely, leaving the villagers a wide escape route. Without their chief to direct tactics, most townsmen reacted to the opening and elected not to fight, but took their women and children and fled into the swamps to the south. Warriors managed only a rear-guard fight, in which some were captured.

Jesup had won the battle with little effort, and now discovered a welcome bounty. The village contained a rich supply of corn and other staples, plus a hundred head of beef cattle. Now he wouldn't have to return to Fort Mitchell, and could continue the trek south to meet up with General John Moore's force of Alabama Guards at Irwinton.

❖ ❖ ❖

BEFORE HE COULD RESTART his column, Jesup received another dispatch, this one from Fort Mitchell. Scott, on an inspection tour there, found Jesup's letter.

"Damnit!" Scott cursed to his attending officers. "General Jesup is sabotaging the entire campaign. He is going to chase every last Indian to hide out in the thickets where we will never find them."

Infuriated anew, he dashed off a second letter demanding Jesup cease his current tactics and hold his position. This time, Jesup could not ignore Scott, so he decided to travel to Fort Mitchell to explain his actions and reason with his superior.

"General," he addressed Patterson, "you have command while I'm gone. Controlling your Alabama troops and our Creek allies won't be easy, but you have my full confidence. To aid your task, I'm leaving most of the regulars with you as a precaution."

Jesup assembled a company of militiamen, peppered with a few regular army officers and men, and rode to Fort Mitchell to convene with Scott. Upon arrival, he found Scott had returned to Columbus. However, probing for supplies, he discovered at the fort's river landing a steamboat loaded with eighty thousand prepared military rations, which he confiscated.

Angry with what he perceived as Scott's ignorance of conditions in the field and lack of tolerance, Jesup composed another letter. In it he justified his actions as necessary tactics to save lives of settlers on the Alabama front. He also accused Scott of treating him with a condescending attitude, which he didn't deserve. He termed it *a degree of harshness which is cruel in the extreme.*

Despite the exchange of caustic letters, Scott and Jesup got together on June 21st. Scott listened to Jesup's explanation, and, though not quite believing the latter's claim of saving citizens' lives, he accepted his insistence he had acted out of necessity. Jesup, in turn, pledged to follow Scott's directives for the remainder of the campaign.

UPON RETURNING to resume his command, Jesup gathered his forces and headed south, but ran into minor skirmishes that diverted him from his route. He found farms ravaged by raiding parties and sent squads, often entire companies, to pursue the perpetrators.

Meanwhile, General Moore received rumors Indians were making ready to flee to Florida, so decided he couldn't wait for Scott. He marched up from his post at Irwinton to unite with Jesup. As a combined force of several thousand soldiers and Upper Creek allies, plus a few Lower Creek recruits, the two commanders set about routing the Euchee rebels and taking many prisoners.

General Jesup, with limited successes in South Alabama feeding his ego, convinced himself he had effectively ended the war. With the capitulation of Upper Creeks and their leaders, the capture of key rebel chiefs, and the flight of multitudes of Indians into Georgia on their way to Florida, Jesup reasoned the Indians' resistance to government control could not regain traction.

However, in the wake of Jesup's victories, raids and atrocities reignited, often more violent than ever. Revenge, as a strong motivator, fueled many attacks, giving settler farmers and families a renewed sense of fear.

Across the Chattahoochee, county militias chased bands of Creeks attempting to migrate to Florida. Skirmishes resulted, usually ending with the militiamen retreating to safety when the battle heated up. In the aftermaths of most of the tiffs, the Indians continued on or hid in forest lairs or impenetrable swamps until the way cleared.

BACK IN COLUMBUS, General Scott was delayed with a sudden illness that had him bedridden for several days. When he finally got underway on June 21st, the same day he met with General Jesup, he found the same lack of discipline among Georgia recruits under his command that Jesup was experiencing with his Alabama charges.

Since General Scott arrived in Columbus, he had struggled to equip and arm the multitude of citizen volunteers who beckoned his call. In the same period, violence on both sides of the river had surged. Scott sent the first few hundred men he could make ready downriver to man the forts and other outposts Governor Schley had commissioned to guard river crossings.

Finding arms, ammunition, and provisions for his campaign proved taxing for Scott. His ill spell set him back, as well as the difficulty of culling enough capable soldiers from the four thousand volunteers who appeared in West Point and Columbus. He needed far fewer men and had barely enough supplies for those. Evaluating the excessive personnel, many incapable of soldiering, slowed his progress further. He found himself stuck in Columbus until able to depart on the twenty-first.

Upon finally reaching the south of the region by way of travel down the Chattahoochee's eastern bank, Scott found Jesup and Moore absent. General Moore, following his move north to ally with General Jesup, did not return to Irwinton to man his previously assigned position. Jesup turned over his forces to General Patterson and went back to Fort Mitchell to prepare the removal encampment for emigration. Patterson remained in the upper swamps to search for and combat fugitive Euchee rebels.

The fractured campaign had dispersed the enemy to protective swamps and thickets, and had alerted them to the armies' master plan. The original scheme, as formulated back in Milledgeville, now seemed impractical. In addition, Jesup's and Moore's armies had been fragmented across the region in such a way that reassembling them into one colossal, unified army for a mass march north was hardly possible.

Only days after Scott arrived in the Irwinton area and not finding the allies he expected, he marched his troops back across the Chattahoochee having engaged the enemy with scant action. Since he had faced few Indians, his professional ego told him they were frightened by the threat of his force and had fled and given up the fight. He returned to Columbus by way of touring the river outposts on the Georgia side of the Chattahoochee. Upon arrival at home base, he declared he had won a great victory and virtually ended the war.

With the 'campaign' concluded, or rather decimated, General Moore departed for Montgomery to report to Governor Clay and release his conscripts at the expirations of their enlistments. General Jesup arrived in Fort Mitchell with a large group of Euchee prisoners in tow.

Therefore, Scott's and Jesup's grand campaign to end the war never materialized.

❖ ❖ ❖

BOTH GOVERNOR CLAY in Alabama and Governor Schley in Georgia were furious.

"Damnit!" swore Clay. "I lent my state's forces into the hands of General Jesup in exchange for his promise of scrubbing the land of hostiles. What did he do? He depleted Alabama's military and scattered our militia units." Clay continued to rant. "Jesup's campaign made the situation worse. Damn him! And damn General Winfield Scott! And damn that treacherous Governor Schley, too! We are further now from ending this dastardly war than we were, and it's all their doing."

Schley shared Clay's anger, but more at General Scott than Jesup. "I'm not convinced Scott even made it down to South Alabama as he claimed. From reports, he certainly defeated no Indians, but wasted the arms, equipment, and provisions Georgia supplied him. Now our Chattahoochee crossings are more vulnerable than ever."

Chapter 24

Federal Road, Late June, 1836

"YO!" THE LEADER OF THE CAVALRY detachment threw up a hand to signal a halt. He and his charges pulled up in front of a modest farmhouse. "This looks like a good place to stop for a while."

"Obliged, Sergeant," said a soldier as he dismounted. "Road dust was getting to me. We need a break."

"We're in no hurry. Nothing on this miserable road, anyhow, but wreckage and blood."

The squad of regular army troops was one of several dispatched from Fort Mitchell by General Thomas Jesup, upon his return from South Alabama, to search for blockages along New Road and Federal Road. They were to survey damaged traces and bridges, wrecked stagecoaches and wagons, and other debris on the roads left by recent attacks. Crews would then be dispatched to repair bridges and surfaces. The routes had to be reopened for safe passage and, more importantly, for mail and freight transit to resume between New Orleans and Washington.

Additionally, the squad was to search for rogue Indians who had been scattered through the area by recent purges of nearby Muskogi villages, and to apprehend and transport them to Fort Mitchell. So far, this contingency had found no stragglers and seemed happy to have encountered none.

"I'm so tired of this horrible country and the heat," complained one tempered veteran. "Worst duty I've seen. Shore will be glad to get back home to Massachusetts."

A younger soldier sneered. "My enlistment is up in a couple of months. Then I'm going home and never leave Indiana again. Ever!"

"I cotton to that," said the sergeant, "but for now we're stuck with the chore at hand." He looked around and focused on the house. "Looks deserted. In decent shape though, as appears." He pointed to several of his mates nearby. "Go knock on the door. Maybe somebody's about. Then look around back and see if there's a branch or other water source. The horses need a drink."

The men returned in ten minutes. "No one's home, Sarge. Barn out back looks like it's been stripped of everything, hay, tools, livery gear, everything. No sign of livestock. Also, the folks' vegetable garden has been ripped up. Nothing left there, either."

Reported another, "No branch, Sarge, but there's a nice well aside the house. Water trough, too, for the horses."

Twenty minutes later the horses had drunk their fill. So had the men, reeling up bucket after bucket and passing the gourd dipper from man to man. After every soldier had refilled his canteen, the sergeant beckoned them to make ready to resume their travel.

A man wiped his mouth and sighed after a second pass with the dipper. "Man," he declared, "that's good water. I 'preciate a nice 'freshing well."

As the squad prepared to remount, an old man walked up, seeming to materialize out of nowhere. "Howdy, soldiers," he greeted. "Glad to see you fellas riding this road again. It ain't been rightly pleasant 'round here in past weeks."

The sergeant paused to face the man. "This your place?"

"Naw. I live down the road a piece, back in the woods so them wild bucks can't find me."

"Then whose farm is this?"

"Did belong to Josiah Smith."

"Did belong? Where is he now?"

"Dead. Them mean Indians kilt him 'bout a week ago."

"The Indians killed him?"

"Yep. Shore did. And dumped his body down that thar well over thar." He pointed to the well the men had just finished drinking from.

The sergeant and his men stood stunned, staring at the man. Then several began pouring out the contents of their canteens. One hardened soldier gagged and headed for the bushes.

❖ ❖ ❖

DAYS EARLIER, General Jesup arrived at Fort Mitchell leading a string of rebels he had captured in South Alabama. He meant to combine them with the large number of Muskogis already awaiting removal.

"Lieutenant," he summoned the first officer he encountered, "is Captain Page about? Have him report to me immediately." He gestured to the shackled Indians being guarded by his soldiers. "And throw these savages in with the others."

Jesup, feeling a false sense of success from his recent campaign, like General Scott, declared the war almost at its end. He set about preparing for the next step, the transport west of the sixteen hundred prisoners accumulated at the fort. Some of that populace were there voluntarily, but most by force. The general was little interested in pursuing additional rebels for now, though fully aware others were still in the wild.

"Captain," Jesup addressed Page when the latter reported, "how fares the repair of the Federal Roads?"

"Well, sir. Almost done. Already running the mails through."

"And preparations for the emigration?"

"Hard to the task, sir."

Indeed, Captain John Page, the removal superintendent at Fort Mitchell, had been preparing the Indian captives for clearance since Jesup left on his campaign. Blacksmiths hammered out chains and manacles for restraining the more rebellious warriors, as well as shoeing horses and repairing wagons. Page catalogued each Creek prisoner and voluntary emigre, and all family members destined for the journey.

Page had recently been appointed removal superintendent by Secretary of War Cass. He replaced John B. Hogan of Mobile, who had served since early 1835. Hogan also held the dual commission of investigating illegal land speculations and attempting to overturn many of the devious contracts, which had cheated the rightful Muskogi land holders.

Cass, and President Jackson by extension, became concerned Hogan was doing too good of a job in favor of the Indians. He replaced him with Page, a more acceptable representative of white business interests and a true believer in Jackson's removal law. At the same time, while retaining Hogan as investigator of land speculation, Cass appointed two associates for him, apparently to neutralize Hogan's efforts on behalf of wronged Muskogis.

White settlers and farmers gathered at Fort Mitchell to claim livestock, slaves, and possessions supposedly stolen by the Creeks and retrieved by the military. Other citizens came as spectators, from as far away as Columbus, to view and hassle the captives.

"Damn savages! Not so fierce now, are you?"

"Proud you're leaving, you scum. You aren't welcome here."

"Maybe civilized people can live in peace now. Hooray for General Jesup! Hooray for President Jackson!"

Standing proud among the shackled prisoners was eighty-six year-old Neah Emathla, hale as most of the warriors half his age. Observers, especially many newspaper reporters assembled for the occasion, found the old chief a fascinating study. One reporter judged him *peculiarly striking in his countenance* and the only Indian he had ever met that dared *look a white man full in the eye* when talking to him.

When captured, Neah Emathla requested of General Jesup, "Shoot me dead, sir. I prefer to die by your evil gun than be locked in chains."

"Nay, sir," replied Jesup. "I only wish to send you and your kind westward, not to execute you."

ON JULY 2ND, with all preparations completed, the procession in a long line left Fort Mitchell destined for Montgomery. Three companies of state troops escorted the gruesome parade. Captive warriors deemed hostile led off in pairs, each brace of adjacent men iron-cuffed at their wrists and tethered together. A long chain ran down the double column, locked onto the center of the short connector between each tandem.

Next came voluntary, non-belligerent men, which would add along the road Neah Micco and his villagers, followed by women and older children, not hiding their unhappiness. The women wailed and sobbed as they walked, open defiance toward the accompanying soldiers evident with every step. Last in line came wagons carrying the smallest children and the aged or feeble unable to manage the march themselves.

Neah Emathla walked at the head of his village warriors, not complaining or showing discomfort. His guards marveled at the aged, beaten campaigner and his dignity, an impressive man indeed.

WHEN GENERAL JESUP reached Tuskegee on July 7th, he encountered Neah Micco to accept his surrender. Only a few followers accompanied the old warrior.

"With my blessings, most of my townsmen have taken flight," he replied to Jesup's query of the scant group. "They do not wish to bow to your conditions."

"You damn lying savage!" Jesup screamed. "Why did you let your people get away? You broke your pledge of honor, you sonafabitch!"

An angry Jesup sent a company of Alabama volunteers under the command of General Patterson in search of the fugitives. Patterson was successful in running down some, who he dispatched to catch up with the assemblage at Montgomery for removal.

AFTER MORE THAN A WEEK'S MARCH on the newly refurbished Federal Road, the column reached Montgomery and camped at the riverfront boat docks to await the next leg of the journey. While they tarried, the pride and desperation of the captured Muskogis intensified. Some warriors swore they would not leave the homeland.

"Death is more acceptable! It is more honorable than abandoning the homeland of our fathers."

Several prisoners had committed suicide back at Fort Mitchell rather than submit to removal. The threat remained in Montgomery.

A squad of horsemen rode into camp asking for General Jesup. "Sir, we have a warrant from Governor Schley requesting extradition to Georgia of a number of criminal Creeks you might have in captivity."

Jesup scanned the document. "I see. These six men are accused of a variety of crimes. They should stand trial. If guilty, they must suffer punishment. They don't deserve to live in peace in the western territories. Yes, you shall have them."

As the guards culled the six and marched them forward, one held back. He scowled and cursed an oath in Muskogean. When a guard moved to urge him on, he reached behind his back and produced a knife. Before the guard could react, the man screamed another tirade, flashed the knife, and slid it across his throat. He was dead in minutes from a cascade of gushing blood.

An hour later, after the commotion had abated, another warrior stepped to the clearing between guards and belligerents. He pointed a second stolen knife high into the sky, yelled a pledge to his sacred forefathers, pivoted once, and swung the blade in a downward arc into his stomach. As he writhed in the dirt, but conscious, he withdrew the knife and plunged it again. Before guards could react, or perhaps chose not to, he managed to stab himself a third time. Still alive, he struggled for a fourth attempt, but no need. He died as he lay.

Guards and Indians alike gaped at the spectacle. As they stared at the carnage, another captive lifted a hammer off a nearby blacksmith table and approached a guard still ogling at the suicide. He raised it above the man's head.

"Watch out, Lige!" yelled a fellow soldier from across the way.

Too late. The hammer crashed into the top of the guard's skull. An instant later, as the victim fell under the embedded hammer, a fusillade of musket fire shredded the perpetrator.

Passage away from Montgomery had to hasten. Too many tragedies already preceded departure.

FINALLY, ALL ARRANGEMENTS were concluded. The itinerary was to include a downriver voyage to Mobile, a jaunt along the coast to the mouth of the Mississippi River, and up that river to Arkansas. There the emigrants would disembark for final passage to the promised lands of the Indian Territory.

On July 14th, the Creeks were loaded onto two steamboats and a barge towed by each. On those conveyances, 2498 souls of native Alabama soil sailed away from the land they and their forefathers had nurtured and loved for centuries.

Chapter 25

Falls on the Tallapoosa, July, 1836

"WE'RE HEARING STORIES of that army general hauling off all them pore Creeks from Fort Mitchell," said Sam Peavy. He, Perley Gerald, and John McKenzie conversed on the trading post porch. "Took 'em to Montgomery, they say, and somehow slapped 'em on a boat. If that's so, I don't know how they'll get out to the Injun Territory, or wherever they're s'posed to be taking 'em. Boats ain't safe."

His companions scoffed. "I'm hearing the same gab down my way," said McKenzie, up for a visit from his burgeoning downriver plantation. His spread stretched from just below the falls to nearly abutting the Muskogi warrior village of Talisi at the mouth of Yufabi Creek five miles downriver. "Tragic tales, most."

"Reckon they'll do the same with them folks?" Perley gestured to the removal encampment across the way. "When you reckon they'll send 'em along?"

"Oh, I guess when they think they have enough for another drive," said McKenzie. "I'm sure they're still collecting Creeks over at Fort Mitchell and down at Tuskegee. I understand they're holding a few over at Tuckabatchi who've volunteered to go."

Perley scoffed. "Harumph! Yeah, they call it volunteering, but them pore souls got no choice in the matter. For too many of 'em, it's go out west or perish here."

Just then, the conversation was interrupted by a gang of horsemen galloping away from the camp.

"Them fellas never ease out of here," complained Sam. "Always hurrying, like some'ings chasing 'em. Gotta be rough on their horses."

"Looks like they're heading to the Gaunt's Farm Road," noted Perley. "Maybe to do mischief out that way, or they could turn up toward the Saugahatchi settlements instead."

McKenzie sneered. "Don't want them scoundrels coming down my way. We get along just fine with the Creeks, and I don't want that to change. Certainly not because of some raid by that gang."

"Humph!" snorted Perley again. "Most of them fellas been in my store on occasion. Ain't nary one of 'em worth a blighted ear o' corn."

Sam gestured toward the horsemen disappearing into the forest. "That mean'un what had the run-in with the Murphs, uh, what's his name?"

"I think Taggle, or Toggitt, or, oh, I think it's Taggert," answered Perley.

"Yeah, that's it. Taggert. Anyhow, that snake works both as a land thief for the speculators, and a removal agent what goes out hunting pore Creeks to hound into that dastardly camp."

"Some of them others do, too," said Perley. "Don't know how they tolerate their ownselves."

"So far, they've stayed away from our Indian neighbors down my way," said McKenzie. "And they shore ain't bothered them bucks downriver at the Talisi village. I think they might be a mite scared of them fellas. With good reason. Those are fierce folks, not to be dallied with."

Perley and Sam chuckled. "Hee, hee," said Sam, "do my old bones a heap o' good to see that Taggert fella get tangled up with some of them Talisi warriors."

WITH THE DEPARTURE OF THE CREEKS from Fort Mitchell, and then by steamboats from Montgomery, General Jesup revised his assessment of two weeks previous when he deemed the war at a virtual end. Now, he declared, the war in Alabama was definitely over, and he dismissed most of his militia troops.

As much as Jesup wanted to believe his own braggadocio, he had missed again. Many villagers yet thrived in the wild, including the remnants of Neah Micco's town. Hostile stragglers camped in virgin thickets or assimilated themselves among still existing peaceful villages. Opothle Yahola, to avoid trouble with the army, complained to authorities that several belligerents were hiding with sympathizers in his town. Simultaneously, he protested to the same authorities when rogue militiamen, looking for a fight, murdered four friendly Euchees at Big Spring. He and other Indian leaders threatened to cease cooperation if the perpetrators were not caught and punished.

The trouble wasn't over. Hostile Red Sticks and Euchee rebels still resolved to foment mischief when they could. Land speculators yet preyed at will on legitimate Muskogi lot holders, virtually unchecked by government investigators. Removal agents had not slackened their scourge of the region.

General Jesup and Governor Clay, and Governor Schley on the Georgia side of the Chattahoochee, had not seen the last of their woes, or that of their charges.

❖ ❖ ❖

GENERAL WINFIELD SCOTT and President Andrew Jackson, in the past, had been political foes, Jackson a Union-Democrat and Scott an adamant Whig. Jackson had even once challenged Scott to a duel. Now they had come to odds again.

Reacting to dispatches from General Jesup and Governor Schley, and to growing public clamor in Columbus and Washington, President Jackson became concerned about General Scott's performance. Adding to the doubt, The Democrat-leaning *Washington Globe* newspaper published a letter to its editor from General Jesup complaining about Scott's tactics, comparing them partially with Scott's failed campaign against the Seminoles. The *scenes of Florida were enacted all over again*, he had written, citing needless delays and faulty planning.

As a result, Jackson decided to recall Scott from the field and summon him to Washington. He made Jesup the new commandant of federal forces in both Georgia and Alabama.

"That cursed Jackson!" stormed Scott upon receipt of Jackson's order. "I knew he couldn't be trusted. He has no loyalty, and he doesn't recognize leadership." He turned his rage to others. "This has to be Jesup's doing; he's a back-stabbing, treacherous bastard! And

Governor Schley is of little better repute. God's wrath be on both the scoundrels!"

General Scott rode out of Columbus on July 8th, bound for Washington and a confrontation with Jackson. He insisted upon departure he had ended the Second Creek War.

Chapter 26

Stewart County, Georgia, July 22, 1836

PADDLERS AND SWIMMERS made no splash as they ferried one canoe after another containing women and children across the dark Chattahoochee. An absent moon, plus a light overcast, hid a man from mere feet away without other concealment. Working most of the night, more than two hundred fifty Creeks reached the eastern bank before daylight. The site was a scant two miles below Fort McCreary, one of Governor Schley's posts to guard against illegal crossings.

The group, the minority of who were seasoned warriors, was led by one of the Euchee village chiefs, Nulkarpuche Tustenuggee, and included refugees from splintered towns throughout the Upper and Lower Nations. Remnants of Neah Micco's town, and others escaping removal squads, had joined the pack with the intent of making it to Florida. They felt confident once there they could join one of the Seminole tribes.

Nulkarpuchee Tustenuggee thought it folly to immediately head south with the probability of encountering patrolling militias close along the Chattahoochee. Instead, he decided to start northeast to throw off potential pursuers, and then bear east for a few miles before turning south.

The ploy seemed to work until observed by a slave boy gathering firewood in the forest. The lad ran to Fort McCreary.

"Sir," reported a sergeant, "there's a young darky out here babbling something about Indians."

The militia company commander, Major Julius C. Alford, looked up from his paperwork. "Indians? What about 'em?"

"Not sure, sir. He's pretty worked up."

"Okay. Let's have 'im, then."

The aide ushered in a shirtless youngster of about twelve. He walked in with his head down and his eyes diverted.

"What's this about Indians, boy?"

"I seen 'em, suh."

"Where? Mind you, look up at me, boy. Where did you see Indians?

"In the woods, suh."

"What woods? Talk to me, boy."

The scared youth turned and pointed south. "That way, suh."

"Yeah? How many Indians?"

"Mon', suh. Mon', mon'."

Alford turned to the aide. "Sergeant, dispatch a couple of scouts on the south river road and see if they can pick up some kinda trail. Then call out the troops. Get 'em ready to ride in case this little sonafabitch is telling the truth."

The scouts returned at a gallop two hours later. "We picked up a trail, sir," one reported. "They crossed the river two miles south and headed east."

"How many?"

"Had to be a large group, perhaps two hundred or more. They tracked through the woods and made no effort to hide their goings. We followed the trail for a couple of miles until ... uh, this was strange, sir. They seemed to turn northeast, not south like might be expected."

"When? Could you tell when they crossed the river?"

"Best guess, sir, from the signs I'd say they have at least a full day start." He looked at his scout partner, who nodded agreement.

Twenty minutes later, a mounted force of ninety-eight cavalrymen thundered from Fort McCreary in pursuit.

The troops, with Major Alford in the lead, tracked the Indians for fifteen miles over the rest of the day and overnight. The next morning, on July 24th, as they neared a large plantation in Stewart County, a forward scout returned with news.

"We've found them, sir, a mile ahead. Looks like a rear guard party. Don't think they know we're here."

"Well done, trooper." The major turned to a young officer. "Lieutenant, take two squads and attack that party. We'll follow in reserve to move on their full body."

A half hour later, the forest filled with a staccato of gunshots. The troopers had the Creeks' rear guard in flight.

"Forward, men!" ordered Alford. He meant to mop up on his advance troops' work and to push the attack onto the whole of the Indian force. The pursuit emptied onto a broad estate a trooper recognized as the plantation of a Mr. Quarles.

Major Alford was encouraged by the small Creek force resisting his charge. "We have them now!" cheered delighted soldiers. Ahead, on the grounds of the plantation, the commander saw at least a hundred women and children, but few warriors. He urged his troops on, tasting certain victory.

Suddenly, out of the woods, surrounding the troops, poured dozens of screaming warriors firing on the pursuers. Realizing they had been tricked into a trap, the militiamen halted their assault and milled around, confused and frightened, under a hail of gunfire.

"Back into the trees!" "Take cover!" "Set up skirmish lines!" ordered officers.

For over an hour the Georgians fought off skirting movements by Indians on both flanks. The fierce battle raged hot before some random soldier panicked and yelled, "All men, to your horses! Retreat!"

The shocked major stood erect from his cover, waving his arms. "No, no! Stay! Keep fighting!" Up and down the lines, exposing himself to danger, he urged his men to stand fast. "We can't retreat! We have 'em beaten. Soldiers, I order you to stand your ground! Sergeant, stop those men!"

No use. The company was in full flight, racing through the forest on foot, looking to catch their mounts. They headed back to Fort McCreary, disorganized and in a panic. The exasperated leader was compelled to follow his fleeing command, leaving behind five troopers lying dead in the field.

The major's report claimed his company had killed twenty-two of the enemy despite being outnumbered two to one. In reality, excluding Indian non-combatants such as women, children, and the infirm, the Georgians enjoyed superiority of numbers, weapons, mounts, and equipment.

Even with those advantages, the Georgia troops had managed to suffer defeat in the Battle of Quarles Plantation.

HEARING OF THE FIGHT at Quarles, Governor Schley and Major General John W.A. Sanford, now with an increased rank and command of all Georgia militia forces, knew the war had resumed. They had believed the overplayed analyses of Generals Scott and Jesup when they claimed they had defeated the Creeks in Alabama and along the Chattahoochee, thereby ending the war. Based on those reports, Schley had dismissed all Georgia militia units from state service save the garrison at Fort McCreary.

John W.A. Sanford of Columbus trailed an interesting history, mostly one of unsavory doings. A strong Jacksonian, he enjoyed notoriety as a local Georgia politician and self-styled militia leader. After passage of the Indian Removal Act, Secretary of War Cass appointed him as an agent in charge of overseeing Indian land sales in Russell and Barbour Counties over in Alabama. His commission was to protect the Creeks against fraud. Instead, he began to ignore dubious transactions in favor of his friends in Columbus.

In the wake of a series of specious investigations in his role as agent, Sanford ran for the United States House of Representatives in the spring of 1835 and won the seat. Upon arriving in Washington, he absorbed the politics of what was really happening in Creek country. Influenced by factions in D.C. and back in Columbus, he became even more interested in Muskogi land tracts, and not for the benefit of the Indians. He allegedly lobbied on behalf of business friends, including Eli S. Shorter and his Columbus Land Company.

A group of six businessmen in Georgia decided to form their own land speculation and Indian removal supply firm. One of the conspirators was a Mr. J. Beattie, who already sported notoriety as a thief of Creek lands and slaves. His partners' reputations fared little better in the eyes of honest citizens."

Scheming to make his group more appealing to the War Department, Beattie approached Sanford. "We could benefit from a spokesman of your prominence, Congressman Sanford," he pitched. "We would be most honored if you would throw in with us as our representative."

Sanford elected to lobby for the cabal in Congress, even as a member of the body, but soon yielded to the temptation of ill-gotten riches. He resigned his Congressional seat after only a few months in office and headed back to Columbus as an active participant. There, he took charge of 'Sanford and Company' and worked the War Department for various contracts regarding Creek emigration, many of them fraudulent. He also resumed his role as a local militia leader.

In early July, President Jackson, disappointed with General Winfield Scott's performance, recalled him to Washington. When Scott departed Columbus on July 8, he yet boasted erroneously about having defeated the Indians in Alabama and ending the war.

Governor Schley interviewed several militia officers as candidates to fill Scott's void, settling on Colonel John W.A. Sanford. Schley gifted him with a glorified commission of major general and appointed him commandant of all Georgia militia forces.

Now, the burden of a renewed and intensified Creek war faced Sanford and Schley, but also Governor Clay in Alabama and General Thomas Jesup, still on the scene as commander of remaining federal troops in both states.

THE MORNING AFTER the July 24th Quarles Plantation battle, Nulkarpuche Tustenuggee led his assemblage southeast toward the Chickasawhatchee Swamp, a haven in which he knew he could hide to rest and recuperate. Major Henry W. Jernigan of the Stewart County Rangers in Lumpkin, a veteran of a previous skirmish at the swamp, moved to intercept them. Gathering as many of his militiamen as he could reach, he pursued the Indians while sending a request to Fort McCreary for reinforcements. Fort McCreary ignored the plea, but Jernigan persisted for a day and a night without the expected aid.

"Halt the column," the major ordered his aide when a forward scout galloped back toward him.

"Sir, the enemy is ahead, camped at Mr. Jones's plantation. I'm certain we are safe from detection."

"Good. What is the lay?"

"A wide cornfield lies between us and the grounds on which they tarry. Other fields and forestland appear beyond."

Jernigan assembled his officers and drafted a plan. "Spread the men through the cornfield and ease through on foot to the far edge. Total silence. We must attack them unaware, so wait for my signal when everyone is in place."

After waiting an inordinate time for all the men to silently sneak through the corn stalks, the first ones in position became impatient. "I got one of the bastards in my sights," whispered one soldier to another. "Watch this." He pulled the trigger, shattering any hope of surprise.

"What the hell!" screamed Major Jernigan. "Who fired that shot? Well, hell, attack, men! Attack!"

Shots already sounded from those on the edge of the field, and from warriors near the farmhouse. Soldiers still working through the corn now hurried to the edge and assumed prone firing positions.

A furious, sustained battle ensued. Then, in a lull when it seemed the Indian defenses were weakening, Jernigan stood and ordered, waving his sword, "We have em' beaten, lads! Up and lively! Charge!"

Two soldiers started to leap to their feet but hesitated when they saw others not moving. They returned to their cover.

"Charge, I say!" implored Jernigan. "Why are you not on your feet?"

"Because they'll cut us down, Major," answered a voice.

"Damn you to hell, you passel of cowards!"

The momentary dissension in the militia ranks gave a dozen warriors a chance to shuffle to more advantageous positions. From improved firing angles, they launched a fresh volley of musket balls. The attackers began to recede at a crawl deeper into the stalks.

"Fall back and regroup, men," ordered Jernigan. The troops retreated but failed to establish a new skirmish line. They fled through the cornfield in search of their horses, so Jernigan had no option but to order a full retreat. Two of his militiamen were left behind, dead among the cornstalks.

Nulkarpuche Tustenuggee gathered his warriors and hurriedly buried his fatalities. He then broke camp and rushed on to Chickasawhatchee Swamp, and eventually to Florida to unite with the Seminoles.

With this victory to add to the one at Quarles, Nulkarpuchee Tustenuggee could now boast of two key triumphs over the Muskogi Nation's white tormentors.

SCHLEY AND SANFORD FACED a major problem. With increased hostilities on both sides of the Chattahoochee, Sanford ordered numerous town and county militia units to reactivate and reinforce certain vital points, only to be rebuffed. Communities in Southwest Georgia had seen enough trouble and seemed willing to ignore Indian traverses through their area as long as travelers, white or red, stayed peaceful.

The situation became acute. Raids and illicit river crossings overwhelmed the Fort McCreary garrison and the few militias along the river still willing to respond. General Sanford hit on a show of decisive action, and marched four companies of cavalry and an infantry battalion from Columbus to Fort McCreary with himself at the head.

Sanford announced upon departure he would not return without success. "I will pursue the enemy to the south keys of Florida if need be," he pledged. His show of force, however, yielded only scattered results, and the war continued.

Chapter 27

Yufabi Creek, July, 1836

A QUARTER MOON DANCED from cloud to cloud over the night sky, often sailing into clear air to glisten its image off the swift, clean currents of Yufabi Creek. Nothing stirred, the only sounds the hoot of a contented owl and the mournful wail of some distant, distressed forest creature.

The moon darted for another cloud, once again turning the night from very dark to ink black. From the cover of underbrush on the south bank of the stream slipped nearly a dozen men. They glided over the sandbar beach and into the shallow water, and waded without a ripple upstream to reach a similar beach on the other side. As quickly as they had emerged, they hustled across the sand and disappeared into the trees lining the north shore. The moon floated free again.

The men were Muskogis, dressed this night in bright red war paint of their Red Stick fathers of more than two decades ago. The anger of those times had not abated. These young warriors and many compatriots, filled with fury, vowed to resist the oppressive government's intrusion into their ancestral grounds, even to fight as their fathers had fought. If they were to suffer the same disastrous defeat, so be it. They would perish with their honor intact.

A dog barked from the edge of Clem MacCulliver's yard, two hundred yards from the creek. An arrow from the adjacent thicket silenced the bark. A restless horse whinnied in the barn at the rear of the clearing then lantern light shone through the cracks in shutters of the house. The front door opened and a man stepped out. He held a musket in the crook of one arm and a lighted oil lantern in the opposite hand.

"I say, anyone there?" the man called in a distinct European accent. No answer. The hoot of the owl no longer sounded. "Who's about?" No answer. "Here, Tiger. Here, boy." He paused a moment to listen. "Now, where is that bloody cur?"

The gang of warriors stepped from the trees as one, evenly spaced a few paces apart. They boldly marched to the edge of MacCulliver's lantern light, their fronts squared to him and weapons at their sides. The Scotsman leveled his musket at the intruders, pivoting the muzzle from one to another, but not daring to fire. Fearful, he retreated backward to the door and stumbled inside, hastily closing the latch.

"Come out, white man!" ordered one of the Creeks in fair English. "Bring family with you."

After a long minute, the door cracked. MacCulliver peered out. He studied the invaders. Finally, "Nay! Away with ye!" He slammed the door.

Keeping his calm but menacing voice, the leader again implored, "Come, white man MacCulliver. Or we come in shoot you."

The door cracked open again, this time a little wider. "What do you want of me?"

"Come out, MacCulliver. We come burn house."

"Wh ... why?"

"You know why, white man. This our land. You no right here. These grounds not belong whites. You have them not!"

"I ... I bought this property from Mr. Taggert," stammered MacCulliver.

"Taggert stole it. White mans steal our forests and hunting grounds. Whiskey and lies cheat Muskogis."

"But I haven't stolen from anyone. I've been fair to all you Indians. Friends."

"That's why we no kill you if leave tonight."

"You won't hurt my family, will you?" MacCulliver pleaded. "Please don't hurt them."

"We not wish hurt anyone, white man, not you or family. We burn house and barn now and turn ground back to forest."

"Then you aren't going to kill us?"

The Indian leader's composure slipped into anger. "We not murderers, as are white mans. They steal Muskogi land, kill my people. We not wish kill you. Soldiers would ride after us and we must fight them again." The man's patience had expired. "We want you leave this night. Get family out of house. We burn now."

The man gestured to one of his colleagues holding a freshly fired pine-knot torch. The henchman stepped toward the rough board house, hastily built by the Scottish farmer only a month earlier.

MacCulliver yelped and ran to the closed door. He yelled and frantically waved those inside to him, urging and scolding with rapid, panicked instructions. A small boy ran out, followed by a slightly older girl, then a crying woman, and finally a boy of twelve or thirteen. The woman huddled the children together in the yard away from the Indians. Each fearful eye watched the strangers. MacCulliver, still holding his musket, scurried over to assume a protective position before them.

The Indian leader strode to MacCulliver and calmly, without resistance, removed the musket from his arms. He inspected its gunlock, then took a large knife from his belt and pried loose the flint from the hammer. He eased the steel strike and the hammer closed, and threw the weapon to the bare dirt of the yard.

"Move back!" the Indian snarled at MacCulliver. He motioned again to his aide, who glided to the house and began touching the flame to tinder spots. Almost immediately, several fires burned within the house and along the outside walls. The woman and her two youngest children cried.

The Creek warriors whooped and began a dance of celebration. They chanted in Muskogean. The leader did not join in, but stared at the flames until they had fully caught. Soon the several small fires had merged into a single inferno. The crude, half-finished barn was also now afire while several warriors chased MacCulliver's horse, mule, and two cows into the wilderness.

Suddenly, the leader shrieked a frightening scream. Then he turned to his men.

"We leave now!" he ordered. He pivoted to MacCulliver and his distraught family. "You go. Not come back. Next time we kill."

The man waved his party toward the thicket from which they had come. They reentered and disappeared through the woods, silently and stealthily.

The MacCullivers stood shaking in the yard, easing farther and farther from the burning house as the heat grew in intensity. The family clustered together, saying nothing but continuing to cry.

"Clem, what will we do?" finally sobbed Mrs. MacCulliver.

"I don't know," admitted her husband. "The only thing we can do for now is wait for daylight. Then we'll have to make our way north to Mr. Gerald's place at the falls."

Just then the doomed house and barn crashed to the ground simultaneously. The fires continued to burn hot, but now they weren't quite so bright.

Chapter 28

Near Calibee Creek, July, 1836

THE SQUAD OF SPECIAL STATE AGENTS spotted a wisp of smoke far to the west just at sundown. Suspecting it might lead them to their prey, they approached cautiously for the next two hours. They walked their horses on the softest ground possible, dismounted, and led them across gravel and other ground to muffle sound. When they caught a sniff of campfire smoke, they crept on foot for several hundred yards.

"Hold up," the leader whispered to the men directly behind. "I mighta seen it."

The posse of eleven civilian agents attached to the military outpost at Tuskegee had sought a renegade band of Red Stick Creeks since dawn of the previous day. Word had reached the Tuskegee commandant of a raid on a farm a few miles up Yufabi Creek two nights before. He assembled the agents from the contingent assigned to him and sent them in pursuit.

Most of the Tuskegee command, as well as that at the falls and other depots, were regional militiamen. They had been recruited and deputized to help gather indigent Creeks and Indian criminals for transport west in the coming weeks. The Red Sticks, or those pretending to be such and employing their fathers' bloodthirsty tactics against innocent white settlers, were certainly criminals. They had to be suppressed and contained.

The posse leader, Assam Felder, signaled for his men strung out behind to hold positions. Then he waved one, a trained scout, to follow him. The two handed off their reins to the next man, and

Felder again motioned for everyone to stay put. He and the scout dropped low and crept another hundred yards to confirm the flicker of firelight Felder thought he glimpsed. There it was, unmistakably.

A small fire burned less than a half mile away. They detected movement, but the combination of distance and dimming light failed to reveal the number of men, or if they were even Indians. But Felder, confident the band was who he sought, gestured to his accomplice, and the scout nodded back in agreement. They had found their renegades.

Returning to the squad, Felder had the horses hobbled and organized his attack. "Check your rifles and cartridges, men, and freshen the priming." He gestured right and left through the woods. "Three men that way, three more the other. Outflank the camp and wait for my signal. You others follow me. Spread aside at five-yard intervals." He again addressed his men before they deployed. "We wish to surprise the vermin and take 'em with little trouble if we can. Be careful."

Twenty minutes later, Felder's team had crept to within forty yards of the campfire. From there, they confirmed the men were Indians, but counted only four.

Hold your ground, Felder signaled to the four with him, two on each side. He deemed it wise to observe the scene for several additional minutes, lest more Creeks appear from somewhere nearby. Also, he wanted to give the flanking teams ample time to establish positions.

Finally, satisfied the four Creeks comprised the whole of the party, it was time to act. After flashing a hand signal to his accomplices, Felder stood up, his long rifle ready.

"Hark the camp!" he yelled. "Hold your places. You're under arrest."

All four Indians lurched upright, startled. Paralyzed for only seconds, they quickly backed from the firelight. With lightning moves, each snatched up weapons and started a run for the trees, but skidded short. Three men emerged from the forest on either side, shouting orders, and with raised rifles aimed at the Creeks' eyes.

One Indian lifted his musket, simultaneously cocking it and pointing it toward the nearest attacker. The agent squeezed his trigger and the Red Stick catapulted backward, his face catching an explosion and a swirl of burning powder, his weapon flying to the side, and him dead before landing with a rifle ball in his forehead. In the turmoil, the other three renegades broke for the forest.

One of the Indians, with his musket held across his front with both hands, ran headlong into an attacker, knocking him to the ground. He attempted to push past, but the adjacent agent swung his rifle stock into the runner's face with a sickening, bloody *Splat!* The agent then jerked a heavy skinning knife from his belt and slashed it across the writhing man's back. He recoiled to ready a stabbing thrust, but Felder stepped over the man's body and held up a restraining hand.

"Stay that!" the leader yelled. "Don't kill 'im. We need prisoners."

Amid the struggle, the remaining two Creeks escaped to the unguarded side of the fire and into the forest. Three agents who still held charged weapons pursued them through the woods and down a slope toward Calibee Creek. A musket shot from somewhere in the dark morass stopped them.

"Aiiee!" screamed one man as the three dived for cover. "Damn savages!"

"Are you hit?" asked the man next to him while the third returned the shot, firing wildly into the darkness.

"No, damnit! But that musket ball hit the tree inches from my head. The scurvy bastards!"

Splashing water far below told the pursuers their quarry had reached and crossed the creek. Wary of proceeding blind, they returned to the campfire.

"Damn!" cursed Felder. "You let 'em get away."

"Can't chase the sonsabitches in the dark, Assam," reasoned one. "Them scoundrels can see better at night than us in daylight."

Felder cursed again then pointed to the wounded man on the ground, his hands lashed behind his back. "Well, let's get this'n back to Tuskegee. We'll freshen our kits and get after them two again, and the rest of the pack. There's more of that gang what burned down MacCulliver's place than just them four."

"What about the dead'n, Assam?" asked an agent.

"Oh, hell, dig a quick hole and bury him. And smooth over the grave so no one will notice it. We can't leave evidence around. 'Sides, nobody gone be looking for 'im. Who cares 'bout a damn Indian, anyhow?"

While the men dug the sandy soil, working in short shifts two at a time, others fetched the squad's horses. A half hour later, the last of the soft dirt was packed atop the grave.

"Okay, gather everything and let's ride," ordered Felder. "Sid, you first pack the prisoner double on your mount. We'll swap 'im around ever' few miles."

Two men roughly grabbed the wounded, tethered Red Stick and wrested him toward Sid's big stallion. One looked at his hand and wiped it on his pants. Then he glanced at the prisoner's slashed back and checked the bleeding, ugly cut atop his fractured cheekbone and eye socket.

"Assam, this bastard's lost lots of blood and he's still bleeding. What should we do for 'im?"

"Nothing. Damn him. Let 'im bleed. Maybe some of that meanness will drain outta 'im."

THE TWO FLEEING RED STICKS ran through the knee-deep creek and up the opposite slope. They paused behind a thicket of scrub brush to listen for their pursuers. Shouts and curses faintly reached them from a distance. They concluded their foes had conceded the chase, but they jogged on another quarter of a mile and set up at the end of a small clearing. There, they could take time to reload their muskets and shoot from ambush if anyone popped into the clearing.

After reloading and priming, and hearing nothing for many minutes, the two warriors felt revenge gnawing at their craws. Gnashing their teeth and grunting obscenities, they worked their way back to the creek and crept up the slope with little sound. They sneaked to within a few yards of the clearing where they had earlier laid their campfire, and squeezed against two massive pines only thirty yards from the attackers.

The Indians listened and, though not understanding the whites' language, realized they had just finished burying their friend and were preparing to leave. Sneaking a peek, they saw their other compatriot, badly wounded, roughly muscled to a horse and lifted to its back behind the saddle. The two looked at each other and nodded, as if to say, *At least he's still alive.*

With a quick prayer to the spirits, one stalker gestured to his partner with his musket, then gently, quietly pulled back the hammer and lifted the strike plate into position. The second man followed his action, then both kneeled and snaked their weapons around the tree trunks.

Almost together both muskets flashed and boomed, spewing smoke and fire. One of the white men, in the act of mounting his horse with one foot in a stirrup and the other leg swinging over the steed's flank, yelped in agony and pitched backward onto a hard landing. The other musket ball whined harmlessly inches above its intended target, a second agent. The struck victim rolled on the ground, screaming and clutching his right side, a lead bullet in his hip.

"Dismount!" thundered the leader of the whites. His men had not waited for his order. Most were already prone in the grass, their rifles cocked and searching for targets.

The wounded man writhed in agony. "Aaagh!" he bellowed. "I'm shot in my butt. Shoot 'em! Shoot 'em!"

"Fan out!" yelled Felder. "Fire at anything that moves. The sneaky weasels!"

Moot orders, for already the two Red Sticks thrashed through the waters of Calibee Creek, recrossing it at full sprint and again heading up the opposite slope to safety.

Chapter 29

The Murph Compound, August, 1836

"PA, I'VE MADE THIS TRIP dozens of times," argued Anna as she curried her horse. "No sense getting all riled up about it now."

"I know, Honey," countered Saul, "but these ain't normal times. There's lots of folks milling 'round down there now, some of 'em bad."

"I'm aware, Pa. I've seen 'em. But I can handle myself."

"No doubt about that, little girl. I've seen you do it many times." Saul chuckled. He paused in his task of sorting and repairing leather harness and gear and fixed a stern eye on his daughter. "But I'm wary about some of those men."

"I ain't scared of them guys."

"Oh, I know you ain't. Problem is, I think some of 'em might be scared of you and take it up to do something about it."

"Phoo! Well, I'm going anyhow. It's my job."

Traveling to the falls to barter and purchase supplies at Perley Gerald's trading post once a month wasn't exactly Anna's job, but she considered it such. She enjoyed the trip, loving the ride through the forests and along the river, and getting lost in nature. She liked Mr. Gerald and his wife Melissa, and most of those who traded with them. A few neighbors would often drop by while she was there, and she relished the chance to catch up on family news and gossip. 'Supplies Day' was always a fun day for Anna, and she was jealous of retaining it for her own.

Occasionally, maybe once a week, one of the Murphs would have to make a hurried trip to the falls to obtain a tool or other item that couldn't wait for the normal supply list. That person was often

Anna, but such an errand didn't hold the same aura for her as the all-out monthly supplies replenishment.

Saul surrendered. "Okay, Honey, you can go, but one condition. Take Matthew and Holt with you." He looked across the barn where Cal was pitching hay into stalls and enjoying the argument. "Okay if Matthew goes with her, Cal?"

"Shore." Cal laughed. "She won't hurt 'im, will she?"

Saul joined the joke. "She might. Can't guarantee nothing Anna might do."

Anna ignored the teasing. "What good would they do me?"

"Well, for one thing, Missy," answered Saul, "they're both bigger'n you. And you're Muskogi, what some of them thugs don't like."

"Holt's Muskogi."

"But Matthew ain't. That might put some of the rowdies off if they're a mind to sass you."

"Okay," Anna conceded, "I guess I'll let 'em go. But them two smart alecks better behave theirselves or I might chuck 'em in the river."

A SCANT TWO HOURS after the sun had fully risen the next morning, Anna, her cousin Matthew, and her brother Holt approached the shoals crossing three miles above the falls. They led two mules laden with fresh vegetables, nuts and berries, and cured deer, rabbit, and beaver pelts. These would be traded with Mr. Gerald for flour, cooking oil, coffee, and other foodstuffs, as well as various household items requested by each of the Murphs. Also aboard were two large bags of shelled corn to be ground into meal at Mr. Gerald's small mill at the edge of the river rapids below the bluff.

Anna, with one of the mules trailing at the end of a lead rope, urged her horse into the river first. The boys followed, leading the other loaded jack. The water flowed higher and swifter than usual and felt good to the riders' feet. The horses and mules paused in midstream to allow the cool current to splash against their bellies. Their ears peaked as they delighted in the river washing away the rising heat of the August morning.

Reaching the east bank, Anna reined her horse to wait on the others, who wrestled with their balky mule. She giggled at them fussing at the stubborn beast giving them trouble. The boys maintained control, but barely.

Anna glanced upriver and saw a large group of people traveling toward her down the trail from the Saugahatchi region. She continued to watch the group even after Matthew and Holt successfully led their mule from the shoals. They joined her in studying the procession, which they now made out to be Muskogis, all women and children except for two aged men. They plodded along, dressed in tatters and carrying bare possessions.

"Do you know them?" asked Matthew.

"No," replied Anna. "I don't think I've seen any of 'em before."

Anna greeted the group in Muskogean as they came near. They stopped in front of the Murphs, apparently glad to rest, and a young woman stepped forward. She tried to smile, recognition in her eyes.

"You are of the Murphs, are you not?" the woman asked.

"Yes, we are. Pardon, please, but I don't recall meeting you."

"Everyone knows of Mr. Saul and Mr. Cal. They are good people and friends of Muskogis."

"Yes, they are. Thank you. They are our fathers. My name is Anna, and this is Matthew and Holt." Anna perused the group. "Where are you going?" she asked, afraid she already knew the answer.

The woman sighed. "We must join others of our people at the falls. Our men are gone, some dead and some hiding in the woods from soldiers. The ones who have been arrested are soon to be forced to leave in irons. Soldiers promise to take them to new homes far away, along with others camped at the bluffs."

"We know. It is a cruel thing they do."

"All hope is gone, and we must go with our people. We would not survive here, even if they let us stay."

"I'm sorry. I wish we could help. But we would be happy to go along with you on your way. We're journeying to Mr. Gerald's place ourselves."

"Thank you, Anna. Mr. Gerald is, too, a nice man."

"Yes, he is." Anna dismounted and handed her mule's lead rope to one of the boys. She took her reins in hand and fell in beside her new friend to walk the remaining three miles with her. "Let's go." She smiled at the woman.

Over the next mile, Anna learned much about the band of Indians. They had lived on bare staples for over a month at their small village near the mouth of Saugahatchi Creek. Their husbands and older sons had been forced to flee by land speculators and looters, or had been captured or killed by soldiers and agents. Large plots of Indian land along the creek had been swindled away or outright stolen. Land grants promised by the Indian Removal law and government treaties were invalidated or ignored.

Anna knew many of the document deeds given to the Muskogis had been simply thrown away by recipients, ignorant and uninformed of their importance. These rightful land owners were easy victims of speculator predators and squatters. They had either meekly acceded to fraud or futilely fought for months to retain their land. The grantees who knew the value of their deeds were striving hard to keep their property, but most of them, too, were losing the fight to greedy predators and criminals.

As she and the woman chatted, Anna noticed four horsemen riding toward them. She stopped at a wide place in the trail and gestured for the Indian group to move aside to make room for the men to pass.

As the horsemen approached they made no move to ride by, but stopped directly in front of Anna and the woman. "Well, looka here," reviled one of the men. "I do believe it's that purty little Indian squaw from up the river a piece."

"Ah, Rab," countered another, "you know there ain't no such thing as a purty Indian." All four laughed.

"Who's this ugly Indian hag with 'er? And all these other wretches and little savages?"

Matthew and Holt, who had been trailing at the rear of the procession, walked their mounts to the front, sensing a threat. Both cradled rifles perpendicularly across their saddles. They reined to a stop beside Anna, who had pushed the woman behind her.

"Ha, who're you two, and whatta you think you are?"

"Hey, one of 'em is another damn Indian, Rab. Just like the little bitch squaw. But they don't look like they belong with these other scamps."

"Sir," Anna began slowly, fighting mounting rage, "we would like to continue on our way." She ground her teeth. "Would you please stand aside?"

The man called Rab laughed. "No, we won't 'stand aside'," he mocked. "Not for no damn Indians. Instead, why don't we just escort all of you down to the falls and turn you over to Major Elliott and Captain Brodnax at the removal camp? They'll be happy to have new Indian meat to herd out west."

"Sir, you have no right to threaten us," said Anna. Hot anger accented her defiance. Beside her, still on their horses, Matthew and Holt slowly lifted their weapons, thumbs on hammers ready to pull them into cocked positions.

Anna gestured them to ease off. "Settle down, boys," she cautioned. "I can handle this."

"Yeah, she can handle it all right, boys, so don't go getting no notions," warned Rab with a sneer. "We'd hate to shoot you." Behind him, his three henchmen raised long rifles and aimed them at Matthew and Holt. "Now, all of you are coming with us. We'll have those two loaded-down mules as our payment. There might even be a little money reward out for some of you vermin." He laughed again. "I might take the purty half-breed squaw for myself."

A strong voice boomed from the trees halfway up the adjacent bluff. "Don't harbor any such thoughts, gentlemen!" The four men, startled, jerked their rifles toward the utterance, waggling them in a frantic, fruitless search. The invisible speaker continued. "I suggest you ease your weapons and be on your way, for we pledge to shoot dead the first one who does otherwise."

Chapter 30

Near the Falls, August, 1836

THE THREATENING COMMAND from high up the bluff momentarily paralyzed each person on the trail. The man known as Rab and his pals waved their guns in the direction of the voice. They sought the speaker hidden somewhere in the thick forest.

"Where are you?" yelled Rab. "Whattya want?" He pointed his rifle from tree to tree.

"Careful with those irons, gentlemen," warned the voice, level and calm. "They could be dangerous."

"Show yourself, whoever you are, or I'll come find you and shoot yore eyes out."

"I 'spect you'd better do as I'm telling and ease up with your guns. We have the advantage."

"Ha!" jeered Rab as he and his men continued to scan the bluff. Their fidgeting had spooked their mounts, which stamped nervously. "I hear you to be but one man. We gotcha outnumbered four to one."

"Oh, but there are two of us, and I have one of you in my sights at this moment. I'll drop you at a first wrong move. Then I can reload faster than you can find me. Trust me, my man, I don't miss."

"You're bluffing."

"No, I ain't, but try me if you must. Also, I believe your numbers are wrong. Matthew, Holt, train your weapons on them weasels."

The Murph boys, until now indecisive without knowing the identity or intent of the stranger, quickly lifted their rifles and cocked them ready.

"It's Mr. Brayke!" recognized Holt. "Anna, it's Mr. Brayke."

Anna looked up at Holt. "I knew it was him right off," she said.

"Now," called Kaspar Brayke, still concealed, "you four boys who ain't welcome, cock your weapons, point the muzzles high into the sky, and pull the triggers."

"What?"

"Do it or get shot, friend."

Rab grumbled, "You ain't no friend of mine, and you can't order me what to do."

"Yes, he can," said Anna as she poked the muzzle of her long rifle, which she had retrieved from her saddle, into Rab's ribs. He flinched then sneered at her. She pulled back the hammer with a menacing click.

The other three men scowled and cursed as they lifted their guns vertically and fired, almost as one. Each animal, startled, jumped and jerked against their restraints. Most of the Indians, standing by, also recoiled, wide-eyed. Billows of acrid, choking white smoke followed the blasts and engulfed the trail before drifting to the river.

"Now, you!" Anna spat at Rab. Her rifle barrel again nudged his side.

Rab reluctantly pointed the rifle skyward. "You goddamn Indian bitch!" he blurted as he pulled the trigger. He winced at the blast. "Damn you to hell!"

Kaspar Brayke stepped from around a tangle of brush onto the trail, having made his way down the slope. Rube followed a second later and offered a threatening snarl.

"Down, Rube. It's all right." The dog calmed with a wag of his tail. "Are all in good health?" Kaspar inquired.

"All but these four," Matthew gloated. "I opine they've had their feelings hurt." He and Holt laughed.

Rab scanned up the bluff, searching. "You said there was two of you. Where's the other?"

Kaspar pointed to his red hound. "Meet my partner here, name of Rube."

"You sonofabitch!" Rab screamed. "I'm gonna kill you, you bastard!"

"Not today, I fear. Now, gentlemen," addressed Kaspar to the gang of bullies, "I urge you to ride on up the trail and not look back. We're watching you, so don't reload them squirrel irons till you've left our sight." He glared at Rab. "Helpful advice, friend, next time you meet a Muskogi, you should tip your hat and bid him good day. You meet far less trouble that way."

"Hell with you, you damn Indian-loving scum!" Rab blurted. "Rot in hell!"

"Save me a place when you get there," chortled Kaspar. "Now, git!" He smacked the flank of Rab's horse with his hand. Startled, the animal leaped, almost dislodging its angry rider. The Muskogi band moved farther to the side to allow the four men to ride past.

"Thanks, Mr. Brayke," said Matthew as the group continued monitoring the riders to assure compliance with Kaspar's orders. "You saved our skins."

"Yeah," echoed Holt. "I rightly admire how you got the advantage on them guys. How'd you happen on us?"

"Oh, we were out trying to plunk a rabbit for our supper, and I heard a commotion. My camp sits atop the bluff, a short piece south of here. When we saw you, I just thought we'd join the fun. Hope you don't mind us butting in."

"We're obliged, Mr. Brayke," said Anna. She gestured to the band of Creeks. "I'm certain these poor souls here join that sentiment. But we had the situation under control and didn't really require assistance."

"I grant you didn't, Miss Murph. I know you to be quite capable."

"Mr. Brayke," Holt interrupted, "Anna most certainly 'required assistance', as did we all." He grinned at Anna. "Didn't we, dear sister?"

Anna glared at Holt. "Well," she said with a chuckle, "you two may have needed help, but I was getting ready to belt that goon myself."

"Anyhow, sir," Holt persisted, "my sister says 'Thank you.'"

Kaspar laughed. "Well, ma'am, I'm happy to be of some small service. Now, may I join you on the remainder of your journey?"

Anna replaced her rifle to its saddle sling and fell in beside Kaspar and the young Creek woman to walk at the head of the band of Muskogis. Matthew and Holt, leading the two pack mules, resumed their positions riding rear guard. No one hastened to reach the falls.

❖ ❖ ❖

KASPAR INSISTED ON PERSONALLY escorting the Muskogis into the army camp. After parting with the Murphs at Gerald's trading post gate, leaving Rube in their care, he led the band to the compound and sought Captain Brodnax. He rejected turning his new self-acquired charges over to lesser officers or agents.

"Mr. Brayke," the Captain greeted, finally appearing after a long wait. "I've not seen you in a spell."

"Captain Brodnax, I'm obliged if you would indulge me. I have this morning witnessed an unfortunate incident involving four men I believe to be assigned to your post in some manner. Too, I wish you to care especial well for this group from one of the Saugahatchi villages. I fear retaliation against them by those men."

Kaspar related the meeting of the Murphs and the Muskogis with Rab's posse. As he concluded, Brodnax appeared little concerned.

"Mr. Brayke, I have limited authority beyond the scope of my camp. I can't control what transpires up the river or elsewhere in the countryside."

"Even if the offenders are your men?"

"Only if they are soldiers or sworn agents under my warrant."

"Are Rab and his pals sworn agents?"

"I don't accept they are."

"Do you deny them?"

Brodnax pondered for a few seconds. "Perhaps, sir. That's all I can tell you. The remainder is only the concern of the army."

"I see." He gestured toward the Indian band. "At the least of your mercy, sir, please look out for these deserving citizens. Thanks for your time." Kaspar half-pivoted, preparing to leave. He looked back over his shoulder. "Good day, Captain, and God help you."

WHEN KASPAR RETURNED to the trading post, Sam Peavy greeted him atop the porch steps.

"Camp keeps growing, don't it?" observed Sam.

"Bigger and bigger all the time." Kaspar scanned the campground, which had bloated tight with humanity and squalor. "Must be two thousand poor souls out there. Never seen such a sorry doing."

"Rumor is they'll be herding 'em out in a few weeks. The lot of them Indians is bleak now, but heaven help 'em when they start moving west. Ain't gone be nothing but a tragedy, I fear."

"Already is, Sam. Already is."

"Firmed up an opinion of the Captain yet?"

"You mean Brodnax?"

"Yeah. Whatcha think of 'im?"

Kaspar pondered a few seconds. "Oh, I don't know, Sam. Hard to fathom his heart or his head. He's military minded, and is doing his duty best he knows how, I 'spose. Seems to be pretty much in control of the situation, 'spite the layout. But putting up with the likes of Rab and his henchmen don't speak well of the Captain's command."

"Some of them 'sworn agents' are bullies, all right."

"Worse'n that. For a certain, there's highwaymen amongst 'em, and I judge some might've stooped to murder."

Sam nodded with a sneer. "I know so. Army don't seem to be doing much atall 'bout them or the land-grabbers and swindlers."

"Like that fellow Taggart, you mean? Uh-huh. I 'spect he and his kind are working for some well-off speculators with money and power, and Brodnax is a might fearful of troubling them folks."

"I venture you're right, Kaspar, of a truth. May the whole push of 'em roast in hell."

AFTER THE CORNMEAL had been ground and the Murphs' supplies collected and packed onto the two mules, Perley and Melissa Gerald followed Anna out to bid her and the boys goodbye. The early afternoon sun burned brutal with not a single cloud to accompany it. Kaspar and Sam stood on the porch studying the burgeoning encampment across the way and continuing to chat about it. Kaspar broke away and turned to Anna.

"Miss Murph," he said with a tip of his hat. "If it wouldn't be too much of an imposing, Rube and I should like to join you good folks for a piece on your passage back up the river. I trust Mr. Gerald can lend me one of his fine steeds for the afternoon?" He glanced at Gerald, who grinned and nodded.

"That's neighborly of you, Mr. Brayke," protested Anna, "but quite unnecessary. We'll be safe and fine, I'm sure."

"Of that I have scarce doubts, Miss Murph, but such an outing would be my pleasure."

"If you must, Mr. Brayke, then please yourself by tagging along," acceded Anna. Matthew and Holt, standing nearby, jostled each other at Anna's quick concession, uncharacteristic of her.

"Not much of a protest, huh?" observed Matthew.

"Weak," agreed Holt.

Shortly, the four riders plodded the river trail north. Leading one of the loaded pack animals behind them, Anna and Kaspar rode side by side in front. Rube bounded joyfully ahead. Matthew and Holt, with the other mule in tow, hung behind at a discreet distance. Their grins grew wider as the conversation drifting back to them became more animated, accented with giggles and an occasional flirty gesture.

At one point, Holt called out in Muskogean, "Give 'im a little kiss, Anna!" Both boys howled with laughter, trusting Mr. Brayke had not learned enough of the language to decipher the tease.

Anna spun in her saddle, hot red with anger, and glared at the two. "Shut yore mouth, Holt! Mind yore own business, or I'll throw you both in the river like I said I would." Scowling, she glanced at Kaspar, who looked back with a grin. It was never clear to any of the three Murphs whether he had understood the gibe.

Kaspar Brayke's intended accompaniment 'for a piece up the river' turned into a pleasant trip all the way to the Murph compound at Soosquana, where he and Rube were invited to stay overnight. He accepted.

Chapter 31

The Murph Compound, August, 1836

HE MORNING AFTER ACCOMPANYING the three Murphs home from the falls, Kaspar strolled toward the stable to check on his borrowed horse. A bright sun peeped an edge over the eastern horizon. As he neared, with Rube at his feet frisky for the day's adventures, he saw his horse tethered to a post outside the stable. A mop of red hair bobbed up and down from across the horse's flank.

"'Morning, son," Kaspar greeted as he recognized the boy. "You're Alphonso, I believe, Ms. Adelin's youngest?"

"Youngest boy, Mr. Brayke. I'm older'n Louise. I trust you don't mind me feeding and currying your horse."

"Not at all. I'm obliged. But why are you out so early?"

Alphonso grinned, flashing a row of sharp, white incisors. "I like to get at 'em 'fore the sun comes up. The horses like it that way, sir."

"Maybe I can help. What needs doing?"

"There's some hay to throw down, if you're of a mind. Then we can turn the lot loose in the corral."

Kaspar and Alphonso spent the next hour working, talking, swapping stories, entertaining each other long past when the final steed had been serviced. The two hung on the corral fence, enjoying each other's company and watching the horses cavort. Phonso divided his time between playing with Rube and inquiring of Kaspar's travels and adventures. His eyes bugged at descriptions of Charleston, Nashville, and other exotic environs. Kaspar probed the boy for information concerning the surrounding community and the neighbors.

"Several families on t'other side of the river. Only a tad other farms on this side, though, Mr. McAdams downriver and the Colbane family up aways on Kalaidshi Creek being the closest."

"What of Muskogis nearby?"

"Scattered about. Villages on most of the creeks around, especially upriver, then down on the Saugahatchi and up at Kalaidshi; that's the last big creek you had to ford yesterday on the way here."

"How long your family been here, Phonso?"

The boy laughed. "Way longer'n I've been, for certain. My pa and uncle staked out this place sometime afore the army attacked the Muskogis. They didn't like that very much. Still rave against it almighty."

"Yes, I've heard them talk. Miss Anna, too. She seems to get quite riled when the army is about."

Alphonso grinned as he peered into Kaspar's face. "You like Anna, don't you, Mr. Brayke?"

"Of course I do. Why shouldn't I like her? I'm fond of all your family."

"Anna sometimes seems upset with you. For no cause I can see. But that don't mean nothing. I think she likes you something special herself."

Before Kaspar could fully grasp Alphonso's direction, a voice interrupted them. "Ma says for you two to come to breakfast," beckoned Silas in a too loud shout. "They're fixing hot ham with fried eggs. Corn muffins and syrup, too."

Kaspar smiled at Silas, then down at Alphonso, still perched on a fence rail. "We dare not be tardy for that, had we, pal? Let's get at it."

❖ ❖ ❖

KASPAR SWALLOWED THE LAST GULP of coffee, wiped his mouth, and sighed. "Now I reckon that was the best breakfast this man ever ate. I thank you, and my stomach thanks you."

"We appreciate your sentiments, Mr. Brayke," said Adelin, "but you have Delaine and Rachel to thank for your breakfast."

The two girls giggled, and Delaine waved a hand. "That's not true, Mr. Brayke," confessed the fourteen year-old. "Mama and Aunt Adelin did it. We only helped a little."

"They helped a lot," insisted Adelin. "And it was they who suggested you be feasted with a special breakfast. So you see, you have them to thank."

"Well, ladies," announced Kaspar, nodding toward the blushing girls, "I am forever in your debt. It was delicious."

Saul pushed his chair from the table and stood. "I must agree. Ladies, that was an outstanding breakfast." He stroked his belly and smiled at Delaine and Rachel.

The girls smiled back and curtsied.

"Thank you, Father."

"Thank you, Uncle Saul."

Saul turned to his eldest. "Anna, I believe you intend to visit Mrs. McAdams this morning?"

"Yes, Pa, I do."

"Would you not like for Mr. Brayke to ride along?"

"Why, yes, Anna, that's a nice idea," said Adelin. She turned to Kaspar. "Mr. Brayke, the McAdamses are our neighbors to the south. Last week, the missus tripped and injured an ankle, quite seriously it seems. Saul fashioned a special walking stick, which Anna agreed to carry to her this morning. And to check on her and her mister's being, of course."

"So, Anna, would you like Mr. Brayke's company?" asked Saul.

Holt yelped from across the room. "Yee-haw! You know she would. Right, Anna? Come on, own up to it." He and Matthew laughed in derision.

Adelin glared at the boys. "Holt! Matthew! Behave yourselves. Mr. Brayke is our guest and he doesn't deserve your disrespect."

"Well, Anna," Saul addressed his daughter again, "are you going to invite Mr. Brayke?"

Anna turned to Kaspar. "Come if you choose, Mr. Brayke. Makes little difference to me."

Kaspar grinned. "I would be honored, Miss Murph, to ride with you again."

ALPHONSO AND SILAS reveled in preparing and saddling the horses, and shortly Anna and Kaspar trotted them from the compound with Rube racing happily ahead. An hour's casual ride brought them to a small, neat farm with a modest house. Anna dismounted to receive the greetings of a middle-aged, muscular man coming to meet them from a nearby field.

"Happy to see you, Mr. McAdams," said Anna as she shook the man's hand. She turned to Kaspar. "I'd like to introduce Mr. Kaspar Brayke and his dog Rube, friends of my family."

"Please to meet you, Mr. Brayke. Handsome hound you got there. Always an honor to welcome friends of the Murphs. This here beautiful little lady is my favorite young'un."

Anna smiled at McAdams. "I wish to visit with Mrs. McAdams. Pa sent her a gift. Is she in the house?"

"Shore. Go right in, dear."

Anna spent the next hour chatting with Mrs. McAdams while the mister toured Kaspar around his farm, barn, and stable. McAdams showed himself to be a proud, hard-working man. He explained the couple had two sons and one daughter, but all had married and established settlements of their own farther west, near the Coosa River.

"Mr. Brayke, this is a fine land and the missus and I are happy, hardy folks, as are our children. But we rue the current tensions between the government and the native peoples, and don't see them soon resolved. I wonder if a humble farmer can weather such."

"I warrant you can, Mr. McAdams, despite the times. I, too, wish for an end to the troubles, but I fear they might increase."

Later, after the two visitors rode from the McAdams place, Anna pulled up on the trail, still a distance from the Murph compound. She looked around, suspicious of their surroundings.

Kaspar followed her gaze. "What are we looking at? Do you think we're being followed?"

"No," Anna said quietly, checking once more in every direction. "Just making sure we're not. Come on. Follow me."

She reined her mount into a right turn and prodded the steed to push through a tangle of brush. Kaspar followed and found them on a narrow, scant trail leading into dense forest. A mile into the thicket, Anna paused to listen then called out in Muskogean. She listened again before signaling Kaspar to continue slowly.

Another hundred yards brought them to a small clearing, where Anna stopped. Remaining astride her horse, she again beckoned, but in a muted tone. She waited. Kaspar sat motionless, puzzled.

After a full minute, a figure arose from behind a nearby tree. Kaspar recognized him to be a Muskogi. The man greeted Anna with an upraised arm, eyeing her companion. He pointed to him as he excitedly questioned her.

As she talked, the Indian's face calmed. After a few more exchanges, none of which Kaspar understood except for a few gestures, the man turned and signed to the woods behind him. One by one, four more Muskogis appeared from the foliage and rocks. They cautiously walked into the clearing. Anna dismounted and greeted each as a friend, all of whom warmly clasped her hand. Some wagged toward Kaspar as the first man had done. Anna patiently explained away their apprehensions, and they soon relaxed. She lifted her bloated saddlebags from her saddle and signaled Kaspar to dismount and join the group, then introduced him in Muskogean. The men then led their guests to a hidden encampment close by, where they were offered sweet cider and seats on which to rest.

A half-hour later, Anna returned her now empty saddlebags to her horse, and she and Kaspar retraced their path from the remote camp. Upon reaching the main trail, Anna gestured for Kaspar to spur his mount up beside her. She then explained their side trip.

"Those men are hiding from the army and their agents, who wish to arrest them. My father and Cal are happy to grant them refuge. The warrants are unjust, and we consider any help we can provide to be repayment for years of high regard and good treatment from the Muskogis."

Kaspar nodded. "From all reports, your father and uncle have always been the Muskogis' best friends."

"One of those men is Nouskuubi. Agents stole his land, entrapped his family in that wretched camp at the falls, and put out an arrest warrant for him. I believe you were at Mr. Gerald's place the day we attempted to get the family out from down there."

"Yes, I remember. Most unfortunate."

Anna scowled. "Evil tyrants! They wouldn't hear of it."

"How did Nouskuubi fare that?"

"We made him stay behind when we went. He protested mightily, but they would have arrested him on the spot if he had been with us. If we would allow it, he'd dare attack the soldiers alone to rescue his folks, though they would kill him for certain."

"What holds him here?"

"The other men at the camp. Pa made them promise to watch him at all times lest he take off to the falls. Till now, they've held him back. You didn't see them, but two of those men have their families with them. They were at another site a ways on into the woods."

"So, I take it this morning's trek was not just to visit the McAdamses. Your pa directed you to look in on the fugitives? And the full saddlebags? I wondered about that."

"Shelled corn. They needed it. We check on them when we dare. To see to their needs, you understand, and pass on news, information, and supplies."

"How long can you protect them?"

"Don't know. But we have to try as long as there's danger."

THE MURPHS INSISTED Kaspar stay another night. When he finally agreed, the three younger children cheered.

"Yippee!" yelped Silas. "Thanks, Mr. Brayke. Come on, Rube, let's play!" The happy dog, accompanied by the Murph dogs, raced him, Phonso, and Louise to the open field.

Kaspar laughed. "So that's it. It isn't me they wanted to hang around, it's Rube."

The friends spent another congenial evening sharing stories and ideas. The highlight was Anna's report on the fugitive Muskogis and further discussion of the Indians' plight and future.

Early the next morning, after another elaborate breakfast, Kaspar and Rube set out for the falls. Kaspar hoped Mr. Gerald wasn't anxious about the fine horse he had loaned for the trip, which had extended longer than expected.

As he approached the ford three miles above the falls, Kaspar noticed a pack riding from the opposite direction. He stopped on the near bank to allow them to reach the ford and cross first. They didn't hesitate and splashed across in a flurry, pretending not to notice him. Agents! Kaspar realized. He counted eight, two of them Rab's thugs from the encounter two days ago. He wondered if Rab himself was among those he didn't see clearly, as they passed too fast to recognize more.

Rube challenged with a low growl as they thundered by. Kaspar remained stationary. He stared after the group until they disappeared around the distant bend. He still didn't resume his travel, instead indulging in dark thoughts.

Finally, aloud, "Rube, they can't be up to any good." He reined his horse into the river. "Nope, no good at all, I fear.

Chapter 32

The Falls on the Tallapoosa, August, 1836

KASPAR POSITIONED HIMSELF atop his bluff camp with a good view of the river trail while he fixed supper for himself and Rube. He searched the road until dark, looking for the reappearance of the agent group, who failed to show.

"Yeah," agreed Perley Gerald when Kaspar had returned his borrowed horse. Perley stood by chatting while Kaspar curried and fed the horse. "I saw them ride outta the encampment. Looked to me like they meant no good when they left."

"Bothers me. They seemed headed upriver, possibly toward the Murph place."

"Them Murphs can take care of theirselves."

"I know, but they shouldn't be hounded by those goons, if that be their aim." He was also concerned about Nouskuubi and the band of friends hiding him.

Later, at dusk, Kaspar moved his bedroll to his lookout spot. He would rest there all night, listening for the posse. He would awaken for certain at any activity on the road.

Before dawn, Kaspar's mind was set. Except for a few individuals on foot and an old farmer riding a mule, no one had traveled the road overnight. The band of agents had not returned. He decided he must check on his friends upriver, so while the sun was still struggling to rise, he was at Perley Gerald's door begging for the loan of another horse.

"Can't leave it be, can you, Mr. Brayke?" chided Perley. "I figured as much when you inquired yesterday. But I agree with your concern.

Them goons ain't up to no good up the river. If it ain't the Murphs they're after, it's probably some pore Muskogi family like they've done before."

AFTER PUSHING HIS HORSE harder than usual, Kaspar cantered to the Murph compound at mid-morning.

"Good morning, Mr. Brayke," greeted eight-year old Louise, tending to a flower garden near the gate. "'sprised to see you this fine day." Rube trotted up and nuzzled the girl. "Hello to you, too, Rube," she spouted, giggling and caressing the dog.

Kaspar reined his mount to a halt, relieved everything seemed tranquil at the compound. He smiled at the girl. "Morning yourself, Miss Louise. Thought I'd pay you good folks a friendly visit and see to your welfare."

Louise smirked and slanted her eyes into a mischievous glance as she continued to pet Rube. "Uh huh. You came up to see Anna again, didn't you? We're onto you, sir."

"Don't know how you got such an idea, Miss Louise. Miss Anna don't even tolerate me." He grinned back at the girl. "Where might I find your folks?"

"Some in the barn and the stable, I'm sure. Others in the house or the larder. Go on over. You're sure to find somebody. And welcome, sir."

"Obliged, Miss Louise. Proud to be here."

After finding most of the family and exchanging warm greetings, Kaspar sat at a table with the Murph adults.

"I'm surprised to see you again so soon, Mr. Brayke," said Saul, "but you're certainly welcome any time. You say you come back today with a worry? Does it concern us?"

"Perhaps, Mr. Murph. Have any riders been by here since I left yesterday?" He went on to relate his fears about the posse of agents and his thoughts of what they might be after.

"No, we haven't seen them, and I hope we don't," replied Saul. "But I'm afraid your concern may be well-founded. Any time those sorts are anywhere in these parts, I worry. We can handle them, I'm assured, but neighbors and friends about could be in peril of their abuse."

"You think we should check on folks, Saul?" asked Cal.

"Yeah, I do. It's late now, so let's head out at first light in the morning. We'll split up to cover more ground and see more people. Holt and I can backtrack the road and go as far as the west side bluff at the falls. Cal, why don't you and Matthew scout the Kalaidshi Creek area? That may be where those thugs were headed." He paused and peered across the table. "Since Anna knows the hideaway of Nouskuubi and those protecting him so well, and speaks the best Muskogean, she should take Kaspar and patrol the pine thickets downriver."

Everyone but Anna and Kaspar grinned and stared at the two. Anna slanted her eyes at her father, but said, "Well, all right. I guess we can do that."

"All agreed then? Get a good night's rest and be ready early. I'm sure Phonso and Silas will already have our mounts fed and saddled."

Adelin rose from the table. "Now, Mr. Brayke, you will, of course, join us for supper. Rachel and Delaine, at Belle's supervision, are preparing a scrumptious feast."

From the side lawn, the younger kids were running back and forth into the adjacent woods chasing Rube and the Murph dogs. Kaspar thought he had never seen his pet so happy, having children to play with.

Chapter 33

The Murph Compound, August, 1836

PHONSO AND SILAS STOOD WAITING at the stable with six saddled and equipped horses when their riders walked up. The sun was only a smudged hint below the eastern horizon.

"Thanks, boys," said Saul. "Much obliged."

Kaspar beckoned Phonso and Silas. "Boys, I'm leaving Rube with you. Think you can handle him?"

The two lit up. "Oh, yay! He'll be fine with us, Mr. Brayke." Both beamed and reached down to nuzzle Rube, whose tail reached a higher wagging speed. "We may even let the girls play with him," one offered.

"You guys run get some breakfast now," added Cal. "You've earned it. Take Rube with you. Hey, try the turkey sausage. Fine eating."

The group of six sheathed their long rifles, mounted, and rode from the compound together. They would remain as one until they met the Kalaidshi road two miles downriver. From there, Cal and Matthew were to turn northwest on that path while Kaspar and Anna veered into the thick forests along the near river bluffs. Anna still muttered about being partnered with Kaspar, but she held objections to herself.

"Be careful and stay safe," urged Saul for the fifth time or more this morning. "If you encounter land agents or other hostiles, stay away from them if you can. Watch their actions, help whoever might be in their sights, but try not to engage them."

"Right," said Cal. "We want no quarrel with that bunch if we can help it."

Anna scowled and spat at an imaginary enemy. "Those scalawags better hope I'm not seeing them down the sights of my rifle."

Matthew laughed. "Very lady-like, Anna. Don't let that long hair get caught in your gunlock." He and Holt roared while their fathers smiled. Kaspar didn't dare laugh since he had to ride with the lady the rest of the day.

"Okay, folks, off you go," said Saul. "Make your way back to the compound tonight or by morning. And stay safe," he repeated once more.

❖ ❖ ❖

"THERE'S ONLY ONE THING those agents could be about in these tangled woods," judged Anna at mid-morning. "But it appears no one's been here in weeks."

"Except us a few days ago," said Kaspar.

Anna twisted her face at him. He smiled back.

Kaspar reverted to a near whisper. "Are we gonna check the Indians' hideaway?"

"No. And if we drift anywhere near it, don't even cut your eyes that way. We haven't seen anyone, but somebody could be spying us even at this moment, and we can't give 'em any hints."

At highest sun, the tandem stopped in a clearing filled with granite boulders, common to the terrain above the fall line and near the river. Anna retrieved a snack of venison jerky and crackling bread from her saddlebag and passed the major portion to Kaspar.

"Do you like our river lands, Mr. Brayke," asked Anna.

"Very much I do. Fine soil and rich forests, and a beautiful swift river." He studied the girl, who was still a mystery to him. "Home for you, isn't it?"

"Never been anywhere else. Never wanted to be. I not only love the wonders of the land, but I love our neighbors, settlers and Indians alike. Glorious people." She grinned and added, "Them who behave themselves, that is."

They lingered in the pleasant setting longer than intended, but finally decided to move on. After refilling canteens from a nearby spring, they remounted and plunged again into the pines.

❖ ❖ ❖

SAUL AND HOLT cantered up to the McAdams farm before the sun had climbed above the morning haze.

Warm greetings by all, but the Murphs remained mounted. Saul got right to the gist of his visit. "Mr. McAdams, have there been any riders pas …"

He was interrupted by the missus. "Mr. Murph, thank you so much for my wonderful walk cane. It works right nicely."

"Thank you, Mrs. McAdams. Right proud to be helpful." Saul shifted his attention back to her husband. "Have riders passed this way the past two days?"

"Not that we know," answered McAdams. "Our place is off the main trail, so someone could have passed by without us aware. Trouble brewing, Saul?"

"No more than what's been streaming, I suppose. Anyway, we have reason to clear the trail today if it warrants clearing. Thankful you folks are all right. Keep a sharp eye for bad blood around. Any time you feel uncomfortable you are always welcome at our place."

"Thanks, friend. Now, won't you and Holt … My, son! How you've grown. You've shot up into a right strapping young buck, haven't you?"

Holt grinned behind his blush.

"Anyhow, the two of you should stay for one of the missus's delicious meals. She can have a nice stew on the table in no time."

"Thank you, Mr. McAdams, and you as well, ma'am. But we have to move on south. We are to check the several Muskogi villages down the river, plus the two farms along the way."

"Not much remaining of Indian villages anymore since they've been hounded by the army folk."

Saul reined his horse around. "Afraid you're right, friend. We'll see you again soon."

Back on the trail, Holt scanned the sky. "Looks maybe an ugly cloud afoot over to the southwest."

"Yeah," agreed his father. "If we hasten, maybe we can cover our ground and make it back home tonight ahead of what rain it holds."

SHORTLY AFTER TURNING northwest on the trail to Kalaidshi Creek, Cal and Matthew discovered hoof prints in the soft mud of a shallow, drying branch.

"'Pears as if they were galloping," observed Matthew.

"'Bout a day old, I'd say," said Cal. "Matches Mr. Brayke's information. Not being easy on their mounts, either. Hell, we may have found our mob of agents. Let's hurry to the Colbane place."

"Hope they're all right," said Matthew.

"And the villages around, what's left of them. Those may be the agents' targets."

They reached the creek and followed the parallel trail to the first village. With rifles at the ready, they eased their mounts among the nearly desolate houses. A few women tended fires, wove blankets, and dressed small game harvested in the morning hunt. Most looked up at the visitors, but without alarm. Then a matronly lady walked out and offered a raised open hand.

"Greetings, Murph friends," she offered in struggling English. "You ever welcome in our village. You come trade for our wares?"

"No, Amitta. Sorry," answered Cal. "Your wares have much value to us, but we come on other business today." He went on to explain their mission and inquire of any sightings of the posse.

The woman Amitta reacted with increasing alarm as Cal spoke. "We have seen no such men," she said. "But from what you say, we must be on guard. Most our men still on hunt today. When return, I ask our council to post look-ons, uh, look-, uh …

Cal smiled. "Lookouts."

"Yes, lookouts. Our council should station lookouts along trail to stop these men if they mean harm. There has been too much sadness already at hands of such."

A light rain began as a fine mist and increased to small droplets. "Might get worse," mused Matthew. "Clouds are thickening."

Cal and Matthew donned deerskin ponchos as they moved on to the next village, lying only a half-mile distance. Muskogi villages often were established in clusters. Good news in that one, too, and in the next one.

"Strange," ventured Matthew. "We're certain they rode this way. Someone had to have seen them, or if they passed in the night, heard the horses."

"The Colbane farm is next in line, two miles ahead," said Cal. By now, the rain had picked up. "Maybe they know something."

Mr. Colbane opened his door barely a crack and peered out. When he recognized the Murphs he stepped into the yard. Indeed, his family had seen the posse. Wide-eyed, he turned his head from side to side, searching nearby woods.

"Yes, they were by here late yesterday, and I don't think they meant well. They cursed and threatened us when we refused knowledge of the bucks they sought."

"Which were, if I venture to ask?"

"Bastro, the headman of the next village, and his friend Joe-Roy. We didn't tell 'em a mite. Anyhow, a little after they passed we heard rifle shots from up the road. Might have come from Bastro's place. I've kept the missus and the kids inside since. Don't want any part of no feud."

"How far?" asked Cal.

"Only about a mile up the trail. Not many bucks still there, women either, since troubles got worse, like it be in most of the villages."

Cal removed his hat and shook water from it, wiped his face, and replaced the hat. "Guess we've found our agents, Matt. Let's go see what they're up to. Mr. Colbane, keep your family inside and your rifle handy."

The two cantered the mile and eased their mounts into the village, alert for any motion. The only sound heard was that of the rain, increasing steadily. No one seemed about until a voice called out.

"You be of the Murph family," the voice said in cracked English, fear inherent. "Quick, you must shield yourselves from guns in the pines yonder."

A man appeared from around a hut and pointed. Without delay, Cal and Matthew dismounted and urged their horses, reins dangling, to trot off in the opposite direction." They followed the man around the hut to take cover behind a crude log barrier. Four other men crouched there.

"What's happening?" asked Cal, anxious and confused.

"Bad men," blurted the first man, recognized as Bastro, the village leader. "Agents from army camp at falls, we think."

"To be sure. We've been searching for them and their purpose for being upriver."

"Land robbers?"

"Probably not, but friends of the thieves, I would think. Mr. Colbane heard shots yesterday. Anyone hurt?"

"Not of us. But we think one of them is wounded. We heard him scream and grab his hip as he rode into the woods. They said they had arrest warrants for Joe-Roy here and myself, but we caught them unawares." Bastro almost gloated. "They ran to the woods and two turned and shot at us. We shot back, and they took cover behind the trees. Been there all night and today. No shooting since, but we see a man look out at us sometime. Guess they think they're trapped, that we have advantage."

"Why can't they escape through the woods behind them?"

"Steep bluffs back there. Horses no make go."

Cal nodded. "They must be tired and hungry, and now wet. Can't be in much of a civil mood."

After about fifteen minutes as the rain continued stronger, Cal decided the stalemate had to be broken. He hailed the agents' lair, not fifty yards away. Minutes passed before a man called back. "Who be ye?"

"My name is Cal Murph," he yelled across. "I'd like to walk over and talk with you. Can we observe a truce?"

Five minutes later, Cal walked slowly toward the pine cove, waving his hat in a sign of truce. Rain blew hard into his face, almost blinding him. The men scowled at him as he arrived in their midst.

"You a damn Indian lover?" asked the group's spokesman.

Cal ignored the question. "You have a wounded man?"

"Yeah. Them sorry Indians shot him. They ambushed us."

"Is he well?"

"Hell no, he ain't well. He's shot and he's bleeding bad. Been bleeding since yesterday."

"I suggest you fellows leave. I can guarantee your safety as long as you ride straight out."

"We came to arrest two of them scoundrels. With legal warrants. Will you help us with the task?"

"Not a chance of such. You're bounty agents, hired by the army to harass Indians, aren't you? These are innocent folks and friends. They've done nothing to offend you."

"The hell they ain't! They're squatters on government land, damn criminals."

"I suggest you shelve that notion and take your leave."

"The only way to the trail south is right by them huts. That's why we ain't already gone from this hell hole. Them stinking savages gonna shoot at us again when we ride past. Can't trust 'em."

"No, they won't shoot. I'll handle them. You need to get your casualty back down the river for treatment. His wound ain't gonna get better sitting here. The rain ain't helping you none, either."

"We ain't leaving like damn cowards," spat one agent.

"I ain't running from any rotten savages," boasted another.

"You give us them two damn Indians we come after first! We ain't leaving without 'em, and maybe some more of 'em."

"I'm dying," yelled the wounded man, almost screaming. "Get me the hell outta here!"

"Shut up, Rab! Quit whining," the spokesman admonished the wounded man. "We're gonna get you away from this slime pit. Just grit your teeth and stay quiet."

"Damn you, you jerk! I'm dying, I tell you."

Rab, thought Cal, *that's the scoundrel Mr. Brayke and Anna ran off down the river.*

Another man wanted out. "I vote we skedaddle and come back later and shoot up the whole mess of these bastards."

Many minutes of hot discussion among the agents, accented with groans and curses from the wounded man, brought a consensus. They would leave if Cal would station himself between them and the Indians. Cal returned to the barrier and relayed the terms, which were received with joy. Ten minutes later, the posse was gone, breaking into a gallop upon reaching the trail.

"We'll camp here tonight, Matt," decided Cal, "in case some of those hotheads have a notion to come back. I'm sure Bastro can provide us shelter from this fierce rain. A comfortable fire on a wigwam floor and a decent meal will dry us out and tide us over till morning."

Chapter 34

Near the Tallapoosa River, August 1836

ABOUT WHEN ANNA DECIDED she and Kaspar had completed coverage of the river forests to which they had been assigned, and found no suspicious beings or behavior, rain began. It increased from a gentle sprinkle to a torrent in minutes.

"No way we can make it back home in this pour," said Anna. "Come on, I know a shelter we can escape to."

Kaspar reined his horse around and followed Anna to a faint Indian trail along the river bank. A half-mile along through grabbing brush from either side, she turned into a large granite outcrop towering high above. She disappeared under a large boulder.

As she dismounted and signaled for Kaspar to do the same, she explained. "This isn't really a cave; it's a rock overhang. It only extends a few yards inward. Muskogis have used it for centuries for camping during a hunt and for hiding from their enemies."

"Nice harborage," judged Kaspar. "If we were fugitives, no law person would ever find us here."

Anna smiled. "How do I know you aren't a fugitive, Mr. Brayke? We know little about you 'cept you've chased around from place to place these many years."

"You figure me too well, Miss Anna. Could be law agencies from several states are hounding me with warrants right now."

Anna grinned. "I thought as much. You carry genuine outlaw blood, don't you? Now take care of the horses while I build a fire. Rub 'em down and let 'em nibble from the bushes and grass patches at the mouth of the cave. There's a little spring behind that rock back there." She pointed. "It trickles down to the river, so dam it up at the cave mouth with sand so the horses can drink."

"Don't believe the rain's gonna let up. How long can we stay here?"

"All night if necessary. How much food in your saddlebag?"

"Let's see. I think I packed some carrots, raw turnips, and a couple of your folks' delicious apples. I also stole some bacon slabs and sausage from the breakfast table this morning."

"Ah, ha! You are a thieving rogue. But in our predicament, I'm happy to share your thievery. And I have some jerky left, plus another half pone of cornbread."

Anna soon had a small fire going under a natural chimney through the overhang, an opening somehow protected from the rain, and busied herself heating the bacon and sausage. While Kaspar shaped the water barrier to form a pool for the horses, she refilled both canteens from the spring's source.

"Rain's not stopping tonight," Kaspar observed when they had finished the slight meal. "May perhaps by morning."

"A good sleep will send us toward home at daylight, even if the rain is still with us." Anna pointed to a narrow rock ledge adjacent to the fire. "You sleep there, Mr. Brayke. I'll take this spot over here." She walked to the opposite side of the cave, lay down, and covered herself with her poncho. "Good night, Mr. Brayke." She was quickly asleep.

Deep into the night, Kaspar awoke to a chill. The fire had reduced to glowing embers. Never mind it being August, he thought, this wet air, coupled with our still damp clothes, can make for uneasy sleep. He looked across the cave at Anna and detected a distinct shiver.

"Miss Anna," he asked in a soft voice, "are you awake?"

She grunted and squeezed herself tighter. "Yes."

"You're cold, aren't you?"

"I'm fine. Go back to sleep."

"You aren't fine. You've caught a chill." He watched her continue to shake, "Miss Anna, come over here. I'm cold and maybe you can warm me."

After ignoring Kaspar and hesitating for a full minute, Anna, without speaking, staggered over to where Kaspar sat, dragging her deerskin poncho with her. He carefully positioned her next to him and bundled both ponchos around the two of them. She immediately fell asleep, dropping her head onto his shoulder. Comfortable now, and assured Anna was as well, Kaspar dozed off again himself.

Later, no hint of dawn yet about, Anna stirred. Kaspar awoke at her movement. He pulled the ponchos closer around her.

"Mmmm," she moaned, then in a low whisper, "Mr. Brayke, do you like me?" Her eyes remained closed.

"I indeed do, Miss Anna, very much. I admire your spunk."

"Mmmm, what's spunk?"

"Well, spunk's like …"

Anna giggled. "Aw, I know what spunk is. Thank you, sir. I think. I like you, too, Mr. Brayke. You're a nice man and my family's good friend."

She seemed to fall back to sleep, but then mumbled, "Mr. Brayke, would you … would you, well, kiss me?"

Surprised and suddenly wide-awake, Kaspar managed to answer, "It would be my pleasure, Miss Anna."

Anna twisted around and raised her head to Kaspar's face. He gently crooked a forefinger under her chin and lifted her lips to his. The lips were warm. After only one soft second, he withdrew, but Anna didn't. Kaspar went in for a longer kiss and Anna responded with a moan and a smile while still engaged.

When released, she giggled. Kaspar stared at her, her eyes still shut. "Mmmm," she cooed, "one more."

Kaspar did as requested, this kiss the best yet. Emotions he had never known flooded his body.

"That was nice," she muttered, snuggling anew against his body and returning her head to his shoulder. "Mr. Brayke, you are a good kisser." Then, after a few seconds, she giggled again. "But how would I know how good you are at kissing? I have no past with which to compare. Hmmm. However, Mr. Brayke, I still must judge your skill at kissing to be excellent."

With that, she was quickly sound asleep. Kaspar, in mild shock and with an inflamed libido, took much longer, but finally finished the night in restless and confused, but happy, slumber.

❊ ❊ ❊

WITH THE DAWN, the rain had depleted to a minor trickle. Without speaking, both got to work, Kaspar saddling the horses and

Anna preparing a skimpy breakfast from scraps they purposefully saved from last night. They glanced clumsily at each other while eating then extinguished the fire, and returned all equipment to their saddlebags. Finally, they restored the cave to its natural state, including leaving no sign whatsoever of the fire.

Before mounting, Anna turned to Kaspar to speak for the first time of the morning. "Mr. Brayke, did we have a strange dream last night?"

"Can't speak for your dreams, Miss Anna, but mine were beautiful."

She beamed. "Mine, too, sir." She paused and turned pensive. "We are never to speak of that, understand? To no one."

"Yes, ma'am. I shall forever be silent."

"Oh, with your permission, I may someday mention it to Aunt Adelin, but not now. Not anytime soon."

"Yes, ma'am."

They nodded at each other, exchanged knowing smirks, and mounted to ride home.

An hour later, they approached the intersection on the road where the Kalaidshi Creek route cut northwest. "Hold up!" whispered Anna. "Horses on the trail from Kalaidshi. Make ready, Mr. Brayke."

They stopped fifty yards from the intersection and waited in the brush, rifles ready. Two horsemen materialized and prepared to turn north on the main track.

"It's Uncle Cal and Matthew!" exclaimed Anna. "Hey, you two," she shouted, "wait up!"

Cal and Matthew reined their mounts and waited for the pair.

"Hello, there," greeted Cal. "Nice to run into you. Find anybody or anything?"

"Nothing," answered Anna. "Just had to wait out the rain. How about you boys? Anything?"

"Well, yeah, we ran into a little action. Tell you and the folks about it when we reach home. We, too, had to deal with the rain."

"Quite a gusher, huh?" mused Kaspar. "Unusual for this time of year. Don't normally rain much in August."

"Where did you two hole up last night?" questioned Matthew, mischief in his voice.

"In the old granite overhang cave on the edge of the river, if it's any of your business." She sneered at Matthew.

"Oh ho! Together in that close space? That's a tight squeeze. You will tell us all about it, won't you, Anna? She didn't hurt you, did she, Mr. Brayke?" He roared with laughter and spurred his horse forward into a gallop. Cal and Kaspar laughed at Anna's irritation.

"Matthew, you brainless vermin! I'm gonna gouge your eyes out!" She set out to chase her cousin the rest of the way home.

Chapter 35

Tuscaloosa, Alabama, August, 1836

"DAMNIT, THAT FOOL CASS is denying us troops again." Governor Clement Clay threw the letter on his desk and cursed anew. "He even refused my request for authority to swear in state volunteers as federal troops. He now thinks we should do with county militias to fight these damn renegade Indians."

"Sir, can we appeal directly to the President?" asked his aide.

"Hell, I've done that before with no success. Secretary Cass has Jackson's hand in these things. After all the support I've rendered the President, you would think he could send us a regiment or two to get shed of this contemptible Indian war, which has been with us far too long."

"Yes, sir."

Governor Clement Comer Clay had been a congressman in full support of President Andrew Jackson's policies, including Indian removal. He had been swept into office in 1828 with the snowball effect of Jackson's election over incumbent John Quincy Adams. He resigned the House to be elected governor of Alabama in 1835, and inherited the sticky task of rounding up the Muskogi Nation and shipping its people west. The problem seemed simple enough from the environs of Washington, but when he returned to Alabama as her chief executive, he faced more trouble than anticipated. Not the least of these was the seeming desertion of Jackson and Cass from federal responsibility for implementing the Removal Act. Both men were not only Clay's former political allies but also gentlemen he had valued as friends. In Clay's opinion, they were leaving Indian removal to the states and what sources each could muster, and keeping federal treasures and military power close to Washington.

Governor Clay pounded a fist on a sheaf of papers on his desk. He stormed at his office aide and military attaché. "Look at this stack of letters from citizens over where the hostilities are. Farmers, merchants, craftsmen, even militiamen themselves! These folks need protection from those damn rebel Indians. They blame me. They think I can grab up these criminals, load them up in a wagon, and haul 'em west myself."

"Yes, sir," agreed the aide. "I mean, no, sir. You're doing all you can, sir."

Clay picked up a letter. "This farmer complains he is suffering day and night burglary and harassment from Indian raiders, where they only used to bother him occasionally. Like 'occasionally' is all right." He threw the paper down and grabbed another. "Listen to this." He read, "'Savages shot my best hog yesterday and run off two horses and my milk cow.' He goes on, 'Governor, you got to do something. Come down here and run these skunks away.' He adds, 'Please'. Half his words are misspelled, but he got the letter together somehow."

Clay reached for another. "There are dozens of these let ..." A knock on the door interrupted him. An orderly opened it and took a step inside.

"Governor Clay, sir, Captain John Page and his aide to see you. They have ridden up from Fort Mitchell."

"Yes, I've been expecting them. Show them in, please."

The orderly ushered in the two men, dusty from the long trail they had traveled.

"Gentlemen," the governor greeted the visitors, "welcome to Tuscaloosa. We were just speaking of the plight with hostilities against farmers and settlers in your area. You've had a long ride. May I offer you a nice bracer?" He gestured for his aide to serve the men.

"Not a pleasant quandary we're in, if I may say so, sir," said Page. "I fear the situation will improve little until we clear away the remainder of the Creeks. We're still dealing with many vile rebels among them who used to be close citizens. Unfortunate turn."

"Unfortunate, indeed," said Clay. "I dare say most of that turn has been at the hands of the criminal land speculators, of which you, I understand, are charged with controlling."

"Only of a sort, sir. That responsibility mainly lies with Colonel John Hogan."

"Ah, of course. Nevertheless, many unsuspecting Creeks have been victimized by those crooks. Makes me embarrassed sometimes to be a white man."

"We're dealing with greedy, unsavory rogues, sir. And, if I may add, some powerful ones managing most of the thefts. We most dutifully are attempting to quell their activities, with limited aid from Washington, I fear."

"Yes, though we're quite isolated from the carnage up here in the capital city, I have dealt with a couple of the major sponsors of those damn land robbers. They are the scourge of the earth, and stand as the root cause of much of our tragedy." Clay glared at the men. "Hell! I've been the one trying to do something about their grabber schemes."

"We are aware of your efforts, sir, and we're working hard on that problem as well. Colonel Hogan is confronting more of the speculators each day."

"Yes, that's excellent. We need to hang the lot of them, same as the Creek savages. I'm doing my best to rid us of the Indian troublemakers and murderers, but recently I'm seeing nothing from the federal government. Secretary Cass and everyone else in Washington have been of little help." Clay dropped his head and paced a lap around his desk, deep in thought. "Captain, how can we strengthen our forces in East Alabama? I mean, to defeat these rebels for good and ready them for the trail west? And how do we neutralize the land grabbers?"

"Sir, I agree we need more federal help. Without it, I fear it to be a pressing assignment. Colonel Hogan is attempting to control the land thefts. A refreshing sign, however, is the several internment camps are nearly ready for another shipment of Creeks to begin the journey west. Perhaps this will be the last of them. When they're gone, things should ease."

"When do they plan to leave?"

"Not sure, sir. Best I understand, the army is aiming for early autumn. I'm coordinating with them to select the best time and best route."

"Best route? Won't they follow the same as the ones in July?"

"Perhaps, sir, but that hasn't been determined yet."

"I see. Yet a few weeks, huh? Now, back to the land speculators. You say Colonel Hogan has the situation in hand?"

Page frowned and shook his head. "Not exactly, sir. Hogan, along with military and law enforcement, has been able to do little against them. Most of the outlaw land speculators are headquartered across the Chattahoochee in Columbus. That makes it tough for Alabama authorities to act against 'em. Difficult to overcome so many layers of political protection they've cloaked around themselves."

"Yes, same as it has been. Those scoundrels are ruining this state. Well, at least our legal experts are trying to rectify the situation. Probably too late, though. Too many innocent people dead in the wake of their greed. Too much property destroyed, too much treasure wasted."

"Yes, sir."

"Now the burden seems to have fallen to Alabama alone. Governor Schley has his border clogged and refuses to allow any Creeks to cross that river into Georgia. Legally, anyhow." He chuckled. "I hear, though, his border posts leak like a rusty bucket. Indians sneaking by them every day. Ha! Good for them. The more who escape to Georgia, the fewer we have to dicker with."

"Yes, they have had some difficulties with that lately."

"And General Jesup is of little care. Secretary Cass pulled most of his regulars and refuses to assign us more. Also, since Jesup fouled the South Alabama campaign, then bragged the lie about ending the war, I understand he has lodged himself and his troops at Fort Mitchell and ventures not far afield. Is that true, Captain Page?"

Page grinned. "Not far off the mark, Governor."

Clay shook his head. "How can we shuck ourselves from these troubled times? Our citizenry deserves to live in peace." He stared at Captain Page and his companion. "Gentlemen, won't we ever learn?"

Chapter 36

Murph Compound, August, 1836

EIGHT YEAR-OLD LOUISE MURPH awakened to a hot, humid August night. She crawled from her bed clutching her burlap and straw stuffed rabbit, waddled sleepily to the window, and widened the shutter. "Not much better, Ralph," she whispered to the rabbit. "No air swishing around anywhere."

The sky teemed with stars. Louise knew it was well after midnight because the half moon had climbed almost to the top. It illuminated the broad yard well enough to see the buildings across the way.

Louise sensed something wasn't quite right. Then she saw why. A man stood in the road that led across the little bridge behind him and into the woods. She stared wide-eyed at the man, who didn't move. He seemed to be staring back at her.

The girl shook out of her trance and crept to her parents' bed. She tapped gently on her father's arm, then shook it when he failed to awaken.

"Pa. Pa, wake up."

"Mmmph …"

Cal Murph stirred little, but Adelin on the other side of the bed raised up. "What is it, Honey? Can you not sleep?"

"Mommy, there's a man in the yard."

"What? What are you saying?"

Cal, now awake, sat up in a lurch. "A man? In the yard? Doing what?" Cal was already pulling on his pants and reaching for his rifle. "Stay here in our bed, Louise."

He hurried to the window to assure himself of Louise's story, and then moved over and eased the door open part way. He led with the rifle barrel and followed it onto the porch, careful to note no weapon was aimed at him. The man, who still had not moved, apparently wasn't armed. His hands hung to his sides.

"Matthew," he said in a low voice back into the house, "ease over to Saul's cottage and fetch him."

"Yes, sir," he whispered back, and slid past to the side porch. By now, every member of Cal's household was fully alert.

In five minutes, Saul had joined his brother. After instructing the others to scan the woods around the perimeter for potential ambushers, the two walked slowly toward the man. When they neared, Saul recognized him.

"Hey, it's Kimiskbone from the forest hideaway." They rushed to the man. "Greetings, friend, what are you doing here?" Saul cradled his rifle and clasped the man's hand.

Cal did the same. "Kimiskbone, are you well? Is something wrong?"

The Indian didn't speak, only nodded his head slowly. Family members began to join the group.

"Let's get him to the kitchen," suggested Saul. "He needs water, and probably food. Matt, go find either Anna or Belle."

"I'm here," said Anna, emerging from behind the growing crowd of Murphs.

"Anna, see if you can get him to talk. That is, after we get a drink into him."

Ten minutes later, after two gourd dippers of water, Kimiskbone looked around. "Friends," he muttered in Muskogean. Anna sat ready to interpret for those of the family not as proficient as she in the language. "Murph friends. Bad news. Nouskuubi."

Anna looked up, worried, and relayed in English, though everyone had caught the name. She gestured for Kimiskbone to continue. He struggled.

"Nouskuubi gone. He left. We hunt whole day for him. Others sent me to tell you. I walk all night. We know you want to be told."

He went on to tell as well as he could how and when Nouskuubi slipped away from the camp. He had pretended to walk to the spring to fill a cook pot with water, and had apparently kept going through the trees. When his guardians realized he was tardy returning, they checked the spring and found only the pot. They searched hard, but he had too much of a start and they hadn't been able to find him.

"We know where he's going," declared Cal. "Should we go after him?"

Saul didn't answer the question. Instead, "Ladies, cook us up a big breakfast, doubles for our guest. Phonso, you and Silas saddle five horses. Holt, you go with Anna to return Kimiskbone to the camp and make sure the others are all right and back in hiding. You and Anna learn all you can from the others about Nouskuubi's intentions."

"Yes, sir."

"But Anna is in charge, understand?" Holt grimaced. "Cal and I are riding to the falls and praying he isn't there. Matthew, you stay home in case Nouskuubi shows up here, or anyone else does."

"NO, AIN'T SEEN HIM, Saul," said Perley Gerald, shaking his head. "Think I'd know 'im if I seen 'im. Ain't seen any Indians come around here on their own will. Certainly not to that camp over there." He nodded toward the mass of humanity across the way.

Both Saul and Cal looked at Sam Peavy, rocking nearby.

Sam spat a stream of tobacco juice over the side of the porch. "Naw, ain't seen nobody like that. Don't think they'd come here no how."

"Yeah, he would," said Cal. "Nouskuubi ain't a straight thinking man." He nodded to the camp. "His family's over there, and he has some notion he has to rescue them."

Perley shook his head. "Any Indian'll get hisself killed if he wanders in over there, 'less he's giving hisself up."

"We have to check, anyhow," said Saul. "We'll leave our rifles here, Perley, if you don't mind. We don't need trouble with those folks. Come on, Cal."

On the walk across, Saul turned to Cal. "We don't need to get too close to Nouskuubi's woman. If she sees us, she's gonna get all riled and worried. That is, if Nouskuubi ain't with the family."

The two men moved into the camp hardly noticed. They eased into position forty yards away from where they had seen the family before, being careful not to be spotted by the woman. After scanning the scene, they found her only a few yards from her previous location. No man was with her or nearby. Saul and Cal studied each person within yards of the family, lest Nouskuubi had somehow made it in and was hiding from the authorities in disguise.

"No, he ain't here," Saul concluded. "Crazy idea, anyhow. No way Nouskuubi could've gotten in without getting caught."

"Or killed," added Cal. "Think they might have 'im in that rickety stockade?" He gestured to the structure at the edge of the bluff. The two already walked back toward Perley's trading post.

"Hmmm. Naw, he wouldn't go for it. He'd go down fighting 'fore he'd let himself get locked up."

A gruff, familiar voice hailed them from behind. They turned to meet the rough thug Taggert they had encountered before. He snarled at them, as did his two companions lurking behind.

"Well, well, I do believe it's them two farmer boys from up the river." He sneered. "You Indian lovers come down to visit these pore rodents again? Yore kind of people, ain't they?"

Saul stared at the man. "Taggert, ain't it?"

"Yeah, I'm Taggert. I believe I owe you a punch in the mouth, farm boy." Saul didn't reply. "You boys back down here trying to kidnap more Indians?"

"Looking for a friend, not that it's any of your concern."

"Same one you was looking for back before? Hey, we might've seen that sorry buck." He turned his head to his henchmen and sneered. "Think that was him, boys?" The two echoed the sneer and laughed.

"Well, sir, whoever you think you saw, where was it you saw him?"

"Now why should I tell you, farm boy?" He spit toward Saul's feet. Saul didn't flinch. "Pshaw! But you might check on a corpse we saw in the thickets up past the ford."

"You murdered him?" Saul resisted stepping toward Taggert. "You sonofabitch!"

"You damn bastard!" thundered Cal.

"I didn't say I murdered him, I just said we saw him." Taggert snorted again. "Damn no good Indian, anyhow." He laughed and turned. "Come on, boys, I'm smelling Indian stink." All three shuffled away laughing.

Saul and Cal stood still, shocked. Then they noticed a man standing a short way to the side.

"I heard," said Kaspar Brayke. "I'm sorry. I'm sorry even if it's not your friend."

"Thanks, Mr. Brayke. Where did you come from?"

"I saw you pass on the road from my camp place on the bluff. Figured you was headed for Perley's, so Rube and I hiked down to say howdy. Perley and Sam said you were over here."

Saul explained the situation to Kaspar as they walked back to Gerald's store. "We came to search for one of the fugitive, land grant holders who's been swindled, we think by that man Taggert. The Indian was a good friend, and his family is in the camp, the same family we tried to retrieve before. Nouskuubi has been insane with rage, and apparently could wait no longer to attempt something."

"Whether it's your man or not, I'll help you look for the body if I may presume to do so."

"Thanks, Mr. Brayke. Let's hope we find nothing."

THREE HOURS LATER, in a thick tangle, Cal stepped back and grabbed his nose. "Saul, Mr. Brayke, over here."

Cal had found the body they were searching for. Two hundred yards past the river ford, thirty yards into the bush, there was the remains of Nouskuubi. He had been shot several times, approximately the previous day.

"Damn!" swore Saul upon identifying the man. The sentiment was repeated by Cal and Kaspar. "Damn murdering devils!"

The three agreed they should carry Nouskuubi back to the forest to allow his tribesmen to bury him with proper rituals. They wrapped the body in a poncho and strapped it onto the flank of Saul's horse.

The trip up the north trail was a slow, sad, silent passage.

Chapter 37

Falls on the Tallapoosa, August, 1836

POST MIDNIGHT. An ill or hungry baby across the way from the stockade cried quietly, soon joined by another awakened by the unhappiness of the first. Their mothers worked to quiet the crying children. A couple of restless horses stomped in the corral with an occasional neigh. A few scattered dying campfires provided the only light under a dark, clear night featuring no moon and ineffective faraway stars.

Sentries walked the circumference of the camp, a hundred yards apart. One patrolled the stockade fence between the wall and lip of the bluff. His casual stroll and slumped shoulders transmitted boredom and fatigue.

Whap! "Aaghh! The sentry went down from a blow across the back of his neck with a pine limb, his musket flying yards away. He quickly recovered to see two Indians helping a third through a split between two loosened fence pilings. He tried to stand, but received a knee to his chin, which sent him sprawling again.

"Alarm! Alarm!" the sentry yelled. He searched for his musket then saw it in the hands of one of the escaping Indians. All three vaulted a large log parallel to the rim of the bluff and disappeared down the slope. "Alarm!" he repeated. "Escape! Over the bluff! Alarm! Alarm!"

Two fellow sentries and several other soldiers joined him. One ran to the edge and fired. Then a volley erupted from others.

"I think I hit one of the bastards!" yelled a soldier, quickly trying to reload in the dark. "I saw him stumble."

Captain Brodnax, half clothed, sprinted to the group, followed by Major Elliot. "What the hell?" both barked simultaneously.

"You hit one?" asked Elliot. "Get down that hill and find out, and get after the others. How many? How did they get out?"

A squad scampered down the bluff, dodging pines and oaks. The bluff didn't drop as a sheer cliff does, but sloped at a steep angle for two hundred yards to the river's edge. The bluff represented a section of the fall line, of which the waterfalls and rapids belonged.

Halfway down, the soldiers discovered a wounded Indian, almost falling over him in the dark. The escapee attempted to hide, but when spotted, ran away with a stumbling gait.

"Halt, Indian! Stop, you savage, or I'll fire."

The man didn't stop, but was easily caught. A soldier grabbed him and spun him around. The Indian attacked with the only weapon he had, his fists.

Blam! A single musket shot dropped the man with a blast to his throat. He died seconds after he hit the ground.

"Keep going!" yelled the sergeant in charge. "Get after the others. I'll follow in a moment. And be careful; the sentry thinks one of the scamps stole his musket." He turned to two soldiers he had delayed. "Schmidt, Owens, carry this bastard back up the hill and ask the major to send down another squad. Tell him we're gonna need more help. We don't know how many of these vermin we're chasing, or how many of their rotten friends we'll meet in these woods."

He turned and ran a winding path down the precipitous slope to overtake his scattering troops. Reaching the river bank, he faced a choice. Unless the Indians swam the swift river, which was unlikely, they would have turned upriver or down. He quickly decided downriver, as the escapees would have to fight the falls if they fled north.

The sergeant soon caught up with most of his squad and gathered them for checking logistics and strategy. He then deployed them through the trees and tangles as they worked downriver. Five miles along at the dawn of the new day, the squad came upon the Muskogi village of Talisi, from which the falls settlement took its name, at the mouth of Yufabi Creek. With the reluctant permission of the town chief, they searched the village for any warrior who looked as if he had just arrived from a night of flight.

Finding no success, the sergeant gazed across the Tallapoosa to the flat plain on which sat the Muskogi capital town of Tukabatchi. "I wager these sonsabitches done ferried them other sonsabitches across the river in one of them canoes. Ain't gonna catch 'em over there."

Nevertheless, the squad forded Yufabi Creek and carried on for another mile south before giving up the chase. They doubled back and paralleled the creek east for three miles to the main trail leading back to the Tallassee settlement at the falls.

❖ ❖ ❖

BY MID-MORNING, details of the escape had permeated the settlement. At Perley Gerald's trading post, discussion and rumors dominated. Several off-duty soldiers were happy to share their versions of the story.

"Otis said a dozen or more, but couldn't be more'n six. Ain't that many scoundrels missing this morning."

"Only one dead. I saw the body. Should've been more, I wish. Somebody said maybe four others got shot but got away."

"Where do you think they ran to?" asked Perley.

"Who knows? Downriver they say. A patrol chased 'em all night but didn't catch 'em."

"Betting word is they're gonna work their way 'cross the river somewhere, then go up the other side to some shelter place 'bout fifteen miles north. Some Indian fanciers up there would take care of 'em, they say."

Perley and Sam Peavy looked at each other, both suddenly wearing worried looks. Later, comparing notes, they agreed the Murphs had to be appraised of the event, and warned trouble may be spilling toward them. Perley put a coin in the hand of a teenaged kid and dispatched him to summon Kaspar Brayke.

"If anyone can handle the news, and knows what to do with it, it's him," decided Perley.

Sam chuckled. "Yeah, and if we don't send for him, he'll break both our necks."

Before Kaspar arrived at the trading post, a large squad of removal agents galloped from the camp, heading north.

Chapter 38

Tallapoosa River, August, 1836

SHORTLY AFTER NOON, Kaspar Brayke sat astride Perley Gerald's best horse. Perley had him saddled and equipped before Kaspar arrived at the trading post. After Perley and Sam related the events of the previous night and shared what information they had gleaned, including rumors, Kaspar swung into the saddle.

"Thanks, friends," he called. "You're good fellows." He galloped away along the river road heading north, Rube gleefully running alongside off on another adventure.

Kaspar eased his horse to a steady trot to save energy, though he was anxious to get up the road as fast as possible. He searched for signs of the agents, and past the ford began to see fresh tracks of a large group in every soft spot in the road.

Kaspar didn't like what he saw and didn't like how he felt.

"PA, PA! COME QUICK! They got Silas!" Alphonso ran into the compound in a panic. "Buncha men got Silas!"

Cal met him on the run. "Whatta you mean? Who? Where is he?"

Phonso, brushing away tears, pointed to the road. "We were in the field 'bout to finish up. Riders rode up. We said hello, they didn't say nothing. One of 'em grabbed Silas. I ran. Pa, they got Silas!"

"I know, Son. I'll take care of it. You run to the house and warn everyone. And fetch my rifle if you will."

As Alphonso ran toward the house, Cal looked up to see a rider appear on the road, then another, and others. Cal counted eight. One man held Silas across his saddle in front of him. Silas squirmed and fought, but the man was too strong and had no trouble holding the boy.

The intruders walked their mounts into the yard and arrayed themselves into a wide row, several yards of spacing down the line. Silas continued to fight in the arms of a man two horses to the left of the leader.

Phonso came running with Cal's rifle. "Thanks, pal. Now run back to the house and man your post." He looked to the other boy. "Silas, be still."

Silas, obviously furious, nevertheless stopped wiggling. The man holding him laughed, spat off to the side, and laughed again. Cal turned his attention back to the leader. He and Cal stared at each other for hostile seconds.

"'Afternoon, squatter. My name is Taggert."

"Yes, we've met. A couple of times, unfortunately."

"Ha! I remember you, too. You one of them damn Indian lovers what wanted to kidnap that squaw and her filthy brats from the removal camp." He sneered. A trickle of tobacco juice ran from a corner of his mouth to his chin. "Is it you or your sorry pal I owe a punch in the face?"

"The honor was my brother's. I wish it had been me."

"Course you do. I might shoot both of you today. If he's around, that is. Maybe he's more scared than you, or just smart enough to hide when he saw us coming."

"I warrant you, sir, he would relish another tiff with your chin."

"Ha! Then why ain't the damn coward out here? But you're wasting my time. We come on government business. Seems we got word you might be squirreling away a couple of escaped bad Indians, and we demand you hand 'em over."

Cal scoffed. "Now why would we do such a thing? Even if we were hiding someone, which we're not, we certainly wouldn't surrender them to a lizard like you."

Taggert's face flushed and his eyes narrowed. "Watch your mouth, you weasel," he snarled. "Trot out them damn Indians and we'll be on our way."

"Don't think so. Now, you just let the boy down from there and get off this property."

"Ho, ho! Seems we got the upper jump here, fella." Taggert bared his tobacco stained teeth as another stream leaked from his mouth and dripped onto his already badly stained shirt. "If you won't hand over who we want, we'll just take this grimy half-Indian lad with us. He'll do fine, I wager."

"That won't be, I assure you, Mr. Taggert."

"What can you do about it, huh? Look around. There's eight of us and we mean business."

"We mean business as well, sir. I did say 'we'. Right now there are at least six rifles aimed by crack shots centered on your chest and those of your mates."

A hint of fear crossed Taggert's face. "You're lying. You ain't got no guns."

"No? Well, let's see if I can convince you." He turned and signaled to the house. Five seconds later a shot sounded from one of the buildings, followed by a billow of gun smoke. A rifle ball cut through the tree behind Taggert, passing only a few feet above his head. "Trust me, you skunk, there are more shots like that, and they will be on target."

"You're bluffing."

"Oh? Do you need another sample? One a little closer this time?"

"Uhhh …"

"I thought so. Now, order your thugs to uncock their weapons and drop them to the ground, muzzles first."

"Ha! We still got the kid. We ain't dropping no guns. Nope, can't do tha … uhhagh!" He reacted to a sharp pain in his side.

"Sure you can," announced a voice from Taggert's right flank as the barrel of a long rifle stuck into his ribs. "I suggest you do the man's bidding, sir," spoke Kaspar Brayke, looking up at the man and holding steady the cocked weapon.

"What the hell …! Who're you?"

"Don't matter who I am. But I know you by your rotten reputation." Kaspar pushed the rifle muzzle harder against the man's side. "You're Taggert, aren't you, one sorry polecat?"

"What's it to you? And I 'spect you best get that iron pointed somewhere else, or I might just kill you right now. Aaagh!"

Kaspar shoved the rifle hard into Taggert's ribs. "Seems you'll be the first to die." He pushed harder. "I won't tell you again. Let the boy go and drop those weapons, or I'll shoot you dead."

"You … Uhhh …"

"No more talking. I'm going to shoot you, and my friends will pick off your hoodlums. You don't have a chance."

"Taggert … Uhhh …," one of the other men pleaded, fear apparent. Several of the horses stomped around, uneasy.

"Okay, okay. You got the drop on us for now, smart guy. All right, boys, I guess you can lower your guns."

"Muzzles down and uncocked," insisted Cal, enjoying the show from his position out front, his rifle still cradled. "Silas, jump down and run for the house."

As the weapons dropped to the ground, Saul, Matthew, and Holt walked across the yard, weapons pointed forward. Cal now had his rifle at the ready, and Kaspar walked out front after giving Taggert one last poke.

"Be of a mind, friends," warned Cal, "there are others still back there ready to fire at your first flinch. So you best mind." He turned to the new arrivals. "Matthew, Holt, see what you can do with those firearms. We'll keep you covered."

"Yay," both boys spurted, satisfied smiles shining. Matthew picked up the first rifle, extracted the flint, scooped a handful of sand, and poured it into the breech and the barrel. Then he turned the muzzle down and ground it into the dirt.

The next man in line realized what Matthew was doing. "Aaagh!" he screamed. "You can't do that!" He leapt from his saddle and made a dive for his musket lying on the ground. As he reached it, Matthew, holding the first weapon at port, swung it stock first upward into the man's chin, flipping him backward in an arc of blood. The goon landed on his back, semi-conscious, crying and moaning.

With a satisfying grin, Matthew threw the first rifle back to its still mounted owner.

"Grrrr …," growled the recipient as he caught the gun.

"Great job, Cousin," said Holt. "I like your style." Both boys went down the line repeating the process, to the amusement of the onlooking guards and to the anguish of the intruders.

As Matthew and Holt finished emasculating the last rifle and musket, a black-haired, enraged missile flew at Taggert, knocking him from the saddle and tumbling over the side of the horse on top of him. Before they landed, Anna already pummeled the man with her fists. He tried to cover up, but the girl was too violent and too angry.

When Saul pulled his daughter off the man, her fury had not subsided. Saul had to hold her back to prevent her from continuing the attack. Taggert staggered to his feet, sporting two black eyes, a busted lip, and numerous bruises. A blend of blood and tobacco juice cascaded from both nostrils.

"You bitch!" he gurgled. "I'll get you for this."

"No, you won't," said Saul. "Now, the pack of you turn your horses around and ride off. Don't show yourselves around here again or we'll shoot your eyes out." He scoffed. "See, my brother told you we mean business."

As the last rider disappeared into the forest, Cal turned to Kaspar. "I sure was happy to see you, friend. I don't understand. Where did you come from?"

"Oh, I was afraid something was up, so I left Rube and the horse 'bout a hundred yards back in a grove and sneaked in to take a look. Then I decided I could do more than just take a look."

"You certainly did that, pal," said Saul.

"Glad I could help. Fun, I must say, chasing away thugs of their foul nature." He smiled. "Best doing I've seen, though, watching Miss Anna thrash that polecat Taggert. Pleasing entertainment."

Anna, standing near Kaspar, blushed, and squeezed close to him. Kaspar's arm snaked around her shoulders and pulled her close. They smirked at each other, as if sharing a secret.

Matthew and Holt broke out in huge grins. "Hey, hey!" yelped Holt.

"Yeah! Go for it, Mr. Brayke," echoed Matthew. He and Holt slapped each other on the shoulder.

Saul, himself unable to suppress a grin, scolded the boys. "You guys behave yourselves. Mr. Brayke is our guest. Now do something useful and go fetch Mr. Brayke's horse and dog."

Walking back to the houses, watching the younger kids already romping with Rube, Kaspar told the family about the incident the night before at the falls, and why he chased the posse. "They apparently thought the men might be here, but that makes little sense. They haven't had time to get this far upriver on foot."

Saul and Cal looked at each other. "Perhaps you underestimate the stamina of the Muskogi warrior, Mr. Brayke," chortled Saul.

Kaspar, suddenly wide-eyed, said, "You mean, uh, you mean they're here?"

"Arrived about an hour ahead of Taggert's gang. Traveled all day, probably ran most of the way. Lots of scratches and bruises, but otherwise just tired and hungry." Saul shrugged. "They aren't going to be happy about the death of their friend. They didn't yet know what happened to him, only thought he had been wounded and recaptured."

THAT EVENING, over another of the Murph ladies' scrumptious suppers, the family celebrated a victory over evil with their three guests. The two Muskogi warriors, exhausted as they were, ate heartily, the best meal they had for months. The other guest, the hero of the day, also enjoyed himself, especially when Matthew and Holt maneuvered the seating arrangement to make certain Anna was seated next to him.

Chapter 39

Executive Mansion, Washington, D.C., August, 1836

PRESIDENT ANDREW JACKSON greeted Secretary of War Lewis Cass as the latter was ushered through the door of the President's Executive Mansion office.

"Welcome, Lewis, nice to see you on this fine day."

"Thank you, Mr. President. Thanks for inviting me."

"Lewis, I'm to receive General Scott shortly to discuss his arguments concerning the Indian problems in Alabama and Georgia. I wanted you to hear him out as well. You have read his written report, I assume?"

General Winfield Scott, who had served as military commander in Georgia during the summer, had arrived in Washington a month previous. Jackson, dissatisfied with his performance regarding hostile Creeks, had recalled him and reverted control of federal troops in Georgia and Alabama to General Thomas Jesup, and that of the Georgia military to Governor William Schley. Scott's reputation had fared no better with his command of forces fighting Seminoles in Florida prior to his assignment to Georgia.

"Yes, sir, I read his report," replied Secretary Cass. "I thought it counter on some points to dispatches we've received from Governors Schley and Clay, also from General Jesup."

"Same as me. The general's document presents a brighter light on the situation than is perhaps warranted. I'm interested in hearing of the difference."

The two fell into small talk for the next ten minutes when the door opened. An aide stepped inside and announced, "Mr. President, Major General Winfield Scott, sir, begs your audience."

"Show him in, Patrick." General Scott, in dress uniform complete with ceremonial saber, strode through the door. "Welcome, General. Good of you to come."

"Thank you, Mr. President. I would never ignore a summons from the Executive Mansion."

"You know Secretary Cass, of course," said Jackson as he gestured both men to chairs. "General, we've invited you here to follow up on your written report on the Creek uprising, and to expand your comments."

"Proud to accommodate, sir. I vouch for my record and my honor. Both are clean."

"Clean, yes, and honorable. But some items do not seem to mate with other reports we've received. This, for example." Jackson tapped a sheaf of papers he had retrieved from his desk. "You claim you and General Jesup broke the will of the Creeks in your June campaign through Alabama. Governor Clay was not impressed. General Jesup agreed with your sentiments in principle, but he hasn't been kind to your efforts."

"I stand by my conclusions, Mr. President."

"You declared the war was at an end?"

"Essentially, sir, yes. Not much remained to do but execute final Creek removal to the west, according to your wise and thoughtful Act. Once the last procession takes place, and I believe it should be forthwith, few viable Indians will yet be in the area to make trouble. Their morale is broken and those stragglers will soon request passage for themselves to join their tribesmen."

President Jackson stroked his chin. "I see. Nice analysis, General. But I must say your optimism is counter to other principals close to the grounds. Most are still reporting hostilities and deep despair. Some claim the war yet rages and is regaining momentum."

"Sir, General Jesup and I wiped the Alabama fields clean of serious belligerents. Those remaining were without power."

Secretary Cass hurried to comment. "Sir, General Jesup seems to agree with you. He, too, judges the war tamping down. Few others hold that view, however. Militias on both sides of the Chattahoochee claim to be undermanned and lacking powder and ball. Many of the units are tired of the fight, and are declining to respond to calls beyond their locales."

"Mr. President, I stand by the results as I left them. I have no concert with what has transpired since my departure."

"Governor Schley disagrees, sir. His dispatch a month ago was taken by this administration as good tidings. I was much pleased. Then came conflicting news from him a few days ago of renewed skirmishes on his side of the Chattahoochee, caused by Creek bands escaping from Alabama. He attributes that to weakened defenses, having dismissed virtually all militias from state service weeks earlier. He had acted thusly on assurance from you and General Jesup that the war had come to a close. Most of the militias have now refused to return to service or to respond to calls for assistance."

"That's most unfortunate, Mr. President. I assure you I left Governor Schley's defenses in good stead. I regret it if they have not been maintained."

Jackson glared at General Scott in silence, not masking his rising anger. He grunted and shook his head. "General, from recent reports the plight of farmers and other citizens in Alabama and Georgia is distressful, perhaps worse than when you and General Jesup launched your campaign. I've fought campaigns myself, sir, and I contend the results must not remain contentious."

"I agree with that, of course, Mr. President. I believe the situation down there can't be as dire as claimed by dispatches you've cited. Once final emigrations west are executed, few Creeks will remain to cause the good people of those environs further difficulties. The land will be free to thrive and grow."

Jackson stood as a signal the conference had ended. "We can only hope, General, your optimism is well-founded." He reached to shake Scott's hand. "Good day, sir."

After General Scott departed, the President paced the floor for a couple of minutes. Then, "Lewis, who's correct in this tangle?"

"Hmm. I venture no one, sir. The Alabamians are under-manned and their resources ill-used. The Georgians are dissident and disorganized. Our generals have been negligent. Greedy land speculators have sabotaged all efforts to peacefully remove the Creeks west. And the Creeks themselves? Well, they have perpetrated too much unnecessary resistance, violence, and blood-letting." Cass paused for a deep breath. "And, sir, if I may venture our shortcomings, we have underestimated all those factions."

Jackson peered at Cass and frowned. "Lewis, it has been a wretched war, hasn't it? You're correct; many must shoulder the burden of violence, and of delay. There is no excuse for taking six years to free those lands."

"Yes, sir. I spoke to Senator King yesterday on Capitol Hill. He grows in impatience and anger."

"Yes. I fathom that. Now, about the Creeks. When will General Jesup be able to move the bulk of what's left of them?"

"Should be soon, sir. I understand several thousand refugees have been mustered in the various camps. Once they are gone from Alabama, the situation should ease, though many will remain." Jackson glared at him. "Those who cling to their legal titles, sir, and others for various reasons."

Jackson pondered a moment, then walked to his desk and consulted a calendar. "Yes, six years is too damn long since we passed the Act. Hmmm, is September first possible, Lewis?"

Cass pursed his lips and nodded. "I believe the first may be practical, sir."

"Then notify General Jesup. We want those damn Indians out of Alabama by early September."

Chapter 40

Loachapoka Village, August, 1836

OPOTHLE YAHOLA STOOD TALL. His eloquence flowed. He had walked the last hundred yards alone to the Red Stick refuge at Loachapoka to attempt again to convince holdouts to cease hostilities and emigrate west. Included among several Creek headmen were Oakfuskee Yahola of Talisi warrior town, who already leaned toward emigration, and Tuscoona Fixico of Wetumpka village in Russell County, wanted by authorities for his leadership of the fatal stagecoach attacks in June. Several holdouts of Neah Micco's village were in attendance seeking new alliances after their leader acceded to peaceful removal. Also hiding in Loachapoka or in nearby Saugahatchi were fugitives from General Jesup's attack on Neah Emathla's town, plus a myriad of other Creeks from fractured communities.

Opothle Yahola faced four dozen miscellaneous warriors and townsmen seated on the ground before him. A group of their women gathered behind to listen. "There remains no future for Muskogis here," Opothle Yahola argued. "We have lost our homeland. To resist further is futile."

"Why do you say such, Opothle Yahola?" countered a spokesman. "You are the Head Chief of all Muskogis. Why are you not leading the fight to save our people?"

"Saving our people is my concern. I ..."

"You ride with the white army. Is that not treason to Muskogis?"

Anger was rising among the listeners. Opothle Yahola didn't flinch. His voice remained calm but strong. He was known as the most gifted speaker in the Muskogi Nation, and the most poised. "Yes, I am your chief. I have served you well. I am serving you well this day, for now is the harshest trial of our time. It is my duty as your leader to see our people through and to seek a just end."

"Just? Is it just to rob our lands, destroy our homes, kill our people?"

"I do not condone such. No, what the whites have done and are doing is not just. And what our Muskogi brothers who have committed crimes, whether against fellow Muskogis or white invaders, is equally unjust and cannot be tolerated. The chieftain Tuscoona Fixico sits among you today. Because he led raids without excuse or mercy against stagecoaches two months past, he is accused of cowardly murder and crimes against property. Should he be guilty, I shall later join in his pursuit, but that is not my mission today, nor my authority."

An angry Euchee from Eufaula leapt to his feet. "Opothle Yahola, you betray us of the Lower tribes. You convinced your favored Upper townsmen to give in to the whites while you join invaders and land thieves to wage war against Euchees and others of the south. Why do you ride with the white armies and fight us instead? You are a traitor!"

"You cannot call me such …"

"Yes! You *are* a traitor. A traitor to your own Upper Creek brethren. Your own Tuckabatchis, and the Oakfuskees, Atasis …" With each tribal name, the man's shout grew louder and more impassioned than the name before. " …Kalaidshis, Talisis, Hillabees, and other Upper warriors fought bravely and justly against the butcher Jackson in the days of our youth. You among them. Now you turn Upper warriors against Lower tribes who now bravely fight battles you should be fighting, the same battles your fathers fought!"

The man's speech raised a clamor. Several belligerents jumped to their feet, screamed, and shook fists at Opothle Yahola. The uproar continued for a full minute, standees storming at the chief. A few made moves to charge, but were held back by cooler compatriots.

As Opothle Yahola calmly abided for the din to abate so he could counter the warrior's speech, a movement to his left caught the edge of his eye. Simultaneously, the noise waned before dying to silence. In the doorway of one of the village's thatched huts stood Tuskenea.

The dozens of onlookers had to expect a duel, at least a fist fight. Instead, the two political enemies stood and stared at each other. Finally, Tuskenea spoke.

"Opothle Yahola, my lost brother from our birth town of Tuckabatchi, you *are* a traitor as my compatriot spoke true, and of you I'm ashamed in the memory of our sacred forefathers. My father, Tustanagee Thlucco, Big Warrior to your English-speaking masters, were he still with us would join in that shame."

"Your father, Tuskenea, was a peace-loving man, and he would praise my efforts to preserve our people. He would not suffer you hiding here among fugitives and criminals. Tustanagee Thlucco was a man of honor and reason. You, his once favored son, are neither of those."

Another protest arose from the crowd, but Tuskenea quieted them with a slight wave. "You call my brothers fugitives and criminals? You smear those of us who defend the Muskogi Nation against unlawful invaders?"

"Yes, there are criminals in refuge among you. Possibly you, Tuskenea. It is known you resided in this town at the time of the two farm massacres of families Davis and Jones, and the murderers are thought to have come from here." The hushed crowd turned eyes to Tuskenea, who still stood in front of the hut from which he emerged.

"I am guilty of no murders, and I do not deny these brethren are my friends, better friends than from my youth in Tuckabatchi and Talisi. I assure you, Opothle Yahola, you have no allies among us."

"Perhaps you underestimate the Loachapokas and Saugahatchis. There are good people here who are hearing my words."

"Your words are blasphemy."

"My words offer safe passage to new lands westward with our birthrights now stolen. Join thousands of your kinsmen who journey with protective escorts in the coming days. If you do not trust the armies to show mercy and provide sustenance then band with me in the light of next spring as I will lead an exposition myself, with no sponsorship or interference by whites. They have promised to permit such, and it will be so."

Tuskenea scowled. "None here will follow you, Opothle Yahola."

"I trust many will. That is my message." Opothle Yahola turned his attention back to the crowd. "I mourn the loss of our sacred and beloved homeland, for it is indeed gone. I now leave you with good will and deep affection, my brothers forever."

With that, the Head Chief of the Muskogi Nation turned and walked away to rejoin his two aides tending their mounts on a knoll a hundred yards away. He never looked back.

Chapter 41

McKenzie Plantation, August, 1836

JOHN MCKENZIE SAT ASTRIDE HIS HORSE next to one of his cotton fields watching his hired hands and slaves work the rows. This time of the growing season weeding was essential to the health of the crop. McKenzie's attention was suddenly diverted to a commotion at his partially completed plantation house a half mile away.

He watched a half dozen horsemen ride up to the house and speak to a slave sweeping the yard. After a few moments, the pack reined around and trotted toward him. McKenzie recognized them as militia soldiers, several of them members of the local Tallassee Guards.

"Good morning, John Highland," greeted John Brodnax when he pulled his mount to a halt. "Your darkie at the house pointed you out."

"'Morning yourself, John. What brings you our way this day? I thought you fellows at the camp were too busy for social visiting."

"To be sure, we are. I regret this is not a social visit, for I'm certain it would be hospitable. These are frightful times, and we yearn for a finish to the unfortunate affairs that plague us." Brodnax's expression turned serious. "John, the army has need of four of your strong wagons, plus teams to draw them. We are readying the next, and I hope last, trip west for the hostiles and the camp is lacking enough transports."

"Hostiles, John? How many of them poor souls are really hostile?"

"Too many, I fear, but the majority are there by their will."

"You know that not to be a truth, John. Those people yearn to live out their days on the soil that birthed them. And they deserve that God-given right."

"Times have changed. The land belongs to those who till it now. Like you, John. Look at your holdings."

"My land is fully compensated for, and relations with my neighbors quite cordial. The Creeks seem to have no truck with me."

"I'm certain that's so, John. But still, we whites are here to stay and the Creeks are no longer welcome."

"John, that is a cruel thing to say." McKenzie paused, his irritation building. "And no, you can't have my wagons and teams."

Brodnax reached into his shirt and produced a paper, which he handed over to McKenzie. "John, you have no choice. This is a warrant from Major Elliot at the camp requiring you to comply."

McKenzie studied the document, then looked up at Brodnax. "This is no warrant," he declared. "This is nothing but a military order. No more than a request, considering I'm a civilian."

"Don't matter, you …"

"Hell it don't!" Sudden anger erupted. "John, you and your men are welcome on my property anytime. You are not welcome to my possessions. Now, you go back and tell your major to obtain his transports elsewhere."

A FEW HOURS LATER, a mounted full squad of half regulars and half militia thundered down the road to the McKenzie plantation. The owner met them in the house's front yard.

The officer at the head dismounted and confronted McKenzie. "Mr. McKenzie, I am Major Basil Elliot. I understand from Captain Brodnax you declined to honor my order this morning to borrow your wagons and teams."

"Yes, Major, I did. You have no right to my equipment and stock."

"Sir, we do, in a military emergency. Now, be kind enough to show us to what we require."

"No, sir, I won't. As I understand the law, civilian possessions cannot be confiscated for military use, even in time of war."

"Should you be correct, Mr. McKenzie, we shall ignore the law you claim. Stand aside. We'll find the wagons ourselves." Elliot remounted and spoke instructions to his men. Several started in the direction of the large barn.

Around the corner of the house, the horsemen stopped. In a row, a dozen men, some white, some slaves, several Creeks, confronted the squad.

"Mr. McKenzie!" barked Major Elliot. "Order your men to stand aside."

McKenzie walked up and stood beside his workers. "What if I don't, Major? Are you going to shoot us? You can see we're unarmed. Oh, except the one man with the pitchfork. Or mayhap my saddle horse groom threatening you with his currycomb?"

"Push through, men," Elliot ordered. He spurred his horse to walk into the line and force its way between two men. Other cavalrymen followed, also shoving aside the plantation men, none of whom moved voluntarily.

A half hour later, four brightly whitewashed wagons rolled from the barn, a militiaman driving each two-horse team. The rest of the posse trailed behind, looking as if afraid they might be ambushed. McKenzie's farmhands, free and slave, since joined by others from the fields and barns, pressed close. They scowled as the wagons passed. Elliot paused where McKenzie stood.

"Major, you are violating the law and your commission," said McKenzie. "I mean to file a complaint on this theft."

"Not a theft, sir. Your transports and your teams shall be returned in a few weeks. Be patient, and know you are rendering your country a patriotic service."

"Bah! Major, your sense of patriotism, and that of your politician masters, is counter to mine. In my eyes, and the eyes of my Indian friends, this is just another in a long slate of crimes committed in the name of the President's removal act."

Elliot tipped two fingers to his hat bill. "Good day, Mr. McKenzie." He pulled hard on his reins and galloped away to overtake his squad.

Chapter 42

Falls on the Tallapoosa, Late August, 1836

SAM PEAVY LOOKED UP from dozing in his rocker on the trading post porch to watch three riders enter the gate. Trailing behind on a lead was a pack mule loaded with fresh vegetables, smoked venison, tanned deer skins, and other trade goods. Sam roused himself and stood to greet the visitors.

"Why, hello, Mr. Cal. And who are these two beauties following you around today?"

Cal Murph beamed at the question, but before he could answer, Perley Gerald emerged from the front door.

"I do declare!" Perley said. "I wager we have a bit of the Murph clan here."

Cal laughed. "Yep. Brought two of the better Murphs with me this morning." He dismounted and handed his reins to one of his companions. "This young lady tending my mount is Delaine. That other'n is Rachel." Both girls, behind big smiles, nodded.

"Welcome, ladies," said Perley.

"Girls, this is Mr. Perley Gerald. You remember Mr. Peavy, I'm sure."

"Shore nice to see you again, misses." Sam touched his hat brim. "Was up to yore place only a few weeks ago, but I believe both of you have growed a foot apiece since. And gotten prettier by that same much."

"Thought I should introduce them to how we get some of our victuals," said Cal, "what ones we don't grow ourselves, plus other needed supplies. Since they do a right smart of the cooking—and what fine cooks they be!—we figured they needed to learn how we get the goods."

"We usually see Miss Anna come down to supply up," observed Perley. "Not today, though?"

Cal laughed. "Anna's still working off her mad. She'll be back, but we figured it best she stay away from folks over there for a while." He gestured to the camp across the way. "We hardly want her beating up somebody else."

"Oh?" pondered Perley and Sam simultaneously, as all worked to unload the mule.

"Haven't heard about our little skirmish, huh? Well, I must tell you of it. Not surprised Taggert and his gang stayed tight on the details. Bet lots of his ilk have asked him about his manglements, and he ain't telling about it."

Carrying saddlebags, the girls walked onto the porch from tending the horses at Perley's watering trough. Sam walked the freshly unburdened mule to the trough.

"Go on in, girls," said Cal, "and meet Mrs. Gerald. She'll give you everything you need."

Melissa Gerald stood in the door, until now unnoticed. "Absolutely," she said. "Come in, ladies. We'll have a nice time together. I'm Melissa."

"Take all the time you need, girls," said Cal. "I have a big story to unfold for these two gentlemen."

Rachel grinned as she and her cousin walked across the porch. "Don't lie too much about it, father," she said with a twinkle.

Cal settled himself into a rocker between those of Perley and Sam. Both leaned in close, expecting an epic tale.

"It all started," began Cal, "with Phonso—he's ten—running in screaming terror and murder. You see, Silas, age nine, had been grabbed by ..." He went on, without exaggeration, to tell about the Taggert posse invading the Murph compound and the events that developed. His two listeners laughed hard when he described Matthew and Holt spiking the gang's firearms.

Sam slapped his thigh. "Serves them varmints right good," he said. "Hope them muskets blowed up in their ugly faces when they tried to shoot 'em again."

"But that ain't even the best part." Cal continued with an animated account of Anna's attack on Taggert. With that, and especially with Cal's description of Taggert's wounds, Perley and Sam could hardly control the hilarity.

"Best thing I've heard this summer," Perley managed between gasps and giggles.

"Can't give a man his desserts better'n that," added Sam. "I see why you can't trust that little wildcat to venture down here for a while."

With the story finished and chortles and chuckles subsided, Cal wanted to know the news concerning the removal camp. "Any word on when the army plans to move those poor people? Summer's winding down, and they ain't gonna wanta move 'em much later than a month or so from now."

"Rumor says within a week or less," offered Perley.

"Really? Any signs to show that might be so? And how they aim to do it?"

"Yeah, could be. More agents have ridden in and attached themselves to the army. That says to me they're about to round 'em up and drive 'em away. A militiaman in here t'other day said they planned to snake the line of 'em down toward the bend of the river to meet up with other camps. Where they would go from there he warn't shore. Prob'ly to Montgomery like the other bunch."

"Well, we Murphs will want to know when it happens. One of us will probably ride down every day or so to keep up and learn the latest."

Delaine and Rachel appeared in the store door, laden with bloated saddlebags. Melissa followed, carrying two full burlap bags and beaming as if she were the girls' proud mother hen.

"Whoa here," exclaimed Cal, "I don't think our animals can carry such a load."

"Aw, Pa, you jest," said Rachel. "We only bought things we needed. You'll see."

Ten minutes later, the horses and mule were loaded and the travelers mounted. "Thanks, friends, we'll be in touch," said Cal.

"Thank you, Mrs. Gerald," called out Delaine as Melissa waved from the porch. "That was so much fun."

Perley shook Cal's hand. "We'll see what we can learn for you, Cal. Meanwhile, hug Miss Anna for us, and offer her our heartmost 'gratulations and thanks." Perley again laughed out loud.

GENERAL JESUP WAVED A LETTER at Captain John Page, the removal superintendent at Fort Mitchell. "Another dispatch from Secretary Cass," he said. "He suggests—more than suggests—we expedite the next emigration. He and the President want the Indians gone by early September."

Page whistled. "General, sir, that will be difficult. Possible, but difficult."

"Make it so, Captain. How many days do you need?"

"Most gear and provisions are already packed and loaded. It's a matter of preparing the prisoners for the march. And we are short of personnel, sir."

"Two companies of Tennessee militia are due tomorrow. They are to aid the expedition all the way to the territories."

"Yes, sir. They are of a need."

"The tone of Cass's letter leaves no quarter. It is obvious they expect results. Cass even details a suggestion of a route."

"Sir?"

"Apparently, Cass is unfamiliar with the geography of this area. He proposes we march our camp and that of Tuskegee to the one at Tallassee at the falls and join forces there. Then journey on to the docks at Montgomery as a unified mass."

"Sir, that would be folly."

"Exactly. Such an unnecessary diversion would cost us at least four days travel. Perhaps more, considering we would have to push approximately four thousand people an extra fifteen or so miles northward along the river, then bring them back down the same route. That is not practical, so let's plan otherwise."

Jesup and Page moved to a map table and pondered the possibilities. After two hours of studying the geography, inventory, personnel, and tasks yet to be undertaken, they were ready to trace a route and project a date of departure.

"Captain, are we agreed?" posed Jesup. "We leave Fort Mitchell with our two thousand charges on September 3rd. Two days' travel takes us to the junction of the Tallassee River Road and Federal Road about three miles south of Yufabi Creek. It should require a day's travel by the Tallassee and Tuskegee camps to arrive there and merge with us on September 5th. I understand they have over a thousand Creeks each rostered for the trip."

"That, too, is my information," confirmed Page. "General, I believe we have a solid plan. I shall draft dispatches for your signature immediately to the commanders at Tallassee and Tuskegee outlining your instructions." Page paused. "Sir, it indeed will be a joy to rid ourselves of this rabble. The land might now find some peace."

EVERY OTHER DAY for the next week, different tandems of the Murph family trotted down the road to the falls. Perley Gerald fed them what updated bits of news he had been able to squeeze from citizens or soldiers. Finally, on Thursday, he thought he had reliable information.

"The army plans to move out at first light Sunday morning," he told Cal and Holt, the visiting Murph team of the day. "Word is the column will meet up on the Federal Road with camps from Tuskegee and Fort Mitchell and maybe some other places and carry on to Montgomery. They say from there the Muskogis will load onto steamboats like before."

"Yeah, boats?" puzzled Cal. "Why are they using river boats?"

"They say a float down the Alabamy River to Mobile is the artful way to go. Don't know how that's gonna get 'em out to the Indian Territory, but that's what they say. Can only 'magine what's happened to that first load down that big river, and where they's wound up to by now."

Chapter 43

The Falls of the Tallapoosa, September 4, 1836

May angry corns beset their toes,
'Till blood at every step may flow,
And narrow shoes their feet to wear,
'Till savage yells are heard no more.

IN FAYETTE COUNTY, Georgia, Larkin Burnitt published this poem with a dedication to the "land stealers of the Creek nation." He may have been presaging the Muskogis' impending forced walk west from their stolen lands.

BEFORE DAWN, five members of the Murph family galloped the miles from the compound to the falls. They arrived at Perley Gerald's post as the first hints of light peeked over the eastern horizon. Kasper Brayke stood on the porch with Perley, Sam, and Rube to greet the Murphs.

Activity was already at full pitch in the removal camp. A column of about thirty prisoners, shackled at the wrists, waists, and ankles, awaited at what appeared to be the front of the line. Two mounted guards, plus several at post, watched closely. Other agents and soldiers scurried around organizing the Indians into various categories along what was to be a long line. Teams had already been hitched to wagons, some of which were piled high with goods and gear. The remainder were being loaded with children and some women and aged men who could do little traveling afoot. Four of the wagons sported John McKenzie's blue logo on a bright white finish.

"That's a pitiful sight," offered Sam. "Pore souls ain't done nothing wrong. Don't deserve such treatment."

"Damn that Jackson!" swore Saul. "This is all his fault, the sonofabitch! He's who oughta be sent off in exile, not these good Indian citizens."

Shortly, the column began to move, Major Elliot and a squad of mounted regulars leading the way, followed by the shackled prisoners, then other groups stretching more than two hundred yards. Wagons rolled at the rear, accompanied by another squad composed of removal agents. By the time these last left the camp, the front of the column already worked their way down the wide bluff trail, heading south toward Yufabi Creek five miles downriver.

"Let's move yonder to the overlook," suggested Perley. "We can see them down the river road from there. No need to bother the horses. We can walk over."

Ten minutes later, the group stood at the lip of the slope overlooking the modest creek at its foot. The bluff wound around from the falls, both being parts of the geomorphic fall line. To the right lay the steep trail down the hill and across the creek, the one Kaspar had first climbed months ago on his arrival in Tallassee. Square miles of flat, arid farmland stretched out before the observers, most of it worked by John McKenzie's new plantation. The road south was already filled with the slow-moving column of sad but proud Muskogis.

The group of seven men and one woman atop the bluff watched in mournful regret. Not a word was spoken until the last native Alabamian had disappeared from sight three hours later.

ALONG FEDERAL ROAD, General Jesup and Captain Page led the column from Fort Mitchell toward the rendezvous with the Tallassee and Tuskegee factions. They had left the day before, on Saturday the third, and stood to make it more than halfway by the end of this day. Arrival at the agreed upon meeting point should be achieved sometime late tomorrow or the next day.

Jesup had calculated Tuskegee could make the trip to the meeting place in one day, Tallassee in two with a hard drive. From Fort Mitchell he hoped to reach the point in three days, but it would require a good tempo and perfect weather. Overcast skies had thwarted the heat somewhat, and no rain threatened, so progress had been good.

"Captain," queried General Jesup as they rode abreast, "I warrant you shall be pleased to see this passel of Indians gone from your midst. Do I pose correctly?"

"You do, sir. But I fear there are more bad ones yet to be collected." Then Page remembered Jesup's boasts about the war drawing to an end. He quickly added, "Your campaign cleaned out most of them, sir, and those who persist will surely see the futility of further resistance." He chuckled with an apologetic blush. "They will soon give up the fight, and be glad for it."

Jesup glanced at Page and grinned. "Thank you, Captain. You are a loyal soldier."

"HO-OO," SANG MAJOR ELLIOT as the head of the column approached Yufabi Creek. He raised an arm as a signal to halt. Across the creek and fifty yards downstream stood a band of Indians on foot holding high a white banner. The leader held up a hand in a gesture of peace.

"Wait the column here," Elliot ordered his aide. He and a small squad carrying a regimental flag splashed across and approached the men. The group awaited him in silence.

"Peace, friends," greeted Elliot. "What be your business?"

The tall leader ignored the question. "I am Opothle Yahola, Head Chief of the Muskogi Nation."

"Yes, sir, I know of your friendship and your honor."

"I come in peace with a sacred request."

"My pleasure to grant it if it be within my ability. I have been appraised of your trustworthiness and alliance to our cause."

Opothle Yahola bristled. "I do not subscribe to your cause, Major, or to Mr. Jackson's law. But you have left us with little hope. To fight longer would be death to more Muskogis, and my mission as their leader is to save my people."

"To be sure, sir. My apologies."

Opothle Yahola gestured to the bundle he held in both arms. An oiled deerskin wrapped it, and it was obviously heavy. "Here be the seven sacred plates of Muskogi ancestors. We unearthed them from the soil of the council oak at Tuckabatchi, where they were buried by ancestors centuries ago. Since the Muskogi Nation thrives in Alabama no longer, these symbols of purity and courage must be carried to faraway land to bless the spirits of our future new Nation."

"I understand. We will be honored to care for them." Elliot reached for the bundle, but the chief drew back.

"No, no, sir, you must not touch. I desire you to send over top three Muskogi village headmen in yon column. I will place the plates in their care and swear them to sacred commitment."

"Yes, sir, we can do that." He turned to the lieutenant with him. "Go back and fetch the three most respected among the chiefs."

It took a while to identify the best candidates, but twenty minutes later, three Muskogis waded the Yufabi ahead of the mounted lieutenant. Opothle Yahola and his band gathered into a solemn conclave with the three and performed rituals understood by only them. The bundle passed into the hands of one of the headmen, who walked it back across the creek. Flanked by the other two, he rejoined the line, clasping the prize tightly and lovingly.

Opothle Yahola watched the three handle the sacred treasure, sad but satisfied they would do it the proper honor. He again addressed Elliot. "Sir, I further beseech you for special protection of the sacred plates and custodians of same, and to permit them to march at the head of your column."

"It will be done. You have my pledge." Elliot reached to shake hands with Opothle Yahola. "I understand you are to follow to the Territory in a few months. I will be honored to greet you there. Good day, sir, and Godspeed."

AT DUSK ON THE FIFTH, Jesup's exhausted column arrived at the junction of Federal Road and the Tallassee river road. The Tuskegee faction had been there for hours, and the Tallassee contingent arrived only an hour before. General Jesup, as the superior officer, decided one night's rest was necessary, and perhaps another day encampment to reorganize such a huge and ungainly conglomerate. Then the march to Montgomery would require another four or five days.

Steamboats and barges awaited the Muskogis for another voyage to the unknown trials and perils of the far-off Indian Territory.

AFTER THE DEPARTURE of the column, the Murphs and their friends had lingered on Perley Gerald's trading post porch, conversing little, with the Muskogi emigrants still in their thoughts. Occasionally, one strolled to the edge to gaze across the way and shake his head at the abandoned field and stockade.

"Mayhaps they won't carry any more Indians to that place," pondered Sam Peavy on one survey of the area. "Prob'ly will, though. Still bunches of young, mean bucks out there doing mischief, and some old war bloods still around to egg 'em on. Makes it tough on the good fellas about."

"John Brodnax will yet be around. Be a blessing if his warrant ain't renewed."

"He'll still have command of the local Guard," offered Cal, "but at least those removal agents are gone."

Anna sneered. "Let's pray the rotten scoundrels stay in Indian Territory. Better, maybe some of them will reap their just desserts out there; not nice desserts, either, I'm wishing."

Another fifteen minutes of brooding followed until Saul broached an idea. "Time to lose our angry faces, folks. Everyone is invited up to our place. We'll ask the ladies to cook up a feast for us, and we can toast our departed Muskogi friends with a jug of fresh plum cider. What say you, Perley?"

"Obliged for the offer, Saul, but I have to stay and help Melissa tend the store."

"Sam?"

"Thanks, too, but I'm just gonna ease up my old bones the rest of the day."

"Mr. Brayke?"

"I would love to once again be your guest, Mr. Murph, providing Perley wi …"

Gerald interrupted. "Yes, Perley will loan you a horse. Anytime you wish to visit the Murphs, the horse of your choice is yours."

Later, six riders walked their mounts at a leisurely pace up the road toward Soosquana as the sun neared its fall in the west. Saul and Cal rode in front, side by side. Anna and Kaspar followed then Matthew and Holt. Rube proudly pranced alongside, occasionally dashing into the woods to chase some critter before returning to resume his strutting duty.

The horses of the middle pair stayed close, sometimes brushing together, as their riders chatted. Giggles arose from Anna, and she occasionally reached over and playfully touched Kaspar's arm.

Matthew and Holt restrained themselves—no teasing, no hooting, no laughing. They rode in silence, fascinated with the two to their fore. They stared and smiled, proud of Anna and proud for her. Anna, the radiant symbol of the Murph family since 1814.

Postscripts

THE SECOND CREEK WAR was far from over. It persisted into 1837 and beyond, in Alabama and Georgia. However, most skirmishes involved fugitive Indians fighting to survive or militias attempting to prevent bands from escaping across South Georgia to Florida.

No more mass removals occurred with the Creeks of East Alabama, though similar emigrations were staged from Gunter's Landing on the Tennessee River in North Alabama. Smaller scale deportations continued for several years. Many Muskogis later left for what became known as Oklahoma in modest to large groups on their own volition. These included Opothle Yahola, who led approximately eight thousand of his followers to the Indian Territory about a year after the September, 1836, forced emigration. He died in Kansas on March 22, 1863, at age eighty-five.

President Andrew Jackson retired to his Heritage plantation near Nashville, Tennessee, where he remained interested in politics and was vocal on many issues. He died on June 8, 1845, at seventy-eight, and is buried on the Hermitage grounds next to his wife Rachel.

Martin Van Buren won the election in November and assumed the Presidency on March 4, 1837. He shifted the emphasis on the Indian 'problem' from Creek removal to that of the Cherokees.

Lewis Cass resigned as Secretary of War on October 6th. The cabinet position remained open until President Van Buren selected Joel Roberts Poinsett, a physician and former diplomat and congressman from South Carolina, for the post upon inauguration.

❖ ❖ ❖

In late 1836, Senator William Rufus King of Alabama, the interim president pro tempore of the Senate, was officially elected to the office. He served a distinguished career as a senator, interrupted by two years as Minister to France, until elected the thirteenth Vice-President of the United States in 1852 as Franklin Pierce's running mate. By then, unfortunately, King suffered from tuberculosis. Awaiting inauguration, he resigned from the Senate on December 20th and sailed for Havana, Cuba, for treatment. In March, 1853, he became the only American elected official to be inaugurated on foreign soil. He then returned to his plantation in Alabama in April, where he died only two days later on the eighteenth. King was sixty-seven years old at his death.

❖ ❖ ❖

Despite his recall from Georgia in 1836, Major General Winfield Scott was appointed commander of removal forces in 1838 by President Van Buren to supervise the Cherokee emigration. He went on to involvement in various military campaigns, including the Mexican War. As an acclaimed national hero, he became the Whig Party nominee for President in 1852, but was defeated by Democrat Franklin Pierce. Scott died in his eightieth year at West Point, New York, on May 29, 1866. He is buried in the Academy cemetery.

❖ ❖ ❖

Brevet Major General Thomas S. Jesup, after his stint in Alabama, was appointed commander of all forces in the continuing Seminole War in Florida. Afterward, he returned to his official position of United States Quartermaster General. He died in office on June 10, 1860, at age seventy-one, having held the position for forty-two years.

❖ ❖ ❖

Alabama Governor Clement C. Clay resigned his governorship in the summer of 1837 upon being appointed by the state to the United States Senate, where he served until 1841. He died on September 9,

1866, aged seventy-six. Present day Clay County, immediately to the north of Tallapoosa County, is named in his honor.

Georgia Governor William Schley only served one term, not being reelected in 1837. He died in Augusta on November 20, 1858, at age seventy-one. A county in southwest Georgia carries his name.

Judge Eli S. Shorter, the land speculator, died in November, 1836, age forty-four, cause unknown, but probably from his long illness.

The dates of Menawa's birth and death are in dispute. He was born in 1765 or '66, and is thought to have died somewhere along the way to Oklahoma in late 1836 or early '37. He would have been seventy-one, perhaps seventy-two.

Tuskenea, after a few run-ins with authorities and at least one brief arrest, may have made his way to Florida to join the Seminoles.

Tuscoona Fixico was eventually arrested for the stagecoach attacks. He and five of his associates were tried, found guilty, and executed on November 25, 1836, at Girard (present day Phenix City, Alabama).

Jim Boy agreed to join General Jesup's campaign against the Seminoles in exchange for a promise of protection for his family and his followers. Upon his return from Florida he found he had been betrayed and his family shipped west. Four of his nine children perished when the steamboat *Monmouth* exploded in the Mississippi River. Jim Boy then emigrated to Oklahoma and became a long-time leader there among his people.

Bibliography

Ellisor, John T., *The Second Creek War*, University of Nebraska Press, 2010

Golden, Virginia Noble, *A History of Tallassee*, Tallassee Mills, 1949

Goss, Bill, "Menawa (Hothlepoya)," *The Tallassee Tribune*, February 28,2008

Goss, Bill, "Opothleyaholo," *The Tallassee Tribune*, February 28, 2008

Hudson, Angela Pulley, *Creek Paths and Federal Roads*, University of North Carolina Press, 2010

Hughey, Debra Taunton, "A History of the Native Americans of Tallassee," *The Tallassee Tribune*, February 28, 2008

Johnson, Myra Singleton, *Tukabahchi Remembered*, 2017

Martin, Joel W., *Sacred Revolt*, Beacon Press, 1991

Matte, Jacqueline Anderson, *They Say the Wind is Red*, NewSouth Books, 2002

Pattillo, Edward, *Carolina Planters on the Alabama Frontier*, NewSouth Books, 2011

Wadsworth, Dr. E.W., *A History of Tallassee*, Auburn University master's thesis, 1941

Williamson, Larry, *Tallapoosa*, NewSouth Books, 2001

Plus numerous internet sites and articles

About the Author

LARRY WILLIAMSON grew up in Tallassee, on the banks of the Tallapoosa River in the heart of the sacred ancestral lands of the Muskogi Creeks. An Auburn engineering graduate, he is now a retired high school math teacher of thirty-six years, who also coached football and track. He currently teaches Writing Your Novel Workshop for the Outreach Program at Auburn University.

Larry's first book was the historical novel *Tallapoosa*, about the Creek Indian War of 1813-14. *Muskogi Sunset*, concerning the Second Creek War of 1836, is the sequel to *Tallapoosa*. Among his other works are *Over the River, Long Ago*, a collection of tales about growing up in the textile mill town of Tallassee in the 1940s and '50s, and *Legend of the Tallassee Carbine: A Civil War Mystery*. *Legend* is a historical novel about the Confederacy's late war attempt to manufacture a new weapon in the mill at Tallassee.

Contact Larry at soosdog@gmail.com.

Made in the USA
Columbia, SC
16 February 2019